JEAN HARRINGTON

KILLER KITCHENS

W⊕RLDWIDE®

TORONTO • NEW YORK • LONDON
AMSTERDAM • PARIS • SYDNEY • HAMBURG
STOCKHOLM • ATHENS • TOKYO • MILAN
MADRID • WARSAW • BUDAPEST • AUCKLAND

To Irma, Mary and Elsie
who ran killer kitchens all their lives

Recycling programs
for this product may
not exist in your area.

Killer Kitchens

A Worldwide Mystery/February 2015

First published by Carina Press

ISBN-13: 978-0-373-26931-0

Printed in U.S.A.

Acknowledgments

My heartfelt thanks to Design Group West of St. Louis for their creative interior design ideas, to American Rare Coin Inc. for US currency facts, and once again, to attorney Carolyn Alden for her legal expertise.

Thanks, too, to Lethaladies of KOD for their many thoughtful online critiques. To Carina Press's executive editor Angela James for encouraging Deva Dunne to enjoy yet another romp with Lieutenant Rossi. And to my gifted developmental editor, Deborah Nemeth, for all her skill and patience.

ONE

ROSSI SNIFFED THE air and grinned. "Smells great in here. Chip's secret sauce?"

I nodded, watching his reaction, waiting for more.

"Looks great too," he said, glancing around. "You did a wonderful job."

Perfect. I threw my arms around him and hugged him tight. My friend Chip's restaurant, La Cucina, was the first commercial space I ever designed, and to be honest, I needed a little reassurance.

As we strolled into the dining room, a server sprang to attention and led the way to an intimate, white-topped table. He unfolded our napkins and placed them on our laps. "I'm Enzo. Chip sends his apologies for not greeting you personally but—" he winked, "—he's going crazy in the kitchen."

"We understand," I said. Before opening his doors to the public tonight, Chip had invited Rossi and me to an early private dinner. That he was now backstage making sure everything would be perfect for showtime wasn't surprising.

Enzo held up a bottle of pinot noir for our inspection. "With the chef's compliments."

We nodded and in no time at all, Rossi and I were clinking glasses. His eyes, all liquid Italian fire, did what they always did when he looked at me. They tuned out everything else within range. At the moment that included the menu, and with the aroma of secret sauce in the air, no easy feat.

I used to think Rossi's habit of concentrating solely on the object of his attention was a detective's ruse for gaining something. I still did. He used those penetrating eyes of his like a secret weapon to squeeze out the truth. For sure, I had never been able to lie to him about a thing. Damn it.

He raised his glass. And an eyebrow. "To Deva Dunne, the best interior designer east of the Rockies. West of them too." He took a celebratory sip before adding, "Seriously, the place looks terrific."

"You really like it?" I guess I needed to keep the compliments coming.

"Yeah." He grinned, showing me a flash of even white teeth.

Damn. Rossi always knew what I was thinking, what I needed. A trait that made him maddening, not to mention rather irresistible at times.

I blew out an exasperated breath and hoisted my wineglass. As I sipped, I glanced around, enjoying the view all over again. To tempt the appetite of anybody who strolled in, I'd painted the dining room Tuscan tomato and the bar area merlot. Striped carpeting in merlot, tomato and taupe echoed the wall colors. For drama and bling, I'd filled ornate gold frames with black and white photographs of Italian street scenes and hung them *everywhere.* And to enhance the photo colors, black Chiavari chairs surrounded tables draped in white linen. No checkered cloths for La Cucina.

Startup costs had been high, so I insisted Chip pay me only when he could. If that never happened, it would be okay. We were friends, and besides, I owed *him* for giving me such a high-profile project to add to my design portfolio.

Rossi picked up one of the brand new menus and handed it to me. "Food? Red walls make me hungry."

"That's the whole idea." Pleased, I took the menu from him and leaned in closer. "You know something?"

He flashed a wicked smile. "Yeah, your neckline looks great when you do that."

I sat up straighter. "This is like being on a date with a Mafia don."

He frowned. "Why's that?"

A while ago he'd told me his Uncle Beppe had mob connections, but he'd refused to tell me how Beppe died. So right away you think concrete overshoes. But on that particular topic Rossi wouldn't give out details, so who knew? "There's no one else here except Enzo. It's like you reserved the restaurant just for the two of us."

Rossi sampled the pinot noir again. "I don't get it. What's the Mafia connection?"

"Remember the scene in *The Godfather* when Al Pacino takes Diane Keaton to the empty restaurant?"

"No, I never saw it."

"Unbelievable. You're the only person I know who didn't."

He shrugged. "I hate mob movies."

"Well, anyway, Pacino's booked the whole place for the night, and there's nobody there except the wait staff." I spread my arms wide. "Like here."

"You have a very fertile imagination," Rossi said, poker faced. "Now how about we pick an appetizer?"

Not wanting Chip to think I couldn't find anything I liked, I wasted no time scanning the offerings. "How about the Dynamite Shrimp?"

"How's that Italian?" Rossi's brow creased.

"Think Italian-Thai. Chip isn't doing the same old, same old. He's innovating on the traditional dishes."

Rossi glanced up, giving me the full impact of those

eyes. "Italian movies are one thing. Italian food's another. I like traditional."

"Right." Funny, too, coming from a guy who all by himself kept the frozen pizza industry going.

As Rossi studied the menu, I stole a glance at him sitting there handsome as sin in one of his signature Hawaiian shirts. Like his taste in food, it was awful. Purple and yellow hibiscus blooms against a cloud blue sky. He wore his Hawaiians as a ploy so he'd seem less intimidating to crime suspects, and he'd gotten into the habit of wearing them all the time. His philosophy was if it worked with suspects, why not with everyone? He was a superb detective, but still, his shirts were so appalling I loved busting him about them.

"So, Mr. Traditional, tell me something. Did your grandfather wear Hawaiian shirts?"

He eyed me over the top of his menu. "Point made. Dynamite Shrimp it is. And how about an antipasto?" He skimmed the selections and sighed. "No tomatoes. Water chestnuts. Jeez." His glance dropped farther down the page. "Ah," he said as if he'd just discovered a murder clue. "Look under entrees." He tapped the page. "For the Traditionalist. Mama Luigi's Sunday Lasagna." He slapped the menu onto the tabletop. "That's for me. I hope Mama Luigi didn't innovate a damn thing." Then he looked up, stricken. "She didn't do fusion, did she?"

"You have nothing to fear, Rossi, except your own lack of taste buds."

"That isn't true. I have superb taste and a subtle appreciation for the finer things in life." His eyes went darker than ever. "Which is the reason I'm sitting across from a gorgeous redhead." He took my hands and, holding them steady and firm, stared across at me with those dark, hooded eyes. "You're very—"

Whatever he was about to tell me never got said. An earsplitting blast cut off his words, and the building rocked on its foundation. The explosion sent the kitchen doors ricocheting into the dining area and the tables and chairs spinning in the air. The impact flung me out of my seat and hurled me across the room.

I landed on the floor with a bone-jarring thud and lay there stunned, too disoriented to move. In shock, trembling with fear, I watched smoke billow out of the kitchen.

Ears ringing, eyes stinging, I ignored the pain in my backside, gripped the leg of an overturned table and pulled myself into a sitting position. Where was Rossi?

Rossi. Omigod, Rossi.

I wanted to scream, but the blast had knocked all the air out of my lungs. I couldn't breathe, never mind yell. Suddenly, his face bloodied, Rossi bent over me and yanked me up. His arm around my waist, we stumbled past overturned tables, crunching on shards of glass and smashed gilt wood frames. Blown off its hinges, the front door lay in the middle of the street. Trying not to inhale the smoke, we staggered out through the opening and gulped in the clear, fresh air.

Fire trucks wailed in the distance. Enzo, so suave a few minutes ago, sat hunched on the curb with his head in his hands, staring into space.

Rossi cradled me in his arms. "It's over now, Deva," he murmured in my ear. "It's over."

I looked up. A thread of blood trickled down his cheek, and his eyebrows were gone. I held him tight, afraid if I let go the rest of him would disappear along with his eyebrows.

"We made it out alive, Rossi. But oh my God, where's Chip?"

TWO

THE NEXT MORNING, feeling as if someone had taken a hammer to every muscle in my thirty-three-year-old body, I leaned on Rossi's right arm and together we limped into Naples Community Hospital to see Chip. He'd survived the explosion, but just barely. Second-degree burns covered his chest, and he'd inhaled so much smoke he was in danger of respiratory failure.

In addition to a mild concussion, Rossi had ten stitches in that gash on his head, thanks to the fancy bottle of wine we'd been enjoying at La Cucina. It struck just above his right eyebrow or what was left of it. Not only was he sans eyebrows, his lashes were singed to stubs. The force of the explosion had thrown me clear of the flames, so I was still the proud owner of eyebrows and lashes, but I had some spectacular purple bruises, one the size of Rhode Island on my left thigh.

We rode the elevator to the second floor in silence. I hadn't had much sleep, and from the look of Rossi he hadn't either. Somewhere around midnight, it had occurred to me that the explosion might not have been accidental after all. But if not, then what? A deliberate act of violence? That didn't make sense. A big teddy bear like Chip didn't have an enemy in the world. Who on earth would want to vandalize his brand new business? For that I had no answer, and head aching, body aching, I followed Rossi off the elevator and down the hospital corridor.

Outside Chip's room, a red No Visitors sign hung on the

door. I pushed it open a few inches and peeked in. Chip lay flat on his back on a narrow hospital bed. A tube fed into one hand, and another snaked from his nose into an oxygen tank. I caught my breath at the sight of him lying there so lifeless, so—

"May I help you?" a nurse asked in a crisp, no-nonsense tone. She stepped forward, wedging herself between me and the door, blocking my view. A name tag pinned to her collar read Nora Reynolds, R.N.

"Naples police," Rossi said, using his official voice and showing her his badge. "We're here to see Chip Salvatore."

"He's not allowed visitors," she said, peering at the ID, then giving me the once-over. "And you are?"

"She's with me." Rossi's stared at her, stern-faced. The nurse squared her shoulders and stared back. Rossi's stare held. A flush whipped up her face, she faltered and stepped aside. "A minute or two."

We thanked her and slipped into the room. At our approach, Chip's eyes fluttered open for a second then closed.

"Deva," he whispered, his voice a hoarse croak. "You okay?"

My heart swelled into my throat. "Oh, Chip. I'm fine, and you will be too." Tears lurking behind my lids leaked out and ran down my cheeks. I flicked them away before he noticed, and gently touched the fingers of his left hand, the one without the IV. His skin felt cold and dry.

"What happened?" he asked. "Nobody's telling me anything."

"There was a gas leak," Rossi said. "The propane truck exploded while they were filling your tanks. Luckily you were the last stop of the day. If the truck had been full, it would have been worse."

With a noticeable effort, Chip turned his head to peer up

at him. "I've been cooking with gas my whole life. Never happened before."

"Somebody left a car running nearby. Or maybe tossed a cigarette. A spark caught. So far, that's all we know, but we're investigating it. So just rest now, buddy."

Chip closed his eyes without answering then swept them open again. "How's Tomas doing? And Enzo?"

"Tomas is in good hands," Rossi answered, smooth as silk. "And Enzo's fine. Just shook up is all. Save your strength. We'll talk some more tomorrow."

I gulped and stared down at Chip's bruised face. Tomas, the sous chef, had been the one closest to the propane tank when it exploded. Thrown against an exposed pipe, he'd died instantly, his skull crushed like an eggshell. Chip had been in the meat locker at the time of the explosion. The steel doors saved him from the worst of the blast. But not the driver of the truck. Like Tomas, he hadn't survived.

Tired out from the effort of talking, Chip dozed off. Rossi crooked a finger, and we tiptoed from the room. Outside, in the hall, the same nurse approached us. "I was just coming for you. He needs to sleep."

Rossi nodded. "Thanks for letting us see him."

"A terrible accident," she said, her face full of sympathy and a bit of curiosity. She lowered her voice. "Rumor has it foul play was involved."

Rossi stiffened. "As of now, there's no evidence of that."

She shrugged. "It's what people are saying."

"People need to say less. False rumors are harmful."

Giving Rossi an uncertain nod, she walked into Chip's room without responding.

Rossi took my elbow and marched us toward the elevator faster than my sore muscles wanted to move.

"Something happens people don't understand and right away they form an opinion," he said, his voice still gravelly from the smoke he'd inhaled. "A half-baked one," he added. "No pun intended."

I groaned. "Hey, how about slowing down? I've got a stitch in my side." I stopped to bend at the waist and catch my breath.

He exhaled and jabbed the call button. "Sorry. I over-reacted." We stepped into the elevator. "Alone at last," he said. He even smiled.

At ground floor level, a little lightheaded, I made it out-side to the hospital entrance and stood leaning on him. One of the retirees who volunteers at the hospital drove a cour-tesy golf cart up to the portico. "Want a ride to your car?"

"Yes," we said in unison. Our collective aches and pains had caught up with us. Grateful for the lift, we held hands and enjoyed the breezy jaunt to the far end of the crowded parking lot. In season, tourists packed Naples, and like all the locals, I looked forward to the quiet summer months when traffic was light, you could park anywhere and get a restaurant table without waiting. But this was April, and we still had a few months to go before our summer hiatus.

Slow and stiff, I gingerly eased behind the wheel of the Audi.

"Drop me off at the station?" Rossi asked as he settled into the passenger seat. "I'll get a lift home."

"But you're hurting too. You need to rest—"

He shook his head. "I want to be there when they ques-tion the driver of that car."

"Okay." I let out a sigh. From experience, I knew argu-ing with Rossi about his work would do no good. A few months earlier, when a Monet masterpiece had been stolen and two people killed for it, Rossi had pursued the case re-lentlessly, hardly stopping to eat or sleep until he'd caught the thief and murderer. This would be no different, and I had no right to expect that it would be.

He rested a hand on my thigh, the one without the bruise. "I'll be working late, so I won't call you tonight. You need to sleep."

"You do too," I said, pulling out of the parking lot without any more protests. This was what a detective's life was like. Crazy schedules. Danger. Secrecy.

I glanced across the passenger seat at Rossi's resolute profile. With his jaw too sore to shave this morning, his chin bristled with a two-day stubble. He looked like an ad straight out of GQ. Or he would have if not for his virulent orange-and-brown Hawaiian.

I couldn't help but wonder what life would be like for a woman with a man like him. Never knowing from hour to hour if he was safe or in harm's way.

A car swerved out of a side street, barely missing my right fender. I stomped on the brakes.

"Hey," Rossi yelled out the window. "You driving or picking flowers?"

His second blowup in the past ten minutes. "You're worried," I said.

He nodded. "Two men are dead, Deva. We don't know for sure what happened. Arson hasn't been ruled out yet. And if it's arson, it's also murder."

THREE

THE NEXT DAY, with the help of three aspirin, I managed to bend over long enough to shrug into a pair of green silk capris and matching cropped top. The aches soon subsided, but my bruises were in full bloom, including the sensational one on my upper thigh. Worse, my left cheek was purple, a shade as close to aubergine as human flesh can get, and my left eye sported a Technicolor shiner.

Figuring everybody in town had read or heard about the explosion, I didn't bother concealing the damage with makeup. Just getting dressed and driving downtown tapped my tiny reserve of energy.

In Fern Alley, a quaint little byway three blocks from the La Cucina disaster, my shop Deva Dunne Interiors still stood whole and intact. At the sight I didn't know whether to blubber like a baby or whoop with joy. Somewhere deep inside I must have been scared the shop might not be there.

I walked past Off Shoots, the neighboring boutique, and as I gripped the handle of my Boston green door, an enormous sense of relief overwhelmed me. It was so intense my hands shook, and my heart rate skyrocketed.

Post-traumatic stress syndrome, I told myself, but no need to let what happened destroy everything. Despite the explosion and the tragic deaths it caused, through some kind of weird, wonderful luck, Rossi and I had survived. I glanced around my little domain—the shop was fine too. I took a deep breath, stashed my bag behind the sales desk and snapped on the overheads.

These morning moments when the shop sprang into life always pumped my adrenaline. Going into business had been one of the best decisions I ever made, and maybe, just maybe, after another year or two of solid sales, DDI would be an entrenched, successful enterprise. At least that was my goal.

I strolled the shop, tidying the displays, adding a few crystal pieces to the shelves, filling the Sheffield tray with cookies from Fresh Market. The bunny-shaped treats were an homage to spring. Besides, they tasted delicious.

I placed the tray on one of the four skirted display tables. To keep things looking seasonal, I changed the skirts every few months. Crimson and gold for Christmas. Apricot for Halloween. Blue and white stripes for summer. This month they were hyacinth for Easter and spring.

As I fussed over the tables, it dawned on me that I was actually caressing everything, stroking each object, each piece of glass, each silk pillow, grateful that they hadn't all gone up in a puff of smoke like Chip's restaurant. Poor Chip. After work I'd stop by the hospital to see him.

Hoping for the first time ever that business would be slow today, I settled down with a sigh by the front window at the *bureau plat* I used as a desk. About then a black stretch limo purred down the alley and stopped outside my door.

A built guy with sofa-wide shoulders, in a gray chauffeur's uniform, visor cap and all, sprang out of the driver's seat. Snapping to attention like an aide-de-camp, he opened a rear door.

I put down the cookie I was about to bite into and watched, mouth agape, as a short, swarthy man emerged from the bowels of the limo, followed by a tall, striking brunette, clearly half his age and at least a foot taller. I popped the bunny in my mouth and bit off his tail.

The aide-de-camp lunged for the shop door and held it open. The man and the woman swept in.

"Oh, cute," she said, looking around. She had a little girl's voice and a big girl's assets.

"Remember what I told you. No comments," the man said. "I'll do the talking."'

She swept her mahogany-colored hair over one shoulder and shrugged like she didn't care. "Okay, sweetie."

He strode up to me and stuck out his hand. "Francesco Grandese." He pointed to the girl. "This here's my wife, Julieta. Jewels for short."

She waggled a finger, the diamond flash setting off a light show that bounced around the shop.

I swallowed the bunny tail and put the rest of the cookie on one of my signature napkins, white paper monogrammed with DDI in Winthrop green.

Holding a hand flat out, duchess style, I said, "I'm Deva Dunne. How may I help you?"

Mr. Grandese seized my fingers in a sweaty palm and eyeballed my bruises. "You were in that explosion the other day." He tipped his chin in the direction of the burned-out restaurant.

"Unfortunately, yes."

His eyes narrowed as he studied me, checking out the damage. "I read about you in the papers. Otherwise I'd think your old man let you have it."

I squared my shoulders and stood erect, back military straight. At five six plus stiletto heels I towered over him. "I beg your pardon."

"Figure of speech is all," he said casually, waving his hands in the air.

"Don't worry about those bruises, honey. L'Oreal has a great cover-up product." Jewels spoke like she really knew.

Her husband glanced at her sideways and frowned. "What did I tell you?"

"Oh, sorry." She suddenly developed a passionate interest in a table display of Herend figurines.

"I don't have time for no chitchat," he said.

Oh no?

"I'd love to hear the name of that product, Mrs. Grandese," I said in my best Boston accent.

"Oh, sure." To give her credit, she didn't look at her husband for a go-ahead before launching into a topic she obviously knew a lot about. "It's called L'Oreal Concealer, and it works really well."

"Does it come in different shades?" My pen poised over a notepad, I waited for her to go on.

"Yes, it does. I use bronze concealer, but you might need light contouring. Though if you get it too pale, it doesn't cover. So go a shade darker than your usual foundation."

"I don't use foundation."

Like a dermatologist in the making, she studied my skin. "No, you don't need it. When you're not beat up, that is."

"Well, thanks, but I do have freckles."

"Nothing wrong with freckles. They go with your red hair. Like ham and eggs or something."

"That's so sweet."

"Girls—"

Girls. "Just a moment, Mr. Grandese." I held up a palm. "Can you spell L'Oreal for me?" I asked Jewels. She did, painstakingly, starting and stopping several times. When I thought Francesco's fuse was ready to hit the TNT, I put down the pen and gave him a megawatt smile.

"And now, sir, how may I help you?"

Deva Dunne Interiors needed all the business it could

get, but I hated bullies and sometimes, as they say at Harvard Law School, a girl's gotta do what a girl's gotta do.

"I just bought a house," he said, plainly not sure whether or not he should be pissed.

"And?"

"I want it decorated. Top to bottom. Head to foot."

Music to my ears. "Tell me about the house." Judging from his behavior, I suspected he'd bought one of those bloated monstrosities that had sprung up around town lately, too large for the lot it sat on, pretentious and tasteless, crowding its neighbors like a gigantic toad on a small lily pad.

He shrugged his fleshy shoulders, straining the material of what looked like a custom-tailored suit. "What's to tell? It's on Rum Row."

I nodded, pretending to be cool while my heart did flipflops. Rum Row also known as Multimillionaire's Row, was a winding, shade-filled street in Port Royal, Naples's most affluent section. Built thirty or forty year ago, the houses there were low-pitched, elegant structures that exuded understated, old-money grace and charm.

I'd kill to design the interior of one of those babies and eyed Francesco carefully. Had I misjudged him? Was he really a wife beater and a thug or merely crass? I gave a mental shrug. I had no proof of either one, and besides, judging Francesco wasn't my job. Interior design was, and dangling in front of my eyes like a luscious carrot was the chance to redecorate a whole, elegant house.

"An interesting proposition, Mr. Grandese," I said.

"Call me Francesco. I'll call you Deva, okay?"

"Of course."

"So you want to take a look at the place?"

"I'd love to, ah, Francesco. But I'm curious. Why have you chosen Deva Dunne Interiors?"

"I didn't choose you yet," he said.

Chalk one up for Francesco. "True. Excuse me."

He waved a hand, dismissing my apology. "It's okay. I'll answer you. Any broad…woman…who gets out of an exploding building alive and goes to work the next day has guts. I like that in a female."

Ha!

"I also figure you started a business, so you know what you're doing." He glanced leisurely around. "I like the looks of your store. You got taste. Class. And that's what I want." He held up two fingers. "Taste and class."

Emboldened, or maybe feeling she'd been quiet long enough, Jewels ventured, "I love these table skirts. I had a prom gown like that once. I like the bunny figurines too."

Francesco pointed to them. "These guys, Jewels?"

Her eyes shining, she nodded, a little girl who senses a treat coming.

"We'll take one in every color," he said to me. Without attempting to lower his voice, he added, "Whatever else you do, don't listen to Jewels. I don't want her doing any decorating. She's not a decorator. She *is* the decoration. You get my meaning?"

He'd wrecked his sweet gesture with an insult but, remaining cool, not letting him see what a prick I thought he was, I opened my appointment book. "I'm free after five."

"No, too late. Let's go now. Donny's out there waiting."

Get in a car with a total stranger whose chauffeur was built like Jesse Ventura?

"Sorry, Francesco," I said. "My shop doesn't close until five."

He rubbed his jaw and frowned. "Too bad. I'm waiting on a call. It comes through, I'll be heading to the East Coast in a couple hours. Got business in South Beach. Maybe you didn't understand me." He let go of his jaw and pointed to the Herend collection. "I didn't come here just for rabbits. I want a whole house redone." He shrugged, straining the suit jacket again. "Like I told Jewels, I got no time to waste. So? You want to look at the job or not?"

I tapped my toe and frowned, pretending I had trouble deciding. The truth was he'd just won round two, but if I refused, I'd lose the job before I even landed it. I had to cut my losses—either cave or lose. So I caved. This time. But no way was I getting in that limo.

"Very well," I said. "Since time is so tight for you, I'll close up shop for a while."

"Good. Now how much for the Herends?"

He knew the name of the porcelain maker? That was a surprise. "Give me a minute to wrap them for Mrs. Grandese, then I'll add up the total."

Jewels helped by carrying her favorites to the sales desk. I cocooned each one in tissue and placed them in one of my special DDI gift bags—white glossy stock with Winthrop green handles and monogram. Francesco paid me in cash and in no time at all we were good to go.

"I'll follow you in my car," I said, taking out my keys. "The address is?"

He opened his mouth as if to protest, but for some reason didn't. "Two fifty Rum Row. We'll be waiting."

Why did that sound like a threat? I grabbed my purse and fished for the cell. I was probably being silly and a little jumpy from the explosion, but still I'd leave the address on Rossi's voice mail.

Just in case.

FOUR

A HALF HOUR later I had fallen madly in love.

Francesco owned my dream house. One of those white-timbered James River designs from the Virginia Low Country. A gracious distance from the street, its slate roof shaded by giant live oaks draped with Spanish moss, the house nestled on its spacious lot like a baby in his mother's arms.

I forgot all about my aches and bruises and hurriedly parked the Audi. The limo slowed to a stop ahead of me and Donny-The-Door-Opener hurried to do his thing.

"A fantastic property, Francesco," I enthused as he climbed out of the back seat.

"You gotta see the inside," he said.

"I can't wait."

While Donny slid behind the wheel and drew the limo onto the side driveway, Francesco removed a key from his pocket and strode up the brick walk. Julieta followed him, clattering along on gladiator sandals with five-inch heels that set off her super mini to perfection.

Heart pounding a little faster than normal, I brought up the rear. After a few moments of difficulty with the key and a muttered "Something else needs fixing," Francesco unlocked the door and with a surprisingly gallant sweep of his arm said, "Have a look."

I took a few steps into the foyer, glanced around and gasped. My dream house had turned into a nightmare. With my teeth on edge and the Grandeses trailing me, I silently toured all the empty, gaudy rooms. Every one had been painted a different high-gloss color. Pink, violet, orange, green, blue, yellow.

When we hit the lilac kitchen, I whirled around to Francesco. "Who did this?"

"The jerk I bought the place from," he said, waving his arms. "Can you believe the guy? No taste. No class. It looks like a goddamn kindergarten in here."

"I kind of like it," Julieta offered.

"See what I mean?" Francesco asked me, shaking his head. "Two years in Rhode Island Junior College and for what? That's why I tell her no comments."

"Oh, Frannie," she said and giggled.

Back in the living room, head whirling from the visual overload, I said, "I think I can guess what the previous owner had in mind. Just a theory but it seems to fit."

"Yeah?" Francesco looked skeptical but ready to listen.

"The rooms are all painted in preppy colors."

"Preppy?" Francesco's brows meshed together.

"You know, the colors prep school grads wear."

"I heard of them, but nobody on Federal Hill—that's in Rhode Island," he explained, "would be caught dead in them."

"Everybody wears jeans there. Or black," Jewels said. "Black doesn't show the dirt. And it goes with everything."

"Everything being your other pair of jeans," Francesco retorted with a smirk.

"If you're lucky," Jewels added, looking serious all of a sudden.

"Well, anyway," I said, bringing the conversation back to the house, "I don't think these vivid colors are accidental."

"What's your point?" Francesco asked, looking like he really wanted to know.

· "Whoever painted the walls this way may have been tying in to an old tradition."

"Which is?"

"Royalty. Centuries ago noblemen used darker versions of these pinks and greens and blues on their shields and flags. Paints and dyes were luxuries, so the colors were a status symbol. A lot of people still believe certain colors are." I turned to Julieta. "In clothes, think Lilly Pulitzer."

"Who?"

But Francesco got the point. "So the previous owner thought he was tapping into a high-society look with this mess?"

I shrugged. "Just guessing, but could be. People still buy in to the preppy look. Especially on the East Coast."

Francesco looked at me with a newfound respect. "The guy I bought the house from? He told me he went to Yale. Almost the first words out of his mouth." He shook his head. "Go figure. It's enough to make me gag."

"Me too." Francesco and I were on the same page. "No question, the interior is deplorable. But fixable. In fact, the house has tremendous potential," I added, heading into designer mode—partly creative, partly psychological, one-hundred-percent sales pitch.

"I'm listening."

"High ceilings, well-proportioned rooms, fabulous moldings, and a floor plan that *flows*. Paint errors are the easiest to correct. You could have a showstopper here."

I meant it too. U-shaped, the house opened with a spacious central foyer that led to a living room and beyond to a terrace and pool. The right wing held a study with a working fireplace, a powder room and a master bedroom suite. The left wing a dining room, combined kitchen and family room and, in back of that, two guest bedrooms and baths. This was my favorite layout in the whole world. Restoring it would be a labor of love as well as a risk. With a chauffeur who looked like a bouncer, and a wife who looked like a stripper, no telling what Francesco would want me to do with the place.

I blew out a breath and told myself to relax. He hated the current appearance of the house as much as I did, and had seen past its flaws to its hidden possibilities. And since when couldn't I convince a client of the soundness of my ideas? *Right.*

"Francesco," I said, "I'd love, *love*, to work on this house."

"I thought so."

So okay, he was a little lacking in the finesse department.

"How soon can you get started?"

Finesse wasn't everything.

"Tomorrow. I work with an excellent painting contractor. Once these walls are a base white—and that may take more than one coat—it will be easier to make other decisions." I cleared my throat. "What we do, of course, depends on your budget. New bathrooms and a new kitchen will add considerably to the cost. And then there are furnishings and accessories."

"Money's not a problem."

"No," chirped Jewels, looking happy about it. Who could blame her?

"I've already bought some stuff," Francesco said.

Uh-oh. "Stuff?"

"Yeah. Everything's in storage. I got pictures I can show you."

"Fine," I lied. What on earth had he bought? Whatever it was, I'd probably have to work with it, or at worse, around it. My enthusiasm dimming a bit, I said, "I'll have to let the painter in to measure the rooms and give me an estimate.

In the meanwhile, I'll draw up a layered proposal for what I believe needs to be done. For that, I—"

"No layers," Francesco said. "Give me the top estimate. Go for broke. Kitchen, baths, the works. I'll break the costs down myself."

Before I could ask, he reached into his pocket and removed a key. "You'll need this."

"As soon as I have the painter's estimate, I'll fax it to you."

Again, no need to ask, he reached into his jacket pocket, removed a business card with his thumb and a stubby forefinger and held it out to me.

The third reach into a pocket produced a silver money clip, very plain, very Tiffany. He peeled off a thousand dollars in hundred dollar bills and gave them to me. "To get you started. Who travels with checks anymore?"

"But you don't know my hourly rate."

He flashed me a toothy grin. "Whatever it is, you're worth it."

Men. Geesh. I thanked him and tucked the money in my purse.

"Tell the painter guy not to waste any time. Call me when he's done and have your proposal ready ASAP so I can see what you got in mind." He snapped his fingers at Jewels. "Let's go," he said, heading for the door.

She teetered after him, her high-pitched voice floating behind her. "Frannie, you're letting her paint all the walls white? The house'll look like a refrigerator."

"What did I tell you?" he said. "No comments."

I followed them out, locked up and drove back to Fern Alley. How I missed Lee St. James, my wonderful shop assistant. Six months ago, when she and her husband left for New York, I hadn't had the heart to look for a replacement. Though I needed to and soon. Closing shop midday was poor policy, but I clung to the hope Lee would return to Naples after her husband finished his stint at the Art Students League.

The painting contractor I gave all my business to, Tom Kruse—it sounded the same, but no, he wasn't *the* Tom Cruise—answered on the first ring. "Good timing, Deva," he said after I told him why I'd called. "I'm finishing up a job nearby, on Whiskey Lane. I'll phone you tomorrow as soon as we're through."

Good. I'd have something positive to tell Francesco. And maybe by tomorrow I'd feel up to staying in the Rum Road house long enough to do some in-depth planning for that top-of-the-line proposal he wanted.

Now all *I* wanted was to sit still, not think, not move. I sat down at the *bureau plat* and lay my head on the top. I must have dozed off. When the antique Yarmouthport bells on the shop door jangled, I came to with a start.

Jerking to attention, I sat up, pretending to be wide awake.

"Hi, welcome," I murmured sleepily.

A slim young blonde in skin-tight jeans and a butterfly top hovered in the doorway. That hesitancy was familiar. Some people weren't comfortable around interior designers, fearing they'd be talked into bizarre-looking rooms they didn't want.

"Come in," I urged.

She stepped inside and slowly approached the desk, her expression changing from uncertainty to shocked surprise. "You've been hurt?"

I nodded. "An accident."

"Oh, I'm so sorry."

She didn't mention the explosion. Maybe she hadn't

heard about it, though if she lived in Naples it must be under a rock. "How may I help you?" I asked.

"I'm hoping you can find someone for me. A man, actually."

"Well, I don't know—"

"He came into your shop earlier today. I saw him."

Francesco.

"His name is Francesco Grandese. Can you tell me how to reach him?" Her lower lip trembled, and she caught it with her teeth.

I shook my head. "Sorry, a client's address is privileged information. But the police might be able to help."

She shook her head so hard her hair whipped around her cheeks. "No, this isn't a police matter. It's personal."

She bent over and rested her palms on the desktop, trapping me in place. "Please. This is important. He was staying at the Inn on Fifth. You know, the one across the street."

"Yes," I said, wondering how she'd found out. Had she been stalking him?

"But when I asked for Mr. Grandese, they told me he'd just checked out. Then I got lucky and saw him leave the hotel in a limo and drive to your shop. That took me by surprise. He's usually in a Ferrari. But before I could get back with everything…" her voice trailed off, "…he was gone. And I've got to see him. It's urgent."

Whatever bothered this girl caused her voice to rise a little higher with every word. Speaking softly to give off calm vibes I didn't feel, I said, "Why don't you have a seat, Miss, ah…?"

"Mimi." She backed off, though I could tell she didn't want to, and perched on the edge of the zebra settee across from my desk. "So can you help me?"

"What I can do is take your name and number and let my client know you're trying to reach him."

She half rose then thought better of it and slumped back. "No, that won't work."

The desperation in Mimi's eyes made me uneasy. I pushed my chair away from the desk and stood. "Then I'm afraid I can't help you. Now if you'll excuse me."

"Will you be seeing Francesco again?" she asked, ignoring the hint to leave.

Not wanting to lie, but worried about where this was heading, I gave her a noncommittal, "I may."

"That will have to do. Be right back."

She sprang off the settee and hurried out of the shop. I was tempted to lock the door behind her but didn't. That was no way to run a business. Still, I felt so drained, I'd close up early and drop in at the hospital to see Chip while I still had the pep to do so. Before I could snap off the overheads, the Yarmouthport sleigh bells jingled again. Mimi walked in carrying a basket covered with a crocheted shawl and carefully placed it on the shop floor.

"What's this?" I asked, pointing to the basket.

"Something for Francesco. Tell him I'd like to keep it, but I can't. It's all his."

"Wait a minute," I said, but she hurried out of the shop, quietly closed the door behind her and ran down the alley.

Strange. I eyed the basket warily. Was this a joke? Or worse, something that would blow up in my face and destroy the shop and everything in it? I didn't know whether to dash outside with my cell and call 911, or contact Rossi, or remove the shawl and see what it concealed. As I stood there trying to decide, the basket moved. It moved again. And yet again.

Frozen in place, as indecisive as ice, I nearly leaped out of my skin when a cry split the air. An unmistakable cry.

An I-want-a-bottle cry. An I-want-a-diaper-change cry. An I-want-to-be-held-and-loved-and-cuddled cry.

I leaned over and snatched the blue shawl off the basket. An outraged baby with big dark eyes and chubby cheeks looked up at me, kicking his legs and arms and howling his head off.

FIVE

Too stunned to move, I stared at the screaming baby. Then I glanced over at the door. It hadn't completely swung closed after Mimi's exit. I patted the edge of the basket and said, "Be right back. I mean it. Just a sec."

I raced outside the shop and scanned the alley, up, down, left, right. Not a person anywhere. Only the boxwood sentinels on either side of my shop entrance and the eye-catching balloons bouncing outside Off Shoots, the boutique next door. Why was I not surprised?

I hurried back inside, my heart pounding, and bent over the still screaming baby. He was dressed in blue pajamas with little white whales and lying on a blue pillow, covered with a blue blanket. The odor of baby powder and baby poop mingled in the air.

"I'm just taking a wild guess here, but I'll bet your name is Francesco." I touched one finger to his tummy. If anything, he howled even louder. I needed to call the police, but they'd never hear me over the screaming.

"You want a bottle?"

Howl.

"How about clean pants?"

A canvas bag was tucked into the side of the basket. I opened it. Sure enough. Pampers and two full bottles of what looked like formula.

"Okay, but it's just you and me, Francesco," I murmured, hoping the sound of my voice would calm him down. "I can't even call for help till you stop screaming."

I lifted him out of the basket and held his small, warm body against my shoulder. Amazing how natural that felt. My late husband and I hadn't had children, a regret I'd carry with me forever. Jack would have been such a wonderful father...and I would have had his child to remember him by. A little boy maybe, with my freckles and Jack's mischievous grin, his... But what was the use in torturing myself over something that would never be?

With one hand, I spread the shawl on the *bureau plat* and laid the baby on it. "You're a stinkapottamus, little guy." *I guess.* "If I smelled that bad, I'd yell too." I tugged off the sodden diaper—yup, a boy—and dropped it on the floor. He kicked and twisted. I held him still with one hand, wishing I'd taken some tissues or paper towels from the powder room before starting this procedure. I couldn't leave him now or he'd roll off.

A yellow arc suddenly spurted up and, with diabolical accuracy, hit me right in the chest.

"Oh hell," I whispered and grabbing a handful of monogrammed napkins, I swiped at my shirt, then grabbed more and wiped the baby clean.

He didn't appreciate any of it. His chubby face turned red, and if anything he wailed even louder. "This is my very first time changing a diaper, darling, so be kind. And just so you'll know, it's the first time I've ever been urinated on too." He ignored me and kept screaming until I rewrapped him in the blanket and popped a bottle in his mouth.

While eyeing me suspiciously, he sucked on the nipple with gusto, and I sank onto the desk chair with him in my arms. Now that it was possible to hear another human voice, I dialed Rossi's number.

"Rossi," he said, still sounding gravelly.

"I'm in trouble," I told him.

"What's wrong?"

"A baby. That's what's wrong."

A crash echoed through the line, like maybe he stood up too fast and his chair flipped over. "Did you say baby?"

"'Fraid so. I don't have time to explain but it's kind of a foundling-on-the-doorstep story. Want to come to the shop? I could use your help, but don't bring a squad of police cars. Now I have to hang up and call Francesco before he leaves town."

"Who's Francesco?"

"The baby's father."

I hung up and, not wanting to disturb little Frannie to reach big Frannie, I searched in my purse for his business card using only one hand. The maneuver took a while, but I found the card and to my relief it listed his cell phone and business numbers as well as the fact that Francesco P. Grandese was a real estate developer. Interesting. I punched in the cell number, was put on hold and sat through a few bars of "Nessun Dorma" before he answered.

"This is Deva Dunne," I said.

"You're a lot faster than I thought you'd be."

"I've got something that belongs to you."

"Yeah? What's that?"

"Your son."

His gasp sucked all the air out of the connection. "Is this a gag?"

"I'm not laughing. You'd better get over here, pronto. I've already notified the police."

IN TEN MINUTES, no more, the limo pulled up outside the shop. Francesco raced for the door so fast Donny didn't have a chance to go for it. At least I'd had the presence of mind to prop the Closed sign in the front window and remove the sleigh bells. Back in the basket, wrapped in the blue shawl, the baby slept like an angel. Poor little guy, he needed to rest, and I didn't want him disturbed. The realization surprised me. Though I'd only known him for a handful of minutes, here I was acting like a mother bear with her cub. Why the surge of maternal feeling? Strange. Very strange.

In the bag, along with Pampers and formula, I'd found a birth certificate. I waved it in the air as Francesco barged in.

"This says you're the father," I announced.

"Oh, yeah? According to who?"

I consulted the paper. "A Mimi Smith."

Averting his eyes, he looked out the window. "Never heard of her."

"She named him after you."

Francesco snatched the certificate out of my hand and eyeballed it. "I paid her off," he howled. *Yelling must run in the family.* "Almost a year ago. She said there wouldn't be any kid."

I pointed to the angel. "She lied, Francesco. She lied. She left you a note too." I plucked the envelope off my desk and handed it to him. He ran a stubby finger under the flap, tore it open and scanned the message.

"She's giving me full custody. Her new boyfriend don't like kids. What kinda animal is that?" He sank onto the settee like his options were either sit down or fall down. "Now what?"

"You're asking *me?*"

The shop door opened quietly and Jewels slipped in. "I got tired of waiting. Oooh," she cooed as she spotted the angel. "I didn't know you had a baby."

"I don't." I upped my chin at Francesco. "He does."

Francesco groaned and slapped a hand to his forehead.

Jewels's eyes widened, two shocked brown pools. "What does she mean?"

Gladiator sandal tapping the floor, arms crossed over her sculpted chest, she waited for his reply. "Well?" she said after a long, silent pause. Clearly she wasn't going to be put off. She wanted an answer and she wanted one *now.* Maybe for the first time in their relationship Jewels had the upper hand, and, intrigued, I watched to see how she would play it.

Francesco had slumped as far back as the stiff zebra skin settee allowed. If it were bigger, I think he would have stretched out flat. "Mimi was a mistake," he began. "We were over before you and I got hitched."

The tapping got louder.

"Over. I swear." He pointed to the baby. "I had no idea or I would've insisted—"

"On what?" A challenge from Jewels. Gentle, but a challenge nonetheless. "You don't like kids?"

"I don't know any." He shrugged. "How can I tell?"

Jewels knelt next to the basket and gazed at the sleeping infant. "A baby's a miracle. You know that?" She stroked the soft brown fuzz on his head then tore her gaze away from him for a second to give Francesco a big-eyed stare. "He's beautiful. He looks just like you."

Francesco struggled off the settee and bent over the basket for a closer look. "You think so?"

She nodded and smiled.

Probably in a last-ditch effort to deny the little reality in blue, Francesco threw his hands in the air and said, "Who knows? Maybe he's not mine. Where's the proof? I'll have them run a DNA. You know, a paternity test."

She turned back to the baby. "If you want to. But whatever it says, let's keep him anyway. I love babies. I would take good care of him and love him because he's yours."

"You would?"

She smiled. "If you let me."

"*Let* you? You won't hit me with divorce papers?"

Jewels swiveled around to look up at him, her eyes luminous with unshed tears. "No, of course not. I'm thrilled. Our little girl has a big brother."

"Our little *what?*" Francesco's swarthy complexion looked decidedly pale.

"I've been afraid to tell you." She rocked back on her heels. "I'm pregnant. Four months. She's a girl."

"I gotta sit down again," Francesco said, slumping back on the zebra skin. "Two kids in one day."

Jewels got up from the floor and sat beside her husband. She put an arm around his shoulder. "You're a daddy," she said, "and I'm a momma. So now there's something you should know."

"Jeez, something else. I can't take any more." He lowered his head to his hands.

Unperturbed, she continued. "I don't mind not commenting on the house." She nodded in my direction. "Do anything you like with the inside. But when it comes to the children," she paused, letting the word sink in, "don't ever tell me not to comment."

He stared at her for a moment then looked in the basket.

"Deal!" he shouted, pulling her onto his lap and squeezing her tight. His shout awakened the baby, who promptly started yelling.

Francesco beamed with paternal pride. "He's a screamer. I like that. In this world, a man's gotta make his wishes known. You know something else?" he said, looking over at me. "Those preppy colors you mentioned?"

"Yes?"

"Put 'em in two of the bedrooms, okay?"

"A pink and a blue?"

"You got it. My kids deserve the royal treatment." He raised a warning finger. "In those two rooms only. No high gloss finishes. And as long as we're talking decorating—" he patted the settee seat, "—don't put one of these racks in the house. It's killing my back."

"Not to worry, Francesco. Right now you have a bigger problem. There's only one bottle of formula left, and you're out of diapers."

JEWELS HAD ALREADY rocked little Frannie calm and quiet when Rossi finally pulled up in the old Mustang he used on the job.

"Where have you been?" I asked him *sotto voce.*

I don't think he heard. He stared at Francesco like he couldn't believe his eyes. "Well, well. Mr. Grandese in the flesh."

"You two *know* each other?" I asked.

"We've met," Rossi said. "So can I assume you're the child's father Deva mentioned on the phone?"

Francesco looked at me and frowned. "I forgot you called the cops."

"I had to."

He patted me on the back. "Sure. I understand. My son needed protection."

"Exactly." I turned to Rossi. "How did you two meet?"

He went all professional on me. I hated it when he did that. "This is an ongoing investigation. No comment."

No comment? "You too?" I asked.

"What do you mean, me too?" His forehead creased, meshing together what was left of his scorched eyebrows.

"Maybe the lieutenant can't comment, Deva," Jewels said, cuddling little Frannie to her breasts, a move that even had Rossi fascinated. "But I can."

I was looking at a newly liberated woman. What a wonderful sight.

"Detective Rossi impounded what was left of my husband's car. Impounded, that's the word, isn't it, Frannie?"

"Yeah, that's the one. They're saying my Ferrari caused the explosion."

SIX

As soon as Francesco and Jewels left the shop with little Frannie, I didn't waste any time quizzing Rossi.

"I nearly died in that explosion. I deserve to know the truth. Is Francesco involved?"

A slight hesitation crept into his eyes. I could tell he was carefully weighing what he could and couldn't say. Finally, he threw me a crumb.

"Technically, yes. And no. Grandese wasn't present at the time, and right now we don't know what set off the blast. Or why the Ferrari was parked at the back entrance with the motor running. Grandese said he sent his chauffeur to pick up some takeout food. Could be. We just don't know. But this Donny character was around the building having a smoke when it happened. He has a rap sheet as long as my arm." Rossi shrugged. "The situation is under investigation."

"Is that all you can tell me?" I asked, hands on hips shrew fashion.

"Yes. Until we know if we're dealing with arson or an accident."

"What's your gut feeling?"

He waggled a finger under my nose. "I have no intention of telling you. Furthermore, gut reactions don't solve crimes. Science and practical application do."

"So you *do* think a crime's been committed?"

"I didn't say that."

"Come on, Rossi. If you can't trust me, whom can you trust?"

He hesitated. Again he was weighing his answer.

"You have to *think* about it?" I asked, on the cusp of being seriously miffed.

"No, that's not it. I trust you implicitly. It's Mr. Grandese who's the problem."

"That's bad news. He's bought a house on Rum Row and wants me to redo the interior. The entire place. Soup to nuts." I sighed. "It's a plum of an offer, but not if I'm dealing with a criminal."

"Right. At the moment we have no reason to believe he is, but my advice is stay away from him. Play it safe. For me, if not for yourself."

"Not fair. Not fair at all. You know I need this job."

Eyes snapping fire, he shook his head. "You're what matters. Not the job."

"But you're not sure he's done anything wrong."

"True. We'll know more tomorrow when the arson squad turns in its report. After I see that, if there's a reason to notify you, I will. Immediately."

Only partly relieved, I sank onto the settee. "I hope to heaven you won't have to. But who knows? The man's such a contradiction. He talks like a thug, his wife looks like a pole dancer, and now you tell me his chauffeur's done time. On the plus side, he paid me a generous retainer, in cash I might add, no questions asked. Didn't even mention needing a receipt."

Rossi treated me to an eyebrow lift. Or what would have been one under normal circumstances.

I eyebrowed him right back. "I gave him a receipt anyway. And he has excellent taste—at least in architecture. Though that stuff he bought remains to be seen."

"What stuff?"

"I don't know yet. Furniture. Accessories." I laughed. "I hope it's childproof." I patted the seat. "Come sit beside me." He did and I snuggled next to him, breathing in his woodsy aftershave. "You like babies?"

"Absolutely."

"Me too. Holding that baby felt right somehow. I never held one before. Can you believe that? Never." Tears pricked at my eyelids.

In the next instant I was in Rossi's arms, my head resting on his chest, my tears soaking into a sunset scene of Waikiki Beach.

"Sorry," I blubbered. "I don't know what's got into me."

"Cry it out, sweetheart," he said softly. "You've been through a lot these past few days."

"Yes, I have," I said, trying not to sniffle. "And before today I never knew how much I liked babies."

He tensed and, putting a finger under my chin, gently raised my face until I was drowning in those eyes that were as black and shiny as sin. "Will you tell me something?"

He sure wasn't after what topping I liked on my pizza, so I just nodded, trying to ignore the sudden knot in my stomach.

"You and Jack never had a child, did you?"

"No," I whispered.

"Can you tell me why?"

He had a certain right to ask, and on some level I had been expecting this question for months. A mirror on the far wall threw back my purple and yellow reflection. I winced and stared down at my hands. I could tell Rossi anything. Still, I held back.

"Was there a problem?" A patient man, a patient detective, he waited for my answer.

I inhaled a deep breath and let it out slowly before trusting myself to speak. "At first, for a year or so, we had each other, and that's all we needed or wanted."

If Rossi flinched at hearing this, he didn't let on. He already knew how much I'd loved Jack and how when he died, I thought my life had died with him.

"Go on," he urged softly.

"Later, when we tried to have a child, nothing happened. We knew we needed to find out why. Jack offered to be tested first. I'll never forget the day he learned the results. No need for me to go through a barrage of fertility exams, he said. He was the problem. I couldn't believe that at first. Jack was always so, so—"

Not wanting to shed more tears, I stopped speaking for a moment to catch my breath and let the memories settle before going on.

"You're only thirty-three. If a child is what you want, you'll find a way to have one. And someone to have one with. It won't be Jack's—" Rossi's turn to pause and see how this struck me, "—but it will be yours. I have no doubt that will happen someday when you're ready for it."

He stood and held out his arms. I walked into them and he drew me close. "You'll make a wonderful mother," he murmured into my hair. "You're so giving, so warm, so beautiful."

His words and, even more, the tone of his voice turned me to mush. I leaned back a little in his arms to peer up at him. "Beautiful? I'm purple and yellow, and the bruise on my thigh is turning that funny absinthe green."

He let go of me with one hand and put a finger on my lips. "Shhhh. You are everything I say you are."

"Aww, Rossi…"

He held me at arm's length and gazed into my face. "Better now?"

"Yes. I loved what you just said to me."

Perhaps someday I would have a child after all. It wasn't too late. That little boy with red hair I'd fantasized about. Or a girl with Latin eyes. Or both. Anything was possible, and for the first time in days I felt like laughing. For years I hadn't given babies much thought, had pushed the possibility of a child to the furthest edges of my mind as being out of the realm of possibility. But now not so.

I gave Rossi a quick hug. "Let me total up the day's receipts, and then I'll be good to go."

Although Jack had been the one with the problem, maybe I'd go to be tested anyway. Just out of curiosity if nothing else.

SEVEN

WHILE ROSSI CHECKED his cell phone messages, I added the day's receipts and put the bank's leatherette deposit bag in my purse. On our way to see Chip, we could swing by SunTrust and I'd drop the bag in the overnight box.

Stress lines etching his forehead, Rossi pocketed his cell. I grabbed my purse, ready to lock up.

"Sorry, sweetheart, a change in plans. I have to get back to the station."

"Oh, no." I groaned. "What about our visit to Chip?"

"If I can, I'll drop in at the hospital later. But why don't you go home? Have a glass of wine. Relax." His hands stroked my arms. I closed my eyes, savoring the touch of his fingers on my bare skin and his whispered, "So smooth." He bent down and kissed my upper arm. "How about it? After the week you've had, you deserve to fall asleep watching TV."

"Very funny." I huffed out a sigh. "But I think you're right." I couldn't remember ever being so tired. An effortless evening suddenly seemed perfect.

"Good." He walked me out to my car. "See you tomorrow. Sleep tight." A quick kiss and he was gone. No point in complaining. That was life with a detective. Take it or leave it. And leaving it wasn't an option I was considering.

As soon as I got home, I kicked off the heels, dropped the tote on the foyer tiles and called the hospital. The volunteer at patient information took Chip's name, and I waited while she checked the computer. After a lengthy pause, she came back on the line. "We have no patient by the name of Chip Salvatore."

"Are you sure? Please check again."

Another pause.

"We have no one listed by that name."

Something was wrong. "Can you connect me with the second-floor charge desk?"

"Just a moment, please."

A crisp voice picked up. "Nurse Reynolds."

"This is Deva Dunne. I'm calling about Mr. Salvatore."

"I'm sorry, I can't give out—"

"We met yesterday, Nurse Reynolds. I was with Detective Rossi of the Naples PD."

"Oh, yes," she said, as curt as ever.

"Could you please give Mr. Salvatore a message for me?"

"No, I can't. He isn't here."

My heart skidded to a near stop. "He didn't die, did he?"

"No, no. He's been discharged."

"But yesterday he could hardly breathe."

"I know." Nurse Reynolds's voice took on a chilly edge. "He left without his doctor's approval."

"Whatever possessed him to do that?"

"I have no idea."

"Did he leave alone?"

"No, with a woman, an AudreyAnn something. Let me check. His file's here somewhere. Yes, here it is, an AudreyAnn Baranski."

"You're kidding."

"I'm sorry that's all the information I have. I hope the police find it helpful."

The police? Before I could explain I wasn't with the police, the phone went dead.

I turned off my cell and slumped on the sofa. Audrey-Ann. Good grief.

Chip owned the condo next to mine in the Surfside Condominiums. Until about six months ago, when she moved out, AudreyAnn had been his live-in love. Chip, the big teddy bear, adored her. I suspect her traffic-stopping double Ds were a major part of her allure. Actually, they'd probably be soft if poked with a finger, which was a good thing because the rest of her was tough as a two dollar steak.

Despite the double Ds, Chip had to be a masochist to put up with AudreyAnn's mood swings. Up occasionally, down on a daily basis. So while she lived next door, my friendship with him had been spotty at best. How can you be friends with a loveable Shrek when his Fiona is a bitch?

Though for sure, he hadn't seen her that way. To fill the crater-sized void she left in his life, he'd thrown himself into starting up his new restaurant, a lifelong dream that had turned to ashes. Literally.

I let out a groan of pure frustration. Pushy in more ways than one, AudreyAnn was now back in both Chip's life and mine.

On the plus side, though I wasn't happy she'd returned, Chip probably was. And that was what mattered. I also wasn't happy that she'd checked him out of the hospital so soon. Still, a hospital wasn't a prison. He had every right to leave if he wanted to. He hadn't broken any law.

One thing for certain, tired though I was, I wouldn't rest tonight until I knew he was okay. So when the lanai slider next door slid open with a familiar *thunk,* the time had come to pay a call. I forced myself off the sofa and went over to ring their doorbell.

AudreyAnn answered the buzzer in a drift of Tabu. She had on her favorite pink T-shirt, the one with *carpe diem* emblazoned on the chest in red letters. Above it, she also wore her usual sullen expression, though truth be told, most people's eyes wouldn't get high enough to notice.

I cut to the chase. "How's the patient?"

"He's asleep."

"With or without the oxygen tank?"

AudreyAnn raised her chin, pointing it at me as if it were a cocked gun. "You a nurse or something?"

"He's my friend. I'm worried about him."

She folded her arms under her breasts. With a shelf to sit on, they ballooned out like flotation devices. "His doctor took him off oxygen this morning. He's breathing a little raspy, but I'll be next to him all night listening."

"That's very reassuring, AudreyAnn. If you need me, give me a call."

"Will do." She closed the door with a snap, and I knew I'd be making ice cubes in hell before I heard from her.

Back in my place I finally poured that wine, wondering why AudreyAnn had come back. Love? *Hmm.* Money? *Double hmm.* With the restaurant in shambles, Chip had financial problems looming on his horizon.

I glanced at the clock. After eight. Rossi must have dropped in at the hospital by now and would know Chip had left. But he hadn't called to tell me so. A half hour later, I wouldn't have heard the phone ring if he did call. I'd fallen asleep like the proverbial rock and stayed asleep until my morning alarm jangled me awake.

The next morning, bright and rested, I drove to work on a day balmy enough to send the palm fronds into a lazy fan dance. On the edge of the highway, hibiscus shrubs sported pink blossoms the size of pecan pies. The show-offs. I loved watching Mother Nature strut her stuff in this gorgeous tropical place, and today the beauty everywhere made me feel fabulous.

Deep inside my purse the cell phone chirped. I pulled over to the edge of Tamiami Trail, dumped the bag's contents on the passenger seat, and grabbed the cell on the fourth chirp. *Rossi.* My heart pounding out a salsa beat, I hit Talk. I hoped he was calling to tell me Grandese was in the clear or…oh, I was just plain glad he was calling, no matter what he had to say.

I went for the clever opening. "Good morning, Rossi."

He plunged right into his message with no verbal foreplay. Not a good sign. The news must be bad. "I have the results of that report you were wondering about."

The breath caught in my throat. "Please tell me it wasn't arson."

"No, apparently not. The propane truck sprang a leak. One spark is all it took. We're calling it an accident."

Though Rossi didn't sound happy giving me the news, relief rolled over me like an ocean wave. "Thanks for letting me know, I'm so—"

"There's more."

Uh-oh. "Good or bad?"

"I'm not sure. A Francesco Grandese is the owner of the building."

"*My* Francesco? What does that mean, exactly?"

"I'm not sure." A chill wind blew through the line. "Though there's nothing sinister about buying a building."

"No, I suppose not." But somehow the information didn't make me happy.

"Sorry to hang up on you, sweetheart, but I have to go. I'm meeting Chip at what's left of the restaurant. He wants to see the damage."

"I'll join you there," I said, signing off before he could protest.

The shop wouldn't open at nine today, but this was more important. I'd been avoiding the La Cucina site since the explosion. Time I checked it out. If a new restaurant were possible, I'd be happy to work with Chip again.

On Fifth Avenue, plywood panels covered the entire front of the building. I pulled around to the rear service entrance and saw much the same, plywood and a rickety padlocked door nailed onto what remained of the back wall.

Chip had arrived first, with AudreyAnn in tow to my dismay, but at least she'd helped him by doing the driving. As Rossi drove up in his dusty Mustang, Chip slowly climbed out of the Taurus's passenger seat. Pale and coughing, he stood leaning on the car until AudreyAnn came around to grip his arm. He was plainly determined to see the damage to the building no matter what it cost him physically.

When I exited the Audi, they both looked surprised to see me. Rossi simply smiled a glad-to-see-you kind of smile. For a brief moment, it lifted the strain from his face. I was getting good at reading him, and my vibes told me he had more on his mind than he'd revealed. *Hmm.*

Ignoring AudreyAnn's "What are *you* doing here?" I hurried over to give Chip a kiss and a hug. Then squaring my shoulders, I strode to where Rossi waited for us by the padlocked door. I wasn't some tourist trying to satisfy idle curiosity. The explosion had tossed me around like a beanbag. I'd earned the right to be here.

Rossi reached into his pocket and withdrew a key with a cardboard ID tag dangling from it. "Be careful," he said, opening the squeaky door and leading us into a scene out of Armageddon.

EIGHT

THE BLACKENED KITCHEN looked as if a giant had reached down in a fit of rage and flung its contents about the room. Tables, stools, pots, pans, dishes, chairs were smashed and scattered willy-nilly. Even the outsized stove had been shoved to one side, the oven doors hanging open, unrecognizable remnants of food still visible on its surface. Ripped from the piping, the utility sink lay smashed on the floor. Next to it sat a dented can. The label read Contadina Tomato Paste.

For Mama Luigi's Sunday Lasagna.

Over all, the odor of charred wood clogged the air like a barbeque gone terribly wrong. Chip's glance collided with mine before we both looked away. "I can't salvage a thing from here. Except maybe the food locker."

The stainless steel walk-in refrigerator appeared intact. Trying not to breathe deeply of the acrid air, I peered inside. It was empty. Someone had disposed of whatever food it once held.

"The kitchen got hit the hardest. You can thank that refrigerator for saving your life," Rossi said, obviously trying to strike a positive note. "And it sheltered the dining room from the worst of the damage."

He walked through an opening that once held swinging doors separating the work space from the public areas. "Be careful," he warned again as we trailed after him. "There's glass everywhere."

At least, with chunks of the roof blown away, we could

see where we were stepping. And like nearly all buildings in Florida, this one had no basement for us to fall into.

Moving gingerly, we followed Rossi into the restaurant dining room. The lovely appetite-enhancing colors were filthy, replaced with soot, stains and gouges. Two steps in, I trod on a photograph of Venice—St. Mark's Square at twilight—and wanted to weep. Chip and I had selected the photographs with such care. Except for one or two torn from their frames, I didn't see any of the others. This time, I didn't dare look Chip's way.

"Hello, hello! Anybody home?"

At the sudden loud voice, we all stiffened and turned toward the kitchen. Francesco and Donny strode in, their shoes crunching on the fallen glass.

"Remember us?" Francesco said, his booming voice echoing off the walls. Donny as usual was silent. A smart maneuver for a major player in this disaster.

"How did you know we were here?" Chip asked.

"I called the house earlier looking for you," Francesco said. "Ms. Baranski here told me you were coming over. I've been waiting to assess the situation, so I owe you one, Ms. Baranski."

"AudreyAnn, please," she said, sending a darting glance Donny's way.

Francesco nodded, his eyes focused on her chest. With a visible effort, he tore his glance away and turned to Rossi. "Now that arson's out of the picture, how about a key to that sorry excuse for a backdoor?"

"Of course. There's one at the station with your name on it. As for arson, it can't be proven one way or the other. That doesn't mean it didn't happen."

"What's that mean?"

"It means what I said it means." Rossi's jaw clenched.

Francesco grunted and looked around at the gutted

room. "Helluva mess in here." He pointed a finger at Chip. "We got some deciding to do."

Chip coughed and shook his head. "My deciding's done." Clinging to AudreyAnn with one hand, he waved the other around the room. "My insurance won't cover this. I'm wiped out."

I sneaked a peek at Donny. If he suffered from remorse, he concealed the fact well. As rigid as a cigar store Indian, he didn't twitch a muscle.

Still holding tight to AudreyAnn, Chip eased over to the bar. "Even the liquor stock's gone. And I bought the best. What a waste."

"Not entirely. Look at this!" On a shelf behind the bar near where the cash register once stood, I spied an intact bottle of Dom Perignon. "It's an omen. For toasting your new restaurant."

He shook his head. "No way, Deva, but at least this looks okay." He ran his hands lovingly over the stainless steel surface of the espresso machine. "Should be, it's a DeLonghi Gran from Italy. Built like a tank. I paid over three grand for it."

"The water line's severed, but otherwise it looks un-damaged," Rossi said. "The food locker's on the other side of this wall. That must have protected it from the worst of the blast."

Glumly, Chip nodded.

"You want me to carry it out to the car?" Rossi asked.

"Why? For a souvenir?" A touch of bitterness crept into Chip's tone. Who could blame him? So far, he'd shown remarkable control, not even sending so much as a dirty look in Donny's direction. How like the big guy to fig-ure an accident's an accident. No one to blame but fate. Caught in the same situation, I'm not sure I would be so objective. So sweet.

Finally, his hands still caressing the DeLonghi, Chip said, "I might as well take it. AudreyAnn likes lattes. Right, honey?"

She gave him a shrug, and with that to go on, Chip pulled the machine's plug out of the paneling in back of the bar.

As he yanked on the connection, wood rubbed against wood, giving off an eerie creak, then with the plug still attached, a piece of the wall paneling fell away and clattered to the floor. The espresso maker nearly went with it, but I leaped forward, steadying it in the nick of time.

Peering over Chip's shoulder, I stared into the opening he'd just created. Light pouring down from overhead shone on the cinder blocks of the inner wall and on something else. Something that gleamed dully.

"Hey, what's this?" he asked, spotting the same gleam. He thrust a hand into the narrow cavity and lifted out a small steel box. A padlock hung from a flange on one side.

I didn't know what the box contained, but my pulse revved up nonetheless. Clearly, someone had hidden it in that wall cavity with care. And people don't usually hide useless trash in their walls.

Chip must have had the same thought. "We need a hammer," he said, wheezing badly.

"No such luck," Rossi said. "But there must be something around here we can use. Ah." He stooped and picked up a piece of twisted metal. Pointing his chin at the padlock, he said, "You want that off?"

Struggling for breath, Chip just nodded. Rossi hit the flange a few times, pounding until the padlock fell away. He stepped aside, and Chip raised the lid on the box. No one said a word as he lifted out an inner steel container and placed it on the shelf next to the espresso maker. This one wasn't locked, and slowly, as if afraid of what he might find, he opened the lid. We crowded in around him and, when that lid came off, the breath rushed out of us all in a collective *aaaaah*.

I thought Chip would faint. AudreyAnn held onto him on one side and Rossi moved in to take his other arm. "You need to sit down?"

"No, I'm all right." Coughing, wheezing, his hand shaking, Chip reached into the inner liner, removed a yellowed oilskin packet and laid it on the shelf. The image of President Grover Cleveland showed through the oilskin in that unmistakable, instantly recognizable shade of green. The one shade of green everybody loves.

No one said a word. There for a while, I don't think we were even inhaling, although we must have been. Donny's hot breath fluttered on the back of my neck. Chip loosened the packet and removed a fistful of money. He flipped through the bills. Every one featured an etching of President Cleveland. Every single one was a thousand-dollar bill.

Chip went weak in the knees, but AudreyAnn grabbed him before he could slide to the floor. He rallied, stood erect and reached into the packet again. He withdrew another handful of bills.

"Every one's a thousand," he whispered.

"Count 'em. Count 'em all," Francesco ordered.

Chip did, with amazing efficiency, stacking the bills on the rickety shelf in five neat piles. "Five hundred bills," he intoned at last. "That's five hundred thousand in cash. Half a million dollars."

This time AudreyAnn missed the catch. Chip passed out and slid to the floor.

Francesco stepped over him and shouldered his way to the money. "I own the building. That makes everything in it mine. I claim the cash."

AudreyAnn got down on her knees and massaged Chip's hands. "Come on, honey, wake up. Come on, honey."

Honey? He wouldn't know who she was talking to. I sniffed. Then my glance fell on one of the bills, and I inhaled a deep breath of the musty air. As every designer knows, the devil's in the details. And what a detail I'd just spotted!

"I don't think I've ever seen a thousand-dollar bill before. May I hold one?" I asked Rossi.

His hand on his cell phone, ready to call 911, he frowned. But I picked up the top bill anyway, and with my thumbnail on the issue date, held it up in front of Rossi. His eyes flared wide.

Before he could dial 911, Chip stirred. All those *honeys* must have reached him after all. With AudreyAnn's help, he sat up, a big grin on his face. "I'm fine now," he said. Obviously, he hadn't heard Francesco's pronouncement.

Rossi pocketed his cell and flipped through the bills before turning around to Francesco. "When did you buy this building?"

"Last year, why?"

"It looks like all these bills were issued in nineteen thirty-four. They may have been hidden here for decades."

"So?" Francesco challenged.

"So they could belong to a previous owner. The police have to be told and the money impounded until a legal owner is determined. If no one can prove a claim, the money will revert to the finder. In my opinion that's Mr. Salvatore here."

"Now wait a minute," Francesco began.

"Yeah," Donny interjected.

"No, you will wait, Mr. Grandese, for the law to decide. Now I intend to escort Mr. Salvatore to a bank. I'll ask that each of these bills be copied for police records, and I'll sign a witness statement testifying to the amount. After that, the money will be held in a safety deposit box until legal ownership is established. In the meantime both of you gentlemen may want to contact your lawyers."

Rossi stuffed the bills back in the oilskin packet and handed it to me.

"Is that wise?" Francesco asked, nodding at the oilskin.

"Yeah." Donny again.

"Yes," Rossi said, "it is." With AudreyAnn's help, he lifted Chip off the floor and walked him out to the car. The espresso machine went next, and then the bottle of Dom Perignon.

AudreyAnn and Chip squeezed into Rossi's cramped back seat and I rode shotgun, the oilskin packet clutched in my lap.

I *knew* that bottle of Dom Perignon was a good omen.

NINE

On our way to the nearest bank, a SunTrust branch on Tamiami Trail, I peered through the rearview mirror, fully expecting to see Francesco and Donny in hot pursuit. *Nada.* I relaxed against the cushions as best I could. Francesco was probably making a beeline for his lawyer's office.

I snuck a peek at Rossi's craggy profile. He didn't look worried, and in the back seat Chip and AudreyAnn were holding hands like teenagers in love. Chip wasn't even wheezing.

When we reached the bank, Rossi turned around to them. "Let me get Deva inside with the money, then I'll come back and help you both in."

AudreyAnn didn't look happy with that plan, but Chip's fast "Okay" settled it.

One hand on my elbow, Rossi escorted me into the bank, strode over to a customer service rep and showed her his badge. "We need a conference room. Please ask the bank manager to join us."

She dropped her pen on the desk and leaped up. "Right this way, Officer."

Rossi gave me a wink, and we followed the girl into a small windowless room with a conference table and several chairs. She snapped on the overheads.

"I'll be right back," Rossi said as he left to get Audrey-Ann and Chip.

Gripping the oilskin packet, I sat down and looked

around. There wasn't much to see. A pelican print and beige walls was about all. The beige was that boring shade that passes for corporate solidity. Why people equated dull interiors with fiscal wisdom I didn't understand. Never did. The room cried for something sunny and tropical—papaya, say, or tangerine. SunTrust Bank, right? Wouldn't an orangey shade work great as a subliminal logo? Or...

"Good morning. I'm Loren Miller, the branch manager. How may I help you?"

Tall, thin and balding, Mr. Miller was one of the few men in southwest Florida unlucky enough to have to wear a suit, shirt and tie to work. My fingers cramping around the oilskin, I upped my chin at the door. "The gentleman who needs your help is coming in now."

Rossi closed the conference room door behind Audrey-Ann and Chip and took care of the introductions before saying, "Deva, show Mr. Miller the packet."

I lifted the bag off my lap and dumped the contents onto the conference table.

For a man used to handling money for a living, Mr. Miller jumped back as if I'd unloaded a live cobra. Initial shock over, he took a step forward and stretched out a hand. "May I?"

Rossi nodded. "I wish you would. And can you authenticate these bills? At least one to start with?"

"Certainly." Mr. Miller turned a Grover Cleveland over in his hands, handling it carefully, almost tenderly. "In all my years in the banking business, I've never seen one of these."

"No kidding," Chip said. "I just found them. All of them. They've been hidden away."

His eyes full of Grover, the manager nodded. "They're so rare, they're collectors' items. Worth more than the face value."

"Wow!" Chip said.

"Depending on condition, of course. But if they're all as clean as this one, they could be worth several thousand each."

"Holy Toledo." Chip turned to AudreyAnn sitting beside him. "Did you hear that, honey? We're rich."

She flashed a triumphant, I-just-won-the-lottery smile around the table, though it dimmed a little when he added, "We'll be able to help Tomas's widow. She's got to be hurting real bad. She and Tomas were crazy in love."

"I believe this is legal tender, but let me test it," Mr. Miller said and hurried out with one of the bills.

"You need an attorney, Chip," Rossi said. "Do you have one?"

Chip looked at me and we both nodded. Simon.

"Simon Yaeger," Chip replied. "He used to live at Surfside. He's a tax man."

"Excellent choice. I know Mr. Yaeger." Rossi pulled out his phone to hunt for Simon's number.

"It's 555-8871," I told him.

"Instant recall?" Rossi frowned a little though he had no reason to.

Simon had lived at Surfside for a while before purchasing a penthouse on Gulf Shore Boulevard North in the brand new Peninsula Building. Originally a sales model staged by a New York designer, his new condo was a gorgeous bachelor pad for a gorgeous, successful…divorced… available Simon. He was a nice guy, too, a very nice guy. We'd dated a few times, but in comparison to Rossi he was just a well-dressed suit.

Rossi handed me his phone. "Yaeger's number's ringing. I think you'll have the best shot at getting him here ASAP."

True, apparently. In a matter of minutes, from his office in nearby Northern Trust Towers, Simon strode into the conference room dressed impeccably as always. Today he wore an ivory silk shirt, hand-tailored slacks and custom-made loafers.

Rossi, on the other hand, lit up the room in a purple hibiscus number. That was fine with me. The conference room needed a jolt of color.

When Simon spotted Rossi, his face fell a bit, but ever the professional, he rallied and shook hands all around, secretly stroking my palm when he took my hand. Or maybe not so secretly, judging by Rossi's scowl.

Rossi cleared his throat. "Chip has a story for you."

Chip had just about finished telling Simon his tale when the bank manager returned with Grover. "This is the real deal. Shall we test them all?"

ROSSI AND I left Chip and AudreyAnn at the SunTrust Bank with Simon and Mr. Miller. The money—all authentic— would be stored in a safety deposit box, the police notified and a search for a possible legal owner begun. After a month of running ads in the nation's largest newspapers and our local *Naples Daily News,* if no one surfaced with proof of ownership, the money would belong to Chip, free and clear.

Except for one tiny detail. Francesco. Chances were he wouldn't give up that much cash without a fight.

"Let him try. We'll be ready for him," Simon vowed with a wry lift to his lips. "Though the best way to preserve the find is to avoid litigation. But that's a problem for another day. For now, let's take care of the initial legalities."

As Rossi and I were leaving, Simon took my hand again, sandwiching it between his own. For some silly female reason I was glad I had worn the snug-fitting sheath in coffee linen and the Paloma Picasso pendant he'd given me last Christmas. And I was glad my Technicolor bruises had subsided.

"Thank you for helping with this," I said.

"My pleasure," Simon replied, gazing deep into my eyes. "Always at your service, Deva. Always."

Rossi cleared his throat, and I slipped my fingers free. "I'll take you to pick up your car," he said. I doubted that this time the gravel in his voice was due to smoke inhalation.

When we reached the restaurant parking lot, we lingered in the old Mustang he used on the job—its dust and scrapes a strategy to fool suspects into believing he was a bumbling, inept operator. Nothing could be further from the truth. Rossi's mind was a sword that could pierce metal. His hooded eyes alone gave him away, and he turned them on me now, full force.

"Your eyebrows are growing back," I said.

"And your bruises are mainly gone. Only a little lavender under one eye." He fingered the spot ever so gently.

I caught his hand in mine and held onto it. "We're healing."

His face sober, he barely nodded. "Can you stay here for a few minutes?"

To try and lighten his mood, I faked a grin. "You want to make out?"

No smiles, just a hesitation, then, "I mean what I said yesterday. You'll make a great mother some day."

"Thank you." But when that day would be I hadn't a clue. The possibility seemed so remote, so magical, I couldn't believe it would ever happen.

"I also meant what I said about the Grandese job. I don't want you to take it."

"Why not?" I asked, really wanting to know. "Arson didn't cause the explosion. You said so your—"

"I said it appeared to be an accident. *Appeared* being the operative word. The arson squad couldn't prove foul play, but questions remain."

"What kind of questions?"

"Donny's unsavory reputation for one. Grandese's business dealings for another. He's a wheeler-dealer apparently. Has real estate holdings here, in Miami and in New England. His affairs are a tangled web. It's hard to believe Chip was targeted, but supposing Grandese was? If so, he's in danger. And that places everyone involved with him in jeopardy too. For your own safety, the less you have to do with him the better."

In his own Rossi way, he was pleading a case. He cared for me and didn't want me harmed. Though the realization was heartwarming, I couldn't give up the Grandese job so easily. Too much was riding on it.

"So far, arson hasn't been proven, and Francesco has done nothing illegal. Right?"

Reluctantly Rossi nodded.

"So what happened to you're innocent until proven guilty?"

"I'm concerned about your safety, not some point of law. What if Donny deliberately tossed that cigarette?"

"You don't know that he did."

"Nor that he did not. The reason he gave for parking by the kitchen door was flimsy at best. And why was he out of range when the explosion occurred?"

"I want to do what you ask, but this time I simply can't. The business needs a cash infusion. You know that. With any luck at all, my work on the Grandese house will get my name into the upscale community. There's no telling what the ripple effect will be. A design business grows on word of mouth. Besides—"

He stopped my tirade with a kiss. One of his best ever.

A long, lingering kiss. A kiss to drown in, to sink into and not care if you ever breathe again. It lasted forever, and when it did, finally, end, Rossi held me at arm's length and gazed at me with those eyes that turned me to mush. To avoid the plea in them, I looked over his shoulder at the temporary plywood wall as if it were an architectural wonder. No question, he had my welfare in mind, but I couldn't give in on this. Not with success so tantalizingly close.

"Well?"

I shook my head. "You're asking me to swim in the shallow end of the pool."

He put a finger under my chin and tilted my face toward him. "No, that's not what I'm asking. I'm asking you to take care. I want you safe."

I forgot the plywood. Gazing straight into his craggy face, I raised a hand to stroke his cheek, feeling its stubble, feeling its strength. "I want you safe too. You live in harm's way every day. But I'm not asking you to give up your work for me."

His turn to look away, to stare at the jury-rigged wall. "My work's my life, though it'll never make me as wealthy as Simon Yaeger. So if that's a problem, tell me. Just don't play games."

He was jealous, an insight that made me happy and sad at the same time. "I do want to play games with you, Rossi. But not head games."

I grinned, trying to coax a smile out of him. No luck.

As always, at the worst moment, a cell phone chirped. Mine this time. I fished it out of my bag and glanced at caller ID. It was the painting contractor. "I'd better get this," I said. "Tom Kruse is calling."

Rossi's jaw dropped. *"Who?"*

He looked so comical I had to laugh. "Not to worry. You're sexier than any movie star on earth."

TEN

Rossi promised to come by with a pizza after work when we'd have a chance to talk at leisure. Armed with that and another long, lingering kiss, I zoomed over to Rum Row only five miles above the limit. Twenty minutes later, I was touring the Grandese house with a shell-shocked Tom Kruse. A trim, sixty-something who took his work seriously, Tom ran Oceanside Finishes, the best painting firm in town. When he wasn't swinging a brush, like today, he dressed as if he were a surgeon, in a white doctor's coat over chinos and button-downs.

As we strolled into the lilac kitchen, he whistled through his front teeth. "Looks like somebody unleashed a paint store in here." He rested a clipboard on the kitchen's purple island. "So what do you have in mind?"

"A clean sweep. The kitchen will be gutted and rebuilt, so leave this for last. Same for the baths. What I'm after in the public rooms is cohesion. A monochromatic look, at least for now."

"Base white on the walls, then?"

"Yes, and a flat classic white on all the ceilings."

"What about those magenta beams in the living room?"

The arched living room ceiling rose to fourteen feet in the center with exposed beams spanning the space.

"The classic white in semi-gloss on all trim and paneling, including those beams. The floor plan is open, so color flow is important. Once we get the walls sanded and primed, we can go from there."

Tom jotted a few notes. "They may need three coats."

"Whatever it takes."

Within twenty minutes, he'd measured all the rooms, promised to fax me a bid that same afternoon, and took off to crunch the numbers. Once his proposal was approved, he would send a crew in immediately.

After Tom left, I toured the house once more, admiring its potential, its grace, its proportions.

I made some notes. For starters all the closets could use organizers. The overdone window treatments with their heavy cornices had to go, the floor tiles in the foyer replaced, probably with marble squares. On the plus side, the hardwood floors were in good shape, only needing to be cleaned and polished.

Until I saw Francesco's furnishings and learned his color preferences, I could do little more today. I'd wandered back to the kitchen, where I'd left my purse, when the doorbell rang, the chimes low and melodious.

At the front entrance I peeked through the sidelights. Holding a covered plate in both hands, a fifty-something woman with the posture of an on-duty sentry stood outside on the slate landing,

I opened the door. "Hello. I'm—"

"My new neighbor. I'm so pleased to meet you at last. I'm Cookie Harkness. From across the way." She held the plate with one hand and extended the other.

Not wanting to offend her, I took her outstretched fingers. "I'm afraid I'm not—"

"Oh, please. Don't worry about not being ready to receive. I'm just a neighbor lady. May I?" she asked, one foot already inside the foyer.

"Well, I—"

Without giving me a chance to say more, she shook

my hand, stepped inside and looked around at the empty, garish rooms.

"Oh my. I'd forgotten how much Drexel loved color. No wonder, my dear, he was such a colorful man himself. Still is, I assume. Last we heard, he was living in the south of France. Aix, I believe, with his fourth or fifth true love. One does have trouble counting…anyway, for a man of his position he always lived modestly. Take this little place, for instance."

Over twelve thousand square feet under air conditioning *little?* Not counting the terraces, the pool, the patios. I held up both hands palms out, the universal signal for Stop. To my amazement, she did. "Mrs. Harkness, I am not your new neighbor, though I'd love to be. I'm Devalera Dunne, Mr. and Mrs. Grandese's interior designer."

Cookie's smile disappeared, and the covered plate— brownies, I guessed—sagged in her hands. "Oh. You should have stopped me."

"I did," I said, trying for a smile.

"These are brownies," she said, glancing at the plate. "My cook made them. It's an old New England custom, welcoming the new neighbors, but…" She was clearly at a loss.

"The refrigerator is still functioning. We could leave them there for the Grandeses and put a note on the kitchen island."

"Oh, a lovely solution. Let's do that."

Clearly she had been in the house before. She strode out to the kitchen without making a single false turn. She wore what my Irish grandmother would have called the Holy Trinity—a Tiffany tank watch, pearls and Ferragamos. I guess Nana would have called Cookie's startling tennis bracelet the Pope. Aside from her sensational jewelry and her shoes, everything else about her appearance was simplicity itself—smooth pageboy hair, face devoid of any trace of makeup, and a sleeveless blue cotton dress that stopped precisely at her knees.

She stashed her brownies in a slightly musty-smelling Subzero fridge, and I scribbled a note, ripped it out of my notebook and propped it on the kitchen island.

"Well, I'm disappointed not to have met the Grandeses. My husband has told me so much about Francesco, but—" she shrugged, "—that's life, Miss, ah, Dunne. Your name's Irish, isn't it?"

"Yes."

"Mother always employed Irish maids. Said they never stole a thing. Nipped a bit, perhaps, but one can live with that if the tippling doesn't get out of hand."

"I wouldn't know, Miss…"

"Mrs."

"Oh, certainly. Mrs. But I've forgotten your first name. It reminded me of a bakery product as I recall." I put a finger on my chin as if deep in thought. "Oh, now I remember. You're Hostess Twinkie. No that's not it. It's Cookie! You're Cookie. But your surname escapes me. Of an unusual ethnic origin, isn't it? Do jog my memory, Miss…"

"Harkness. *Mrs*. Norman Harkness." Shoulders thrust back, chin up, neck stretched taut, she added, "Norm and I are Mayflower descendants."

"Oh really? My ancestors came over on a boat too."

Cookie's already taut jaw froze at the chin line. "That's hardly—"

"Here nor there." I figured I'd finish an interrupted sentence for once. I know, I know. After telling Rossi that the job was all important, here I was shooting myself in the foot. Alienating one of the very people Deva Dunne Interiors needed most.

The problem was I had a terrible temper and certain

types of behavior made me crazy. Snobbery being one. I was constitutionally unable to ignore it or laugh it off or deal with it rationally. Oh no. I had to retaliate, cut the snob's ego down to size, so that my own ego came out on top. That was a terrible character flaw. I needed to work on ridding myself of it, to take the psychological high road and remind myself snobbery was a form of insecurity.

So maybe I should have felt sorry for Cookie-the-Snob Harkness. I was working on it as I walked her to the front door. But not too hard. It was too much fun wondering what she'd be like when she heard Francesco fracture the language. But as she waved goodbye with a "Ta-ta" and strolled across Rum Row, it occurred to me that all she might hear was the sound of his money.

An instant diagnosis. Another flaw in my character—snap judgments. Though in interior design it could often help me quickly solve a problem, analyzing people was a different story. In that arena I had a long way to go. Except for Rossi. When it came to Rossi, my judgment was right on target.

I wandered out to the kitchen for my purse. I'd lock up, go back to the shop and wait for Tom Kruse's fax. From past experience, I knew he'd be pricy but fair and that Francesco would get a faultless job.

Key at the ready, I opened the front door and stepped outside. To my amazement, a flotilla of vehicles clogged Rum Row. Immediately in front of the house, a moving van the size of the *Queen Mary* was easing to a stop. A familiar limo drove up behind it, and behind that a pale blue panel truck emblazoned with Bebe's Boutique in bright pink lettering.

Holy cow. Moving day.

Donny opened the limo's rear door and Francesco jumped out. Then Donny reached in to assist Jewels, who carried little Frannie in a baby pouch across her breast. She'd ditched the gladiator spikes for flat thongs which evened the playing field height-wise for Francesco.

"Hey," he shouted when he spied me in the doorway. "I'm glad you're here. We're moving in, and I want you to see my stuff."

Oh boy. The moment of truth. *Keep an open mind,* I told myself, *no matter how bad his things may be. You can convince him to get rid of what's impossible and work the so-sos into some kind of decent decorative scheme. If he won't listen to reason, return the retainer and walk away scot-free.*

I blew out a breath. That was the last thing I wanted to do.

Two muscular men emerged from the cab of the truck, both hefty enough to give Donny pause.

"This way, Phil," Francesco yelled, and they lumbered up the driveway to the garage. "The king bed and the high-def TV go in the apartment upstairs. My man Donny'll show you where. All the rest of the stuff goes here in the garage."

The two movers loped back to the truck to start unloading. Francesco turned to me. "You surprised we're moving in so soon?"

"A little. The house is far from ready."

"Yeah, I know, but things are working out good. My business on the East Coast can wait, so we decided to move in right away. A hotel's no place for a baby. The dust we'll be kicking up during the decorating won't be good for Jewels or Frannie either, so we're doing a switcheroo. While the work's going on, we'll stay in the chauffeur's apartment, and Donny'll live in the house. That way we can both guard my stuff. It'll be okay in the garage. It's air-conditioned, and I got security in here too."

A radiant Jewels strolled toward us, cuddling the sleeping baby, who was enveloped in a blue blanket and the sweet aroma of baby powder. In that moment I envied her. She'd found her destiny and how many of us ever do?

"Frannie, I'm going to show the man from Bebe's where to bring the baby equipment," Jewels said, walking back toward the waiting panel truck.

As the movers staggered in with a tall, bulky object shrouded in a quilted cover, I followed them into the garage, my anxiety level soaring. This first piece would tell me a lot about Francesco's taste and what I'd have to work with.

"Some of these things've been in storage for years, and I kind of disremember what they look like. Remove the wrap, boys," Francesco ordered. "Show the little lady whatcha got."

The muscles in his arms straining the sleeves of his Harvard T-shirt, Phil unbuckled a series of canvas straps. His helper in a tee from the Foxy Lady Lounge slid the protective padding away.

My heart stopped beating.

"Oh. My. God. Is this a—? No, it can't be. No way." I swiveled around to Francesco then back again. "Nobody has one of these. Do they? It's impossible. I've never seen anything to compare. Not in real life. Not outside a museum." I was babbling and knew it, but couldn't help myself. The shock was too great.

"You like the desk, huh?" Francesco asked.

"Is it a Townsend?" I whispered as if we were in a church. "From Newport?"

"So they told me."

"Who's they?"

"Sotheby's."

I hoped the movers brought in a chair next because I needed to sit down. Now.

I must have turned pale. Francesco reached out to take my arm. "You all right?"

"Yes, stunned is all."

The secretarial desk in Honduras mahogany stretched tall and magnificent in front of us, every line pure and perfect all the way from the bonnet top to the matched front panels to the curved drawers, to the cushioned feet.

Francesco ran a hand over the wood, caressing each curve. I didn't blame him. I would have done the same thing if I dared touch it.

"Original hardware?" I managed to ask.

"Better be. For what they soaked me."

For this piece alone, the security system needed to be up and functioning. And Donny needed to stay alert day and night. And there was a truck full of other furniture still to be unloaded. *Unbelievable.*

I watched, jaw agape, as the men carried in a long narrow object. From its shape I guessed it was a tall case clock. Feeling like a kid in a candy store, I practically drooled while they unwrapped it.

In hand-carved walnut, with a hunting scene painted on the dial face, and marvelous brass finials that nearly touched the garage ceiling, I'd swear the clock was also worthy of a museum.

"English or American?" I asked.

"Federalist."

"Is everything this good?"

"I don't buy junk," Francesco replied. "Wait'll you see the blanket chests. Original paint on them. I beat out Williamsburg for one."

"A chair. I need a chair."

"Hey, Phil," he yelled at the guy in the Harvard shirt. "The lady needs to sit down."

As soon as Phil brought in an authentic Windsor, I slumped into it and watched the floor show.

Francesco had the eye of a connoisseur, all right, and the money to indulge it.

"My grandfather was a cabinetmaker," he said, stroking a Chippendale chest as if it were a woman. "Learned his trade in the old country. Worked for peanuts all his life, but he didn't care. He loved the wood. Me too.

"When I was a kid, he'd take me to the Met two, three times a year. We'd ride the train down from Providence and wander the furniture rooms. You know, the ones from different periods. *Nonno* would point out why a piece deserved to be there. What made it stand out. He'd talk about the skill of the craftsman and show me the details somebody else might miss. Taught me everything I know. About wood. And women." He barked out a short laugh. "Not about anything else, I guess."

"That was a lot, Francesco," I said, sitting there in a daze.

"Yeah, you're right. So you like my stuff?" he asked again.

"I'm in love, Francesco. In love."

As more and more pieces were unwrapped, I realized Francesco had concentrated his collection on museum-quality Early American hard case goods. He had no upholstered pieces, no artwork, no accessories, no rugs. A good thing. That's where I came in.

When the last piece had been delivered, the garage was pretty much packed. Donny would have to park the Ferrari out on the driveway. I rose out of the Windsor with some difficulty.

"You leaving?" Francesco asked.

I nodded. "Your collection has given me some ideas for the house. As soon as my thoughts gel, I'll get back to you. For now I need to get to the shop. The painter's fax is probably waiting for me."

"Whatever he says is okay. Get him started. I'm in a bind here. I got a family to get settled," he said, sounding positively delighted about it.

"Fine." Purse over my shoulder, I headed for the open overhead doors. "Oh, by the way, a neighbor stopped by with brownies. They're in the fridge. Her name is Cookie Harkness."

Francesco nodded. "Oh yeah. That must be Norm's wife. What a guy. He could talk Jesus off the cross." He shook his head. Whether in disgust or confusion I couldn't tell. "Norm tipped me off about this house. The only good tip he ever gave me. He's got a lot of opinions about everything, but when it comes to the ponies, he's got no judgment at all. I musta been nuts giving him a loan for the Preakness. Getting my money back's going to be murder."

ELEVEN

FRANCESCO HAD ME bamboozled. I couldn't fit the various parts of his personality into an understandable whole. Entrepreneur. Lover. Man of taste. Crass lout. Definitely a connoisseur. Possibly a man of questionable dealings. And just possibly the victim of a crime.

For some reason, maybe that Townsend desk, I wanted to believe he was an honorable businessman, a little rough around the edges but in love with his wife and baby and seeking the good life. Not a target on somebody's hit list. And not the person responsible for the death of Tomas and the driver of the propane truck.

So despite Rossi's misgivings, until the police proved that Francesco was guilty, I'd consider him innocent. Besides, not to be a hypocrite, the heart-stopping bonanza I'd just been privileged to see had me panting to work for him. At least until he proved he couldn't be trusted. He should show his intent soon—within a month in fact—when Chip laid claim to the hidden money. How Francesco dealt with that would tell me just about everything I needed to know.

On my way home, I stopped at the shop to pick up Tom's fax. His price was high but he hadn't hit it out of the ballpark. Next stop was Publix Market for fruit and salad fixings to augment Rossi's pizza. I tossed a tray of chocolate brownies in the wagon too. Cookie had started a trend. Funny the way Francesco had referred to her husband. As if he had little to no respect for the man. Another piece to try and fit into the puzzle.

But not the only one. Yesterday I'd decided to go for a GYN exam, and today the sight of little Frannie nestled in his blue blanket was an adorable reminder to follow through and get myself checked out. Why not? Maybe it was curiosity and nothing more, but I wanted to prove once and for all that babies were in my future. Rossi was sweet to try and downplay my worry, but he was a man, and superb detective or not, when it came to this subject he couldn't possibly understand how a woman would feel.

I stripped off my clothes and took a quick shower before climbing into a pair of white shorts and an apricot halter— one of Rossi's favorites—so low cut in front, I never wore it outside of the condo. Just the thing for tonight.

I remade the bed with fresh sheets and arranged a pile of pillows on top. Then I chilled a bottle of champagne I'd been saving for a special occasion. For a finishing touch, a few early-blooming gardenias from the yard soon had the living room filled with perfume.

After turning the condo lights down low, I put on a sultry Julio Iglesias CD. *"Amore, Amore, Amore. La la, la, la. La, la, la, la."*

Oh, give me a piano I can lie across.

My chimes rang with Beethoven's Fifth. The magic moment. Rossi was here. Still humming *"Amore,"* I hurried to the door and yanked it open. "At last…"

"Surprise!"

"Lee St. James!" My mouth dropped open. I know it did. *"Surprise?* I'm shocked. I thought you were in New York. Come in. Come in."

I grabbed Lee in a hug. She clung to me for a moment then wheeled her luggage into the foyer and burst into tears. Her hands covering her face, she stood with her shoulders heaving and sobbed. Only six months earlier, radiantly happy, she'd left for New York with her brand new husband, Paulo St. James. His scholarship to the Art Students' League was the opportunity of a lifetime. They'd both been thrilled, and everyone who knew them had been thrilled for them.

Now this.

"Come sit down," I coaxed. Putting an arm around her, I drew her into the living room. As she sat weeping on the couch, I raced to the bathroom for a box of tissues.

Without a word, I handed her five or six and watched as she soaked through them. Whatever the problem was, she needed to cry it out, but as minutes ticked by with no end in sight, I brushed the hair back from her cheek and gently lowered her hands from her face.

Her nose red, her eyes puffy, she stammered, "I'm s-so s-sorry, but I can't seem to help myself."

"Is it Paulo?"

She nodded. I handed her a fresh batch of tissues and gradually, one shuddering breath at a time, she gained control.

"I shouldn't be bothering y'all like this, but I didn't know where to go except here."

"You're welcome anytime. You know that. But where is Paulo?"

She made a ball of the damp tissues and clutched them in her lap. "Paris. Paris, France."

Uh-oh. "Why Paris?"

She gulped and forced down a new sob. "He was offered an internship at the Louvre, a chance to study with some of Europe's masters. Henri Bertrand asked for him especially."

I shook my head at the name.

"Y'all don't know him?"

"Offhand, no. Sounds familiar though."

"He's one of the best portrait painters in France. Having him as a mentor is an honor. Paulo couldn't refuse but…but…"

"What?" I asked as gently as I could.

"He was about to refuse anyway."

"Why?"

"His stipend didn't include me. And we couldn't afford to have me go with him."

"So Paulo went alone?" That was a greater surprise than finding her on my doorstep. The way he loved the girl, with his heart shining in his eyes every time he looked at her, I was amazed he'd left her alone for any reason on earth.

With a new spurt of tears running down her cheeks, Lee said, "He intended to refuse, but I told him if he did I'd divorce him. That I wanted to be married to a successful painter not a failure." She lowered her arms to her knees and laid her head on them. Though muffled, her words were clear enough. "How could I have said such a cruel thing? I love him more than life. I don't care if he's a success or not. I just want him to be happy, and his work makes him happy. He *had* to go."

At a loss for words, I rubbed her back in a fruitless effort at comfort. Last October when Lee and Paulo were married, they had been so much in love, an aura radiated around them. Now to see her like this made me want to weep too. I searched my mind for something positive to say.

"Paulo knows what you've given up for him. He must love you all the more."

She raised her tear-stained face. "Think so?" The ghost of a smile flitted across her lips for an instant.

"Definitely." I spoke as if I knew. In a way, I did. I knew Paulo's dedication to the talent—maybe even the genius—he was striving to perfect. He would understand Lee's sacrifice better than anyone. Still…

"He was crying when he left, Deva. Imagine. Crying like a baby. So was I."

I could picture the two of them at a JFK parting gate, clinging to each other until the last possible second. "How long will he be gone?"

She shook her head. "I don't know. Until he learns everything he can. Or until his stipend runs out." With an almost visible force of will, she straightened her shoulders and brushed her long blond hair away from her face. "I sold some of Momma's silver to pay for my airfare here, and I put the money Paulo gave me back in his luggage. So if you haven't hired someone else for the shop, I'd surely love to work there again."

A steel magnolia. That was what Lee had been ever since I'd known her. "And I'd surely love to have you. You can stay here with me if you like."

A faint light shone in her eyes. "I didn't want to ask but—"

"No need. There's plenty of room. I have two bedrooms."

Da da da DA.

Rossi.

He stood outside with a pizza box in one hand, a bunch of grocery store flowers in the other, and a big smile wreathing his face.

"We have company," I said.

The smile melted away. "Oh yeah?" he growled.

I was beginning to think smoke inhalation had permanently affected his voice. "It's Lee. She's alone."

He handed me the flowers and raised a singed, quizzical eyebrow.

"Paulo's living in Paris."

"Uh-oh." It was "uh-oh" for poor Lee and "uh-oh" for our romantic evening.

Outwardly unfazed, Rossi strode into the living room, plunked the pizza box on the coffee table and spread his arms wide. "Come to poppa," he said to Lee.

With a little cry of delight, she jumped off the couch and hugged him tight. He hugged her back and kissed her cheek, then held her at arm's length.

"Except for the red nose and the swollen eyes, you're as beautiful as ever. Still Lorelei and Guinevere rolled into one." He let her go and said, "First I'm going to open a bottle of wine so we can have a toast. Then I want to hear everything. And I mean everything." He winked. "Even the things you don't want to tell me."

He was trying to lighten the mood. I knew Lee understood that, but she blushed anyway. "I'll tell you everything my momma would have approved of."

"That'll be just fine." Scooping up the pizza box, he disappeared into the kitchen.

"He's such a darlin' man, Deva," Lee said, managing a watery grin. "Y'all look so cute together."

"Cute?" Rossi yelled from the kitchen. "That's a first."

Were Rossi and I together? I couldn't have answered that if I had to. I'd be lonely without him in my life. He filled the gap Jack's death had created. But I was enjoying my independence—as well as Rossi's company. I had the best of both worlds and felt selfish for even thinking that way. But that was the truth, wasn't it?

As I settled onto the couch alongside Lee, Rossi returned holding an opened bottle of merlot in one hand and two glasses upside down in the other. He went back for one more glass then poured a few fingers of wine for each of us.

"A toast," he said, raising his wine on high and arching his remnant of an eyebrow at me. "To good friends."

I nearly choked. Is that what he thought we were?

Friends? Lee, yes, without question. But I didn't consider Rossi and me as just friends. But maybe he did. Maybe he enjoyed his independence as much as I enjoyed mine.

Whatever he thought about our relationship, I knew he regretted our lost evening and wouldn't stay the night. Not now. Leaving the two of them to chat, I went out to the kitchen to heat the pizza and toss a salad.

Sure enough, after dinner he said, "I have some desk work to clear up, so I'd better get back to the station."

I hated to see him go so soon, but tonight Lee was the one who needed the TLC.

What Rossi needed I could tell the minute I walked him to his car and he pressed against me.

"I'm so sorry about tonight," I began.

With a finger to my lips, he cut off my apology and upped his chin in the direction of my condo. "You did the right thing. That girl comes first tonight. Having them apart like this isn't good. We need to figure out a way to send her to Paris."

"Yes," I agreed, hugging him even closer and, for a sweet moment, resting my head on his chest. "You know something, Rossi, under that tough guy exterior you're really a softy."

"Not at the moment," he said, wryly. "Come to my place tomorrow after work. We'll order in Chinese, talk and…"

He lowered his face to mine, seizing my mouth in a kiss that as far as I was concerned could have gone on all night. Might have, too, but for a croaky, "Hey, love birds!"

We sprang apart, guilty as a couple of teens making out in class. Of all people, Chip came striding, actually striding, toward us, wearing the biggest grin I'd seen on his face since La Cucina's demise.

"How you feeling?" Rossi asked.

"The burns on my chest are still sore but other than that

I'm fine. Never better." Chip took in a deep breath and let it out slowly. "See that. Not even wheezing."

"That's wonderful," I said.

"I've got more good news too. Francesco's hired me to cook for him and the family."

"Is that right?" Rossi said.

"Yeah, until I can claim the money. I don't think he's going to go after it. He knows I'm strapped for cash and wants to help out. He's hired Bonita too. Tomas's widow."

Rossi stepped nearer to Chip and lowered his voice. "I'll tell you the same thing I told Deva. Watch yourself in there."

Chip stared at him, baffled. "Why say that? The guy's only trying to help."

"Could be. Just so you know. I've warned Deva too."

Rossi shot me a glance to see if I'd object, but I didn't. Mr. Macho had my best interests at heart. Why fight it? I tossed him an air kiss.

He shook his head and turned back to Chip. "The cause of the explosion is still unclear. It could be what it seems, an accident. Or something more."

Chip nodded hesitantly, obviously not happy with where this was heading.

"We don't think anyone was after you, but Grandese is another story. Somebody might be after him."

Chip's jaw went slack. "Grandese was targeted?"

"No proof of that," Rossi said. "Just be careful. Another thing. No one knows who hid the money in the wall, or how long it's been there. There had to be a reason it wasn't in a bank. If whoever hid it learns it's been found, anything can happen. Or that person may be long gone. Since we don't know either way, keep your eyes and ears open. And let me know if anything strikes you as suspicious. Anything at all."

"Okay." Chip's elation of a few minutes ago had fled. Once again he looked like an injured man.

"Are you well enough to hold down a job, Chip?" I asked.

"Sure," he said, perking up a little. "AudreyAnn's coming along to do the prep work, so I'll be okay. Getting stronger every day."

He had lost some serious weight lately and he gave his pants a hitch over his nearly flat belly. "It sure is great having AudreyAnn back. That was a long six months while she was gone." His sunshine smile dimmed. "She says she was staying with an aunt, but wherever she was doesn't matter. She's back. That's all that counts."

Was it? A year earlier, AudreyAnn had had a fling with Dick Parker, the former owner of the Surfside Condominiums. Had history repeated itself? If not with Dick, with someone new? For Chip's sake, I wanted to give her the benefit of the doubt. But the question hovered in the air and in Chip's expression. Where *had* AudreyAnn been these past six months?

And a question far more serious: Why would anyone want to blow up Francesco's property?

TWELVE

WHILE I COULDN'T do a thing about Francesco's business dealings, his house was another story. I *could* make a difference there, and I'd start right as you first stepped in.

That meant Zuber scenic murals for the foyer. Just like in the White House. Expensive as sin and beautiful as Eden. Francesco had said go for broke, and the French murals were top of the line—hand-blocked and hand-painted original eighteenth-century designs. Along with a black-and-white marble floor, they'd create a drop-dead entrance.

One scene especially had me captivated. *Les Zones Terrestres,* a tropical dream vista with flamingos, palm trees and a distant mountain reaching for the sky. It held a variety of luscious colors I could pluck out for the rest of the house. Though I'd use Benjamin Moore's subtle Putnam Ivory on the living room walls, above the dining room's perfectly proportioned wainscoting a vivid color would add a jolt of excitement. Maybe a custom-mixed coral with yellow undertones for an interesting complexity. A few words to Tom Kruse and he'd understand the effect I was after. Or if not, he'd be willing to keep mixing until I reached that "aha!" moment. Heavy silk panels at the windows, very simple but rich with—

"Deva, a Mr. Grandese on the line," Lee said.

Busy at my drafting table, I hadn't heard the shop phone ring. "Good morning, Francesco. I'm working on your proposal even as we speak. Should have something to show you in a day or two, but the bids will take longer."

"Ball park figures'll be all right. I want action. That paint crew you hired is hot on the job, and that's what I like. Things are humming over here." A little throat clearing, then, "I'll be away for a couple days, so I'll take a look at what you got after I come back. Want you to know we're throwing a little housewarming party Friday night. Chip's working on the food already. The place is all torn up so we'll eat outside. Under a grapevine like in the old country." He laughed, throaty as a lounge singer. "Seven o'clock. Bring that detective along. *Ciao*."

The phone went dead. I stared at the receiver for a long moment before setting it back in the cradle. Francesco might have thought he was inviting me but what he'd barked out was an order.

I slumped in the ergonomic chair and swiveled like mad. I should tell him to shove it…and throw away what might be the only chance I'd ever get to install Zuber wallpaper. As I sat there swiveling, I knew I wouldn't boycott his party. Every woman has her price, and I'd just been bought, lock, stock and barrel, for a roll of wallpaper. Well, several rolls. Actually about fifty thousand dollars' worth.

I stretched in place, took a deep breath and went back to work. If I could nail the basic design, I'd have the presentation boards ready to show Francesco when he returned. Then I'd have him sign a standard, boilerplate contract. As a financial safety net that meant fifty percent upfront for most purchases, and one hundred percent upfront for the made-to-order, over-the-top scenic paper. I wouldn't risk doing business with him otherwise, not with Rossi's warning echoing in my mind. Carpeting, artwork and accessory items could be filled in later. Naples had world-class art galleries and antique stores, so once he okayed my concept I'd begin shopping.

At one o'clock I looked up, startled, as Lee placed a tuna wrap and a bottle of ice water at my elbow.

"Coming up for air, Deva?" she asked, pale today but composed, a euphemism for miserably unhappy. Lord knows I wanted to help her, but the cure was Paulo. Anything else was only a Band-Aid on the wound.

She wore the black dress and high-heeled sandals we'd bought together a year ago, the same dress she wore the day she and Paulo fell in love. Right in this very shop, a moment I would never forget. How could I? I'd seen the spark leap between them.

"How are you today?" I tried to keep the worry out of my voice.

"I'm fine, Deva," she said, though she looked anything but. "Paulo just texted me. He's found a room with a north light. His landlady…he calls her the concierge…is very nice." A frown furrowed Lee's lovely face. "I wonder what he means by nice?"

"He means she's old and fat and loves the sound of his Jamaican French."

She laughed. "He might mean she's young and pretty. You know they say French girls have a way with them."

The ooh-la-la effect. "No," I said trying to speak like I really knew. "Concierges are always old and fat. It's a job requirement. And besides, to Paulo you're the most beautiful girl in the world."

She didn't deny it but didn't reply either. She was probably remembering when he'd told her the very same thing. The Yarmouthport bells jangled, and she hurried over to welcome a woman searching for that perfect lamp.

Though Lee didn't mention Paulo again, she was even quieter than usual for the rest of the day. At five o'clock I handed her my car keys. I'd be with Rossi tonight, and she'd be alone. As I hugged her goodbye, I hoped she wouldn't be too lonely, but of course she would be. Still she left with a smile and a wave, and I settled down at the *bureau plat* by the front window to wait.

Rossi kept such erratic work hours, I couldn't believe it when he drove down the alley a few minutes later. I wasted no time grabbing the overnight bag I'd packed that morning, locking the shop door and hurrying outside.

"LET'S EAT OUT of the boxes," Rossi said when the Pagoda Gardens delivery boy left. "Chinese tastes better that way."

"A quote from Wolfgang Puck?"

"Yeah, her. I like pizza straight from the box too."

I stared at his smiling face. He was playing a word game with me. "You're a clever guy, you know that?"

He backed up against a kitchen counter and folded his arms, straining the orange plumeria blossoms on his *Miami Vice* shirt to the max. "I used to think so, but now I'm not so sure."

"Why not?"

"I've got you alone at last, and I'm talking Chinese food instead of tearing your clothes off and chasing you through the house."

"Let's be serious," I said, leaning on the fridge for a little support. "I've been meaning to ask you something for days."

"I know. So out with it. What's bothering you?"

"Lately I've been thinking I might want to have a child someday, so I thought I'd go and be checked out. Have a GYN exam. You know, just to make sure everything's okay." I studied him for moment, trying to gauge his reaction, but it's hard to read a closed book and Rossi wasn't opening up. Only the lids of his hooded eyes moved as he looked away from me. "But suppose it isn't? Suppose I have a problem?"

"That's what's been bothering you? Where's the law that says you have to have kids?"

"Don't ask ridiculous questions. This isn't one of your cases."

Hot as flame, his glance seared me. "Oh yes, it is. It's a case of my being crazy about you. So don't go creating barriers between us." He stepped away from the counter. With a few strides, he closed the space and spread-eagled his hands on the fridge, trapping me against the door. "If you try, you'll have a war on your hands. Though the one thing I can't fight is your memory of Jack." His eyes narrowed. "Is that what this is about?"

I shook my head. "No. This is about the future. Don't you want to have a family someday?"

He shrugged. "Sure."

"Suppose just for the sake of argument that you hook up with a woman who can't have children. What then?"

"There are all kinds of families, Deva. Family means a group of people who love each other."

"Oh, please. That kind of family wouldn't be enough."

"For whom?"

"A guy like you."

He lowered his head, shading his face so I couldn't see his expression. "I don't have a choice," he said softly.

"Of course you do."

He raised his head. His eyes bored into mine. "No, I don't. I haven't wanted to bring up the subject…it's too humiliating. Easier to pretend the problem doesn't exist."

"What are you getting at? What problem?"

"Maybe you should sit down."

He had me scared suddenly. He'd been concealing something from me. Something serious.

"All right. The living room?"

We sat side by side on his couch, and he half turned to

face me. The sadness in his expression tugged at my heart. Whatever he had to say, I needed to know fast and clean. No softening the blow. No easing the pain.

"What's the matter? Just tell me. I can't stand seeing you so sad."

He picked up my hand and, holding it tight, said, "I've been seeing a doctor. A proctologist."

"A *what?*"

"No point in keeping quiet about this."

"You can tell me anything. You know that."

His eyes avoiding mine, he said, "The doc found something."

My heart stopped. He was sick. "What is it? What's the matter?"

He hesitated then blurted out the words as though if he didn't do so quickly, he wouldn't be able to. "I can't have children." He took a deep breath and exhaled slowly before adding, "I'm sterile."

"No way! I don't believe that."

He hung his head. "Believe."

I squeezed the hand holding mine. "That doesn't matter. And I never meant anything more in my life."

He flung his left leg over his right knee and raised one of those singed eyebrows. "Gotcha!"

I dropped his hand as if it were a hunk of lava and reared back on the cushions. "There's nothing wrong with you." I wasn't asking a question.

The eyebrow rose higher.

"Not fair, Rossi. Not fair."

"But effective. Now…" His voice was positively chummy. I could have kicked him in the groin. Should have. "Is there anything else you wish to add to this conversation?"

"Yes. You're diabolical."

"Of course I am. I'm a detective. So to end the subject once and for all, find out the truth if you must. Go to your doctor. Ease your mind, but understand this—I'm crazy about you, and always will be, no matter what he says."

"She." All the fight had gone out of me. I wanted to make love not war.

Rossi must have felt the same way. "You know what," he said, reaching out and pulling me against the plumerias. "The Chinese can wait."

THIRTEEN

FRIDAY EVENING WE were a block away from the Grandese house when a booming Italian love song exploded in the air.

"O sole...o sole mio...sta 'nfronte a te! O sole..."

Rossi and I looked at each other and grinned. Rum Row would never be the same.

We rang the bell and waited at the front door. For the occasion, Rossi had donned his most lurid Hawaiian shirt, lavender orchids on a vivid purple background.

"You'd better stay out of the kitchen," I warned. "I'll never find you in there."

Before he could ask why not, a sad-eyed, dark-haired woman met us at the door. "Everyone is out by the pool," she said, gesturing to the brick path stretching along the side lawn.

"Your name is?" I asked.

"Bonita," she said softly. "I was the wife of Tomas." Ah. The woman Chip had mentioned.

I took her hand. "I am so sorry for your loss, Bonita."

An expression I couldn't fathom crossed her face. "No one is sadder than I, *señora*. Inside me is all the sorrow in the world."

"I know," I said. And I did, but there was little more to say, and with a parting smile, I took Rossi's arm and together we walked along the brick path.

"Don't be sad," he said. "Not when you look so beautiful tonight."

With his words ringing in my ears, I strolled onto the terrace where a table draped with a white cloth was set for a party. Francesco dropped a basting brush next to the barbeque grill and rushed over to us. "Right on time. I like that." He eyeballed my halter dress, careening to a stop at the neckline. "Looking sharp, Deva. Green's your color."

"Yours too, Francesco."

He laughed and looked down at his green polo shirt. "Yeah, we're in father and daughter outfits tonight." This was the first time I'd seen him wear anything but a dark suit, white shirt and silk tie. At his ease with black chest hair sprouting out of the neck of the shirt and a pair of white shorts revealing his tree-trunk legs, he was obviously enjoying the role of family man. "Hey, Jewels," he yelled. "Come say hello. I gotta get back to the grill."

Jewels walked across the lawn with little Frannie on her hip. In her loose white shift and thong sandals, she looked like a model for a teen magazine. As she came near, she smiled at Rossi and examined my face. "You look good. The bruises are all gone. I like your dress too."

"And I like yours."

"It's a maternity. I've been dying to wear one. Frannie thinks I don't need it yet, but…" She shrugged and kissed the top of the baby's head. He drooled and cooed, and she cooed "Nice boy" back at him.

I glanced over at Rossi. He was grinning at little Frannie, which I interpreted to mean, "Babies are great." *Well they are,* I told myself, *so don't read into it.*

"I'm not drinking these days," Jewels said. "But why don't you have something?"

A portable bar had been set up by the pool with Donny

presiding. We strolled over to him. "White wine for the lady," Rossi said.

Poker faced, Donny nodded. "Chardonnay? Pinot grigio?"

"The pinot," I replied.

"For you, sir?"

"The same."

So far, that was the most I'd ever heard Donny say. The phrase "a man of few words" must have been invented with him in mind.

As we sipped and admired the garden with its lush tropical plantings, Bonita came outside and took little Frannie from Jewels.

I inhaled deeply. The perfume of night-blooming jasmine and barbeque sauce floated on the breeze along with a booming aria from *La Bohème*.

"A half hour, tops, and Grandese can expect a cruiser in his driveway," Rossi said in my ear.

"I've never been to a party where cops showed up."

"Tonight's the night," he said with a laugh.

"Hey, you two," Francesco shouted from across the lawn. "Why don't you pay your friend a visit? He's slaving away in the kitchen. We're having his home-made lobster ravioli tonight and my special ribs. Antipasto, iced shrimp, tiramisu. How's that grab you?"

Rossi gave him a thumb's up. With wineglasses in hand, we headed for the kitchen, nearly colliding en route with Cookie Harkness.

"Miss Dunne! What a surprise." Clad in bright pink cotton tonight, she seemed stunned to see me.

Accompanying her was a deeply tanned man decked out in an ascot tie, linen shirt and rust-colored slacks embroidered with tiny green palm trees.

Cookie waved a languid hand in his vicinity. "My

husband, Norman Chandler Harkness." She turned to Rossi. "And you are?"

"Victor Giuseppe Rossi." A three name response to a three name introduction. Good for Rossi, but *Giuseppe?* Had he been named for Uncle Beppe of the mysterious demise? Hmm, interesting.

Norm gave me a flabby handshake and pointed a finger at my glass. "You beat us to it. We were just chatting with the chef about the menu. Now we're off to get a libation."

"By all means," Rossi said. "We'll trade places with you."

The kitchen buzzed with activity. By the stove, Bonita held little Frannie on her hip while she warmed a bottle of baby formula. AudreyAnn, in white slacks and a T-shirt under stress, greeted us with a curt nod and kept on arranging an antipasto platter. And Chip, a Coffee, Tea or Me apron over his chef's clothes, was busy dividing a bowl of chilled shrimp into ten individual appetizer dishes.

"Fresh, never frozen," he declared, stopping for a moment to check the oven. "From Biloxi. Best shrimp in the world. And my spicy salsa." He came back to the prep table and ladled a generous spoonful of salsa over each individual shrimp glass.

"You missed one, Chip," I said.

"No, that's Francesco's. He's got a delicate stomach. Anything spicy gives him heartburn." Chip shook his head regretfully. "Too bad, my salsa's famous. Right, Audrey-Ann?"

Without looking up, she gave him a grudging, "Yeah."

Lovely. The woman has all the charm of weeds in a driveway.

"We'll be ready whenever Francesco is," Chip said, putting the rest of the salsa back in the fridge. "He wants us all to eat together. Imagine. The chef, the salad girl…" he shot a quick, alarmed glance AudreyAnn's way, but she didn't bristle, "…Donny. Bonita. Can you believe that? What a guy!"

"Sounds good to me." Rossi swiped one of the shrimp from the big bowl, and we strolled out to the patio where "Nessun Dorma" blasted the peace out of the evening.

Tears running down his cheeks, Francesco basted the ribs yet again. "Hear that aria?" he called to us. "Makes me cry every time."

"Ten more minutes till a cruiser visit," Rossi said to me, enjoying himself enormously. "Care for another drink?"

I shook my head. "I'm good for a while. We've lost our bartender anyway."

At a beckoning finger from Francesco, Donny had replaced him at the grill and was turning the ribs with barbeque tongs. His boss disappeared somewhere, probably back to the kitchen.

"I'll help myself," Rossi said, striding toward the bar.

Figuring this was a good time to tour the house and see what Tom's painting crew had accomplished, I opened a patio door and stepped into the living room. I didn't get too far before voices coming from the foyer stopped me in my tracks.

Francesco and another man. Something agitated in Francesco's tone told me I should leave, but before I could make a move I heard, "This is the last time I'm telling you, Norm. No excuses. I want my money."

Norm murmured something. Whatever he said, Francesco wasn't buying. "It wasn't a goddamn Christmas present. It was a loan. For six months only. Maybe you got trouble recalling that, since it was over a year ago."

Another murmur. I really needed to beat a retreat, but curiosity had me rooted to the floor.

"It don't mean a thing. Stockbroker be damned. You're

nothing but a hustler. Worse. Your pool table's got no pockets. And I don't care if you got pockets or not. I'm giving you till Monday."

"You won't pull any rough stuff, will you?" Terror must have caused Norm to speak up. His question, quavery but clear, echoed in the empty rooms.

"Rough stuff? Don't make me laugh. What we got going is a gentleman's agreement. But I got my ways of collecting. No action by Monday, Cookie finds out."

"No, please…"

No more hesitating, I had to make myself scarce and get out of there before they spotted me. The patio door seemed a mile away. The quickest way out was through the dining room and back to the kitchen. I tiptoed across the living room floor, quiet as the proverbial mouse, rounded the archway into the dining room—and almost smacked into Bonita. Equally stunned, we both gasped, two silent, shocked intakes of breath.

Bonita didn't look as if she were on an errand. Nothing in her hands, no hurrying to get from point A to point B. No, like me she'd simply been listening to Francesco and Norm's conversation. Snooping, in plain English.

"Perdóneme," she said, and before I could answer, she turned on her heel, fled the dining room and hurried out to the kitchen.

Sorrow over Tomas's death had obviously not killed her curiosity. But who was I to talk? Still, I couldn't help but wonder what she hoped to hear.

Back on the patio, I made a beeline for the bar. With Donny still manning the grill, Rossi had stayed on as bartender. And *Manon* had replaced *Aida* on the sound system.

"I'd love a glass of wine now," I said. He poured me a drink from the open pinot bottle. As he handed me the glass, he looked up over my shoulder and broke into a white-toothed grin.

"Officer Batano, good evening."

In the brown uniform of the Naples PD, the biggest cop in the world approached us, a look of utter astonishment on his face. "Rossi! You live here?"

Rossi laughed. "Not on my salary."

"I need to speak to the owner. No one answered the front door."

"We couldn't hear the bell," I said.

Francesco barged onto the terrace and shouldered his way over to us. "Hey, what's going on?"

"I'm Officer Batano of the Naples police. Do you reside on this property?"

"That's correct. What's up, Officer?"

"Your music's too loud for the neighbors. The station's been flooded with calls."

"They don't like opera?"

"Only at the Met," Rossi told him, still grinning.

"Okay, okay. I'll turn off the system. But I'm not happy doing it."

Batano gave Rossi a two-fingered salute. "Have a good evening, Lieutenant," he said and strode off.

Francesco killed the speakers and into the sudden silence yelled, "The ribs are done. Jewels, tell Chip we're ready to eat."

"Okay, honey." She left Cookie's side and hurried indoors.

Glass in hand, Cookie wandered over to me and asked, "Where are the other guests?"

"Everyone's here."

She shook her head. "You must be mistaken. The table's set for ten, but there are only six of us."

Cookie was in for a shock.

"Did you count the cook, the kitchen helper, the nanny and the…" I changed "bouncer" to, "…chauffeur?"

"Omigod," she said, splaying a beringed hand across her chest. The pink diamond was drop-dead gorgeous. "You don't mean that."

"Yes, I do. Is there a problem?"

Cookie drew herself even more erect than usual. "If you don't know, no amount of explaining will help." She gulped her drink. "Right now, I need to find the powder room, but when this charade is over, Norm and I will have a talk."

Yup.

AudreyAnn lit the hurricane lamps on the table and brought out baskets of warmed crusty Italian bread and small saucers of herbed oil for dipping. A few minutes later, carrying a tray laden with the individual shrimp servings, Chip set them about the table, putting the one without the salsa at the head, Francesco's place.

Jewels sat opposite her husband at the other end of the table, the baby in a portable crib by her side. I squeezed in between Rossi and Donny and across from Norm and Bonita. The cooks sat down last.

"How about a little Pavarotti while we eat?" Francesco asked.

"I wouldn't advise it," Rossi replied, smiling.

"Yeah. Don't want the cops here twice in one night. Just shows what kind of neighbors I got to put up with."

I shot a quick glance in Francesco's direction. Did that mean he wanted to leave, wouldn't go through with the restoration?

He caught my glance and read my thought. "Not to worry, Deva. I'm nuts about this place. When Jewels and I are under air, I'll blast the hell out of the sound system. Get the kids used to good music."

Cookie returned from her visit to the powder room and

sat down rather gingerly to the right of Jewels. Then, rigid in her seat as if she feared contamination from some source close by, Cookie sucked on her bourbon and ignored her shrimp.

"You don't care for shrimp?" I asked.

"I'm enjoying my pre-dinner cocktail at the moment."

"I see. Well, when you're ready, they're delicious."

Like the shrimp, I was ignored. The woman sat sipping in silence until Norm whispered something in her ear.

"You did *what?*" she asked, slurring her words ever so slightly.

"Shh."

"You going to eat that shrimp?" Donny asked suddenly. The first full sentence I'd ever heard him utter.

"Are you speaking to me?" Cookie asked.

"Yes. You want the shrimp or not?"

"I beg your pardon."

"That a yes or a no?"

When she didn't answer him, Donny shrugged. "I guess that's a no."

While Donny found solace in his beer, Norman again whispered in Cookie's ear. For Brahmins who worshipped correct behavior, wasn't that rather rude?

This time Cookie didn't say a word but took something Norm handed her and concealed it on her lap. What on earth was that all about?

Oh well. I turned to my shrimp, enjoying every morsel as well as Rossi's hand on my knee, caressing me secretly, giving me bad boy glances from under those hooded lids.

A few minutes later, though he hadn't even touched his shrimp, Francesco announced, "Time for the antipasto."

"These shrimp are scrumptious," I said. "You don't like yours either?"

"I been eatin' them all afternoon. I'm ready for some

provolone and salami and a couple slices of tomato." He tore off a chunk of warm bread and dipped it in a saucer of oil.

What about his delicate stomach? I wondered as Chip and AudreyAnn cleared away the first course dishes. Donny must have taken his boss's impatience as marching orders, for he stood too and, picking up his dish and Francesco's, carried them out to the kitchen.

As we waited for the antipasto to be served, Cookie and Norm sat in glum silence, draining their drinks. She had both hands on the tabletop, so whatever Norm had given her she'd put down somewhere. Her purse probably.

"The party's dying," Francesco declared, jumping up. At the bar, he uncorked a bottle of Chianti, brought it to the table and poured some for everyone without asking if we wanted any.

He returned to his seat and raised his wine on high. *"Cin cin!"* A ray of late-day sun struck his glass, and even from where I sat, I could see the Chianti glowing ruby red in the fading light. "Preppy, huh?" he said to me and laughed.

My glass halfway to my lips, I smiled. There was definitely something about Francesco that—

A scream straight out of a horror movie rent the air. And then a crash. My hand shook, splashing wine all over the white tablecloth.

"Jesus Christ, the kitchen." Francesco leaped to his feet and raced inside with Rossi right beside him. Jewels scooped up the baby and hurried in too. Then Bonita. Only Cookie and Norm remained at the table, and as I followed the others, I heard Cookie say, "The help one gets these days is atrocious."

Hovering in the kitchen doorway as if afraid to get any closer, Jewels stood clasping the baby to her breast. I peered over her shoulder. Ankle deep in antipasto, mouth hanging open, AudreyAnn clutched her cheeks with both hands. Beside the stove, Bonita and Chip ignored the rattle of a steaming kettle and stared at the floor where Rossi crouched beside Donny.

"What the hell happened to him? Did he pass out or something?" Francesco asked, bending over Donny. "That scream scared the shit outta me."

Spread-eagled on his back, his black ankle boots pointing east and west, Donny wasn't moving. His mouth twisted to one side, his normally swarthy skin an unearthly white, he stared unseeing at the kitchen ceiling.

Rossi tried for a pulse, shook his head and whipped out his cell phone. "Medical emergency. Two fifty Rum Row. This is Lieutenant Victor Rossi, Naples PD…I can't get a pulse, and he isn't breathing…I'm not certain, but that could be." The 911 dispatcher must have asked if Donny were dead. "Someone will be at the front door." Rossi pocketed his cell. "They're on their way."

"Chip, the stove," Bonita said.

"What?"

"You need to turn it off."

Chip came back to reality with a start. "Oh sure." He peered into the boiling pot. "Well, so much for the ravioli. It's in shreds."

"You asshole," AudreyAnn hissed between her front teeth. "How can you think of food at a time like this? That's Donny lying there. My Donny."

Her Donny? Since when?

Looking like he wanted to burst into tears, Chip started wheezing. With the baby in her arms, Jewels walked over to the stove and turned off the burners, taking a moment to pat Chip's arm. A sweet girl.

As Francesco knelt over Donny, stroking his cheeks,

urging him back to consciousness, Rossi kept a finger on Donny's pulse, his expression grim.

"He can't wait," Francesco said. "He needs CPR *now*."

"I'll do it," Jewels said, handing the baby to Bonita.

"You know how?" Francesco asked.

"Yes, I think so. I had to once for my mother."

As she went to kneel over Donny's inert form, Rossi caught her by the arm. "I heard a siren. The medics are here. They'll take care of him. The front door, Deva."

Before I could move, Bonita stepped forward. "It is my job, *señor,* I go."

Outside, a siren's screech came to a sudden stop. Rossi let go of Donny's wrist and stood. A moment later an ERU team raced into the kitchen behind Bonita.

Gently touching Francesco on his heaving shoulder, the female partner, a muscular girl of twenty-something with *Alex* stitched onto her uniform pocket, said, "You can stop now, sir." But Francesco didn't stop and kept on in a frenzy, patting Donny's face, pummeling his chest, *willing* him to respond. Willing him to wake up and big-shoulder his way through the kitchen…through life.

The girl nodded at her male partner, who had *Mike* on his pocket. He leaned over Francesco, grabbed him around the middle and lifted him off Donny, out of their way. Francesco slumped on the floor, watching ashen faced as they went to work.

Long moments passed in silent tension before, finally, Mike closed Donny's eyelids and stood. "I'm sorry. There's nothing more we can do. He was gone before we got here."

With a wild keening as the only warning, AudreyAnn flung herself across the kitchen and onto Donny's body. She lay crumpled on top of him, then lifting his head and rocking to and fro, she clutched him to her bosom. But even that didn't bring him back to life.

Alone with him in a world of her own making, not knowing or caring who else was there, she crooned to him. "Oh no. Oh no. No, Donny. No. Don't leave me. Please. Don't leave me."

I stole a quick glance at Chip. Despite the steamy kitchen air, he wheezed so loudly his ragged breathing echoed across the room. Donny was dead and Chip was alive, but had AudreyAnn just killed his reason for living?

FOURTEEN

THE MEDICS COVERED Donny with a blanket and lifted him onto a gurney. Francesco, his head between his knees, stayed on the floor where he'd been dumped. After giving little Frannie to Bonita, Jewels knelt beside her husband and put an arm around him, cooing to him in the same soft voice she used on the baby. Like the baby, Francesco responded, smiling weakly at her one moment, wrapping an arm around her the next. Tears streamed down his cheeks. Facing the grim reality of a loved one's death, he was as heartbroken as anyone I'd ever known, and my own heart went out to him.

Clinging to each other for support, Cookie and Norm ambled into the kitchen, two sheets to the wind as my Irish nana used to say. They must have been ransacking the bar while the rest of us were caught up in the crisis.

"What's the matter?" Norm wanted to know. It came out "Whasha matta?" so nobody bothered to answer him.

"Is there a problem?" Cookie asked. "Ish there a problem?" Nobody answered her either.

"A physician will need to determine the cause of death," Alex said. "Do we have a next of kin present?"

Rossi pointed to Francesco. "Mr. Grandese there was the deceased's employer. You might ask him."

Clipboard perched on her knee, she crouched on the other side of Francesco. "I have a few questions, sir."

"Shoot," he said wincing at his own word.

"What is the deceased's name?"

"Donatello Grandese."

What?

"A relation?"

Ignoring the tears streaming along his face and soaking into his chest hair, Francesco said, "My cousin. He was a good man, made some mistakes in life but paid his dues. I promised our *nonno*…our grandfather…I'd look out for him. Some job I did, huh?"

At that moment I wanted to tell him he *had* done a good job. Not only had he tried to help Donny, he'd reached out to Chip and Bonita too. Whether he knew it or not, Francesco was a nurturer.

Alex murmured a few words of comfort and continued writing on her clipboard. After asking several more questions, she had Francesco sign a release. "As soon as cause of death is determined, the coroner's office will be in touch with you." She stood, gave him a copy of the release form and pocketed her pen.

Mike got behind the gurney, but before he could wheel it out of the kitchen, Francesco sprang to his feet. "Give me a minute," he said. The medics stepped back, and lifting the blanket from Donny's face, Francesco kissed both his cheeks. *"Ciao, bambino,"* he whispered.

Clearly, cinderblock Donny had been a kind of little brother to him. As if he couldn't bear the sight of seeing Donny leave forever, Francesco covered his eyes with his hands as the medics wheeled the gurney out to the waiting ambulance.

Bonita broke the silence that had fallen like a lead weight over the kitchen. "I'll put the baby to bed, *señora?*"

Jewels nodded and said, "Let's leave the kitchen, everybody," and taking her husband by the arm, she drew him outside to the terrace. She eased him onto a patio lounger, went over to the bar and held up a Courvoisier bottle, checking see if there were anything left in it. *Norm and Cookie?* Satisfied that there was, she poured two fingers of cognac into a plastic glass and brought it back to Francesco.

"You've had a shock, honey. Drink this. It'll make you feel better."

He looked up at her with love in his eyes. "You're taking good care of me, sweetheart, not like me with Donny."

"Don't blame yourself. He's in God's hands now."

"Thash right," Norm agreed.

"You still here?" Francesco asked, peering over at him in the half dark. "Why don't you go home? Take your wife with you."

"Thash an insult." Cookie struggled to her feet.

"Just leave," Francesco said. "Party's over."

I blew out a breath. Despite his world class furniture, Francesco wasn't going to be Mr. Popularity in the 'hood anytime soon.

"We'll be going too," Rossi said. "We're sorry about what happened. Call me at the station if you need me. Anytime."

Stretched out on the lounger, looking too used up to move, Francesco took a swig of his cognac. "Appreciate it, Lieutenant."

I patted Francesco's shoulder in farewell and gave Jewels a kiss on the cheek. "If there's anything I can do...anything at all, let me know."

"I will, Deva." And climbing onto Francesco's lap, she laid her head on his chest and snuggled against him.

As Rossi and I walked toward the kitchen, my heart beat a little faster than usual. No telling what shape Chip and AudreyAnn would be in.

Surprise! Peace reigned in the room...or at least quiet. No dish throwing. No shouting. No sobbing in angst. Not

even any wheezing. Chip stood at the sink, scrubbing the
ravioli kettle, while AudreyAnn stacked the dishwasher.

"You guys all right?" Rossi asked.

"We're okay," Chip answered, his voice noncommittal.

AudreyAnn continued to drop silverware into the dish-
washer basket without saying anything.

"There for a while AudreyAnn had a meltdown," Chip
said, sending a guarded glance her way. "Her problem is
she's got a big heart. She loves everybody. Can't stand seeing anyone in trouble."

She shot me a wary-eyed look. Woman-to-woman we
both understood each other. A year ago, when she had
the affair with Dick Parker, the former owner of Surfside
Condominiums, Chip concealed the truth from himself
with the same statement. Almost word-for-word. Was he
so much in love with her he consciously denied she was
a serial cheater? Or so needy he refused to acknowledge
the truth to himself? Poor Chip. Either way, I felt sorry
for the guy and returned AudreyAnn's suspicious stare
with a shrug.

Ever the detective, Rossi asked, "So tell me, Chip, what
exactly happened to Donny? I mean, how did it play out?"

"Nothing unusual. At least not at first." Chip removed
the kettle from the sink and wiped it with a towel. "He
brought in a couple of dishes and stood by the island there
scarfing down Francesco's leftover shrimp. Next thing I
know, boom, he's on the floor. Isn't that right, Audrey-
Ann?"

Wordless, but tearing up, she nodded.

"Just like that? No warning?" Rossi asked, disbelief
in his tone.

"That's right," Chip said. "One minute he's fine, enjoying the shrimp, the next minute he's down. I guess heart
attacks work that way."

The discarded shrimp dishes still cluttered the island.

"You have any plastic wrap?" Rossi asked.

"Sure, in that drawer over there."

Rossi opened the drawer, tore off a sheet of wrap and draped it over one of the shrimp dishes. The one without salsa stains. "If you don't mind, I want to have this examined."

AudreyAnn, big-eyed, stopped filling the dishwasher and stared at Rossi. "Poison?" she whispered.

Rossi shook his head. "Probably just some bad shrimp. E. coli can be toxic. Best to be sure."

"YOU KNEW DONNY was Francesco's cousin, didn't you?" I asked as soon as Rossi and I were alone in what he called his party car, a vintage BMW he kept as shiny as his badge.

"Yes."

"And you don't think E. coli killed him, do you?"

"I'm doubtful. It doesn't work that fast."

"Poison?"

"I hope to God not." He spoke in that professional I-can't-tell-you-anything tone I hated.

"But you think it is."

He sighed. "Deva—"

"A lecture's coming."

He drove as he always did, staring straight ahead, no nonsense, no sideways glances, all attention on the road. "I'm a cop." Well, he did pull his glance off the road for a nanosecond and swiveled it over to me. "There will be times when I can't share information with you. That won't mean I don't trust you. It will mean I'd be violating security. Or placing you in danger. Or both. So bottom line, don't ask. My silence in a police matter will never mean anything personal against you."

I leaned toward him, straining against my seatbelt. "So you *do* think this is a police matter?"

Another sigh, louder this time. "You didn't hear a thing I said."

"I heard every word. But *until* this is a police matter, why can't you answer me?"

I knew I had him. The logic in that was fabulous.

He shook his head *and* sighed. "All right, rather than argue, I'll make an exception this one time." A pause then, "According to what Chip saw, Donny went down fast. No warning. No chest pain. Just a sudden collapse. I'm not saying that doesn't happen, but I want it checked out. The autopsy should clarify the cause of death. If there's any trace of a foreign substance—"

"You mean poison?"

"—in the body or on the shrimp dish we took that will confirm—"

"—your suspicions."

"Or disprove them. Satisfied now?" He turned right onto Gordon Drive.

I wasn't ready to give up my bone. "That's why you didn't let Jewels give Donny CPR, isn't it? Just in case there was poison residue on his lips."

"Yes. Just in case."

"But why would anyone want to kill Donny?"

"If someone did kill him, that's what I'll be paid to find out. *If* being the operative word. He had a long rap sheet plus some creepy pals. Maybe Francesco hired him to help straighten him out. Who knows? And now, Mrs. Dunne, home to bed?"

He definitely took his attention off the road that time.

All along Gordon Drive, night mist from the Gulf enveloped the car, wrapping us in a velvet cocoon redolent with sea salt and jasmine. Alone with Rossi and at peace for the first time in hours, I wanted the road never to end, the drive to go on forever, the moment to last an eternity.

But reality intervened. "I need to get back to Surfside, Rossi. Lee's been alone all evening, last night too. Sorry, but…" To take the sting from my words, I reached over to stroke his thigh. He grasped my fingers and drove with one hand on the wheel. A first. He was breaking his rules left and right tonight.

"I know Lee needs you. This situation won't go on forever."

"No," I murmured, happy that he understood, stretching against the seat belt again to give him a big sloppy kiss on the cheek.

"It better not go on, or I'll be turning into a gentleman caller." He barked out a laugh. "Tomorrow let's grab a bite after work. I want to discuss a plan I have for helping Lee."

I relaxed the rest of the way home, and when we got to Surfside, Rossi released both seatbelts, took me in his arms and kissed me crazy.

By my front door, not wanting to say good-night, I leaned against the building's stucco wall and flung my arms around his neck. He pressed into me. Hard. One more kiss then he dragged himself away. "Call you in the morning. Sleep well."

He climbed into the BMW and drove off, his rear lights glowing like tiger eyes in the night. That was when it hit me, and waving my arms and shouting his name, I ran after the car. He didn't hear me, and I stood on the tarmac watching his lights turn into pinpricks in the dark. All the trauma of the evening must have unhinged me. I'd forgotten to tell him I overheard Francesco threatening Norm. And so had Bonita. Also I wanted to share my theory about what the threat might mean. Francesco was the one who was supposed to eat that shrimp. He was the one who should have died, not Donny.

That meant somebody murdered the wrong man. Could the killer be Norm Harkness?

FIFTEEN

WELL, I SHRUGGED, no point in remaining alone in the dark no matter how velvet the night. I'd go in and text Rossi my big news.

In the living room, the sofa lights and the TV were blazing away. The minute I stepped into the foyer, Lee leaped up, humming with excitement.

"If y'all hadn't come in soon, I'd surely have broken into bits," she said, whirling me around the living room.

Out of breath and dizzy, we collapsed on the sofa together.

"So tell me!"

"Paulo texted me an hour ago."

"And?"

"And—" her eyes sparkled with blue fire, "—he has a commission, his first big break. I'm so thrilled! Some important man wants a portrait of his wife. A few more commissions like this one, and Paulo will have saved enough to send for me." A little crease appeared on her forehead. "He likes Paris. Nobody there notices that he's Jamaican. What he's really saying is nobody cares if he's black." Her blue eyes flared wide. "Why should they? He's so handsome. So kind. So gifted." The little crease on her forehead deepened. "I'll think of that and not about whether the woman he's painting is beautiful…but she probably is. Why else would her husband want her portrait?"

"Why?" Insecurity, that bugaboo of lovers, had obviously sunk its teeth into Lee. No wonder. She had set the man she adored free in Paris of all places. But mentioning that wouldn't comfort her now, so I said, "Because he loves her with every fiber of his being. Because no other woman on earth exists for him. Because he wants her image on his wall, close to him, where he can gaze at her every day… even when she's far away."

I let my words shimmer around us until Lee smiled and said, "You're what my gran used to call a wise woman. And I've been acting like a foolish one. My momma wouldn't be proud. I'm so glad y'all got home before I fell asleep. I was just dying to share Paulo's news." She covered a yawn with a hand. "How was the party? Have a good time?"

"No, we didn't. One of the men collapsed."

Halfway through another yawn, she dropped her hand from her mouth. "Collapsed?"

"Died."

"Oh no. Who was he?"

"Someone I hardly knew. Someone too young to die."

My voice trailed off. In my heart of hearts I didn't think Donny had expired from natural causes. Neither, I felt sure, did Rossi. He was probably at the forensic lab already, demanding the shrimp dish be examined immediately.

Lee stood and stretched. "I think I'll turn in, Deva. The excitement about Paulo has me all tuckered out."

I lay back on the sofa. "Good night, Lee. I'll sit up for a while. I need to send Rossi a message. Then I'll try to relax before going to bed. The whole night's been…a nightmare. I couldn't sleep right now."

Lee turned off most of the condo lamps, and I lay slumped on the couch in the half glow, enjoying, as always, the soft sheen of my Irish furniture. Almost everything in the room had belonged to Jack's Dublin family—the mahogany hunt board, the four-drawer chests, the brass candlesticks, the Sheffield silver, the drop leaf table and, anchoring everything, the inspiration for my peach and taupe color scheme, the Tabriz rug in those muted shades that take generations of wear to achieve. I loved every piece. Each one reminded me of the Jack I had lost. Each one not nearly as valuable as Francesco's stunners, but still valuable enough.

Of course! I bolted upright on the couch. Something else I hadn't thought of had hit me. I'd sell a piece of Jack's furniture. Maybe two pieces. That would yield more than enough money to send Lee to Paris. Drawing in a deep breath, I fell back against the cushions. What a good idea. I could do this. Yes, I could.

But what could I bear to sell? I studied each piece with an eye to parting with it. One of the four-drawer chests maybe? No. Not a good idea to break up a pair. Both then? I heaved a sigh. Instead, how about the Tabriz? Or the rose medallion collection? Yes, definitely the porcelains. And also…well, I'd decide exactly what in the morning. Letting a few pieces go would solve at least one problem if not all the others. Especially not the Donny problem. For that I'd have to wait until Rossi contacted me.

"It was cyanide," Rossi said when he rang the shop the next morning. "At least on the shrimp dish. The coroner's exam will take more time, but I think there's little doubt of the outcome."

"What happens next?"

"We wait for the autopsy results. Until then, should anyone ask, Donny died from a sudden heart attack. Understood?"

"Absolutely."

"Good," he said, sounding relieved.

"Did you get my message?" I asked.

"Yes. Thanks. It's an interesting tidbit. I'll keep it in mind."

Not a very satisfying response to my big revelation about Francesco and Norm, but he had warned me that when it came to his work not to expect much sharing. I didn't like that but could live with it. I gave a mental shrug—as long as I was involved with Rossi I'd have to.

After we hung up, I mulled over what he'd told me. If the coroner pronounced Donny's death a murder, wouldn't the chef be the first suspect? The chef and the salad girl? The salad girl who'd wept over the body of *her* Donny, hugging him to her breasts, distraught and grief-stricken.

An act?

I flung down my pen, all interest in the Grandese presentation boards vanishing. AudreyAnn had left Chip for six long, mysterious months and then made a dramatic return to his ever-loving arms. Had she been living with Donny and been dumped? From her behavior at his death, they were far from strangers. Could she be a scornee still in love with the scorner?

If so, how did that implicate Chip? Had he killed Donny in a fit of jealous rage? Lovable, bumbling, Shrek-like Chip?

Hard to believe.

And what of helpful, sweet Bonita? A widow with sad eyes still grieving for her dead husband. Had she accepted Francesco's help because she needed it, or because she wanted revenge? Moving in and out of the kitchen all evening, she'd had ample opportunity, and Donny would be her logical target. Though the Ferrari had belonged to Francesco, Donny had actually caused the spark that exploded and killed Tomas.

I shook my head at my own stupidity and picked up the

pen again…Francesco was the intended victim, not Donny. So there went my revenge theory.

I stared up at the shop ceiling. Maybe I should change the white to a flattering pink wash. *Hmm.* Suppose some-one slipped cyanide into the shrimp dish *after* it had been removed to the kitchen? Then Donny was the intended victim after all, and I was back to the Chip-AudreyAnn-Bonita theory of murder one.

I heaved a sigh so loud Lee looked up, startled, from the carton of Steuben bowls she was unpacking. Until the po-lice received the coroner's report, speculating was a waste of time. Though no doubt Rossi's mind was already rac-ing with possibilities. He'd probably even drawn up a list of suspects and motives. That the list would include me, I dwelt on briefly. That a list drawn up by someone else in Homicide would include both Rossi and me, I dwelt on far longer. My fault.

Rossi's warning echoed in my brain. If I'd listened to him and refused to take on the Grandese project, neither of us would be in this mess today. To Rossi's credit, he hadn't mentioned that inescapable detail. But the guilt weighed on me nonetheless. Without question, we were both poten-tial suspects, a fact he must have recognized the instant he suspected poison.

Rossi. I couldn't help him with any concerns the chief might have, but his worry that Jack had a lock on my heart I could try to put to rest. One way was to go ahead and see my gynecologist. Find out whether I could have a child. Prove to Rossi that I wasn't holding on to the past, using it as an excuse to cling to old memories.

I wasn't, was I?

No. I dug the cell phone out of my purse and punched in my GYN's number.

Dr. Elizabeth Enright couldn't see me for two months.

In case of emergency, her assistant would give me a referral. Was this an emergency? No. The truth had waited this long, it could wait a few weeks longer. Besides, now that Jack was gone, I had no plans for having a child in the near future—not with Rossi—not with anyone. I had a business to establish, a busy life, a full life. All I wanted from my doctor was the truth.

Actually I had talked myself into feeling a bit better when another call came in on the shop phone and blew my good mood south of the equator.

"For you, Deva. A Mrs. Cookie Chandler Harkness." Lee covered the receiver with a hand. "She sounds mighty fancy."

I wrinkled my nose and took the receiver, wondering what on earth she wanted. "Good morning, Cookie."

"Miss Dunne."

"Mrs., actually. But do call me Deva."

"Oh. Of course. Terrible business last night. Terrible. But you already know what happened, and that's not the reason I'm calling."

"No? Then how may I help you?" I used my Back Bay Boston voice, which I enjoyed hauling out once in a while when the occasion warranted. Like now.

"Well you can't help *me,* but I know a young man…his mother and I were roommates at Miss Porter's ages ago… anyway, that's neither here nor there. His name is Nikhil Jamison, and he needs help decorating his apartment. He doesn't have much to spend so I told him about you. I know your services are cheap."

Cheap? God, the woman set my teeth on edge.

"If you mean inexpensive, Cookie, what gave you that idea?"

"Well, you're hardly Carlton Varney." She laughed, a tinkling, glass-shattering laugh.

I wanted to kill her. "I'm sorry, Cookie, but I'm too busy to take on another client. Do express my regrets to your young man."

"But that's not—"

"I really must go. I'm late for an appointment. *Ciao.*" *The nerve of that broad. I'll give her cheap.*

I hung up and forced my attention back onto the Rum Row project. Family tragedy or not, I suspected Francesco would want to see my concept ASAP.

For major projects like this one, I did floor plans to scale showing all major furniture placements. As soon as I completed Francesco's project and was paid in full, I planned to purchase a new computer and use CAD—computer aided drafting—for big jobs. No more hand-rendered floor plans after this one.

Francesco had given me snapshots of his antiques, including the dimensions of each piece. I spread the photos out on my drafting table and began the selection.

I didn't get too far. Usually I could ignore the foot traffic and distractions of the shop to concentrate on planning projects, but not today. As Lee greeted two customers searching for drapery fabric, I swiveled away from my project to stare unseeing at the opposite wall.

Say Donny's death had been an accident and Francesco was the intended victim. Who at the party wanted him dead?

Norm Harkness would be my first pick. He had a powerful motive. Francesco had threatened him with exposure if he didn't pay back the money he owed him, but from what I overheard, Norm wasn't able to settle the debt.

What about Cookie? Would she actually kill an offensive neighbor when she could simply cut him dead? Or to be serious, what if she knew about Norm's debt? If she did, would she commit murder for her man? Divorce was so much easier. I gave a mental shrug. Who knew?

Then there was Jewels. Caring for one baby, pregnant with another, surely she didn't want her husband dead. Except, of course, that as his widow she'd inherit everything. An evil thought crept into my mind. Though she appeared to love little Frannie, was she harboring a bitter resentment against Francesco for having taken another lover?

As for sweet, grieving Bonita, no way would she murder anyone. She simply didn't have the *gravitas* for such a violent deed…still, why was she eavesdropping on Francesco's argument with Norm?

Phew.

I swiveled around to the desk, but the questions wouldn't leave me alone. Chances were remote that Simon Yaeger's search would turn up a long-lost owner for all those Grover Clevelands. So with Francesco out of the way, the half million plus would soon be Chip's free and clear. Murders had been committed for a lot less. That left AudreyAnn. If she didn't love Chip, her motive for staying with him was security, so her reason for wanting Francesco dead echoed Chip's.

No. I paced around the display tables, searching for solutions, but I was fishing without a pole. Somehow, for either Chip or his squeeze to kill Donny in a fit of jealous rage made more sense than for them to kill Francesco for money he might not even attempt to claim.

That left only Rossi and me on my suspect list. Why would I want to kill a man who had given me *carte blanche* to work on a house I loved? As for Rossi, what possible motive would he have? Ridiculous to even consider him for the suspect list.

No, we were both in the clear. At least I hoped to God

we were, and that the chief wouldn't take Rossi off the case. For if anyone could solve it, he was the man.

Having succeeded in calming myself, I went back to the presentation boards. Definitely historic Putnam Ivory on the living room walls, classic white on the woodwork, and we'd retain the dark walnut-stained hardwood floors. They were in perfect condition. Altogether my plan would create a neutral envelope against which each Federal piece would be as prominent as a five-carat diamond in a Tiffany setting.

The furniture placement did present a design challenge, though. As you entered the living room, the far wall overlooking the pool was all glass. So placing the magnificent Townsend desk straight ahead as the focal point wouldn't be feasible. I'd have to center it on the right wall and place the largest of the inlaid chests opposite. An oil painting over the chest would balance the visual weight of the Townsend…an oriental on the floor…the Zuber paper would give me more than enough color ideas for rugs.

I'd float twin sofas in ivory linen in the center of the room—one facing the pool and one with its back to it. Very sleek, very minimalist, very Juan Montoya. A coffee table in glass would visually disappear, not war with the antiques and yet be serviceable…unless Francesco wanted to use one of the blanket chests for that purpose. No, that wouldn't be sophisticated enough. What if…

The Yarmouthport bells on the shop door jangled, interrupting my fragile concentration. I glanced up. A prince of prep in khaki pants, rep tie and striped shirt, and with a gait like an overgrown puppy, loped over to Lee. Could this be Cookie's friend's son? No. Even Cookie wouldn't have the nerve to send him here when I'd refused to take him on as a client.

Oh, yes, she would.

I flung down my pen again. At the rate I was going, completing the presentation boards would take roughly the same time as finishing the Sistine Chapel.

"Mrs. Dunne handles the designing," Lee said to him. "Right now she's in the middle of a project. But if y'all want to look around for a moment, I'll see if she'll see you. Who shall I say is calling?"

He murmured something I didn't catch and, reaching into his shirt pocket, removed a business card and handed it to her.

Well, well. He looked like a recent college grad, twenty-one or -two at the most. Lee put the card on my desk.

Nikhil Jamison
Licensed Broker
Harkness Investments, Inc.

Harkness? This lad worked for Norm? My interest in Cookie's young friend suddenly shot to the ceiling.

SIXTEEN

Intrigued, I said, "I'll be happy to speak to Mr. Jamison, Lee."

He heard me and crossed the shop to my drafting table with a few long-legged strides. "Mrs. Dunne, I'm Nikhil Jamison. Cookie Harkness sent—"

"—you to me," I finished, trying not to show my exasperation. And clearly failing. His smile faded. Contrite, I stood and extended my hand. This kid wasn't responsible for Cookie's arrogance. "Nikhil's an unusual name," I said, making nice, before sinking back onto my chair.

"I know. My parents honeymooned in Mumbai. Guess they used to call it Bombay. I came along nine months later." He flushed a deep magenta and added, "I have to explain my name to everyone I meet."

Ah, a kindred spirit. "Me too."

He gave me a shy smile. "Yeah, I've heard of divas, but you're my first Deva."

"It's really Devalera. My father wanted a boy and got me instead. He named me for his political hero, Eamon de Valera of Ireland. By the time I was six, I could recite de Valera's whole history."

Nikhil laughed, showing me a big, bright smile and a wealth of understanding.

"Why don't you have a seat?" I indicated the gold Chiavari chair across from my desk.

He perched on the edge and ran a nervous hand through his tousled blond hair, rumpling it even more. How appealing. I liked him on the spot and guessed that like most twenty-something guys, he was uncomfortable in a design shop.

"How may I help you?" I asked.

He gulped in a lungful of air. "I…um…have this girl-friend," he began.

"I'm not surprised to hear that," I replied causing his cheeks to flush deep red again.

"She's coming to Naples next month, after she graduates from Vanderbilt. We met there. I graduated last year…and I…I want to ask her to marry me, but…um…my apartment is such a dump that—"

"You're afraid she'll take one look, turn around and run away."

"Something like that. The way the place is looking now, for sure she won't want to stay."

"If she's in love, she will."

He glanced down at his hands. "I can't take that chance."

With his pink cheeks, his shy smile and the sincerity that oozed from his every pore, I didn't think he had a thing to worry about. But that wasn't what he'd come to hear, so I asked, "Where do you live?"

"On Tenth Avenue. A rental in the Azalea Building."

"I know the area well. Great location. Near all the action on Third Street South."

"Yeah, it's a cool spot. That's why I'm leasing there."

His apartment was in what I called the flower complex. Named for a different blossom, each building part of a cluster of two-story structures set inside a wide swath of grassy lawn. The units were modest but affordable and quiet.

"Tell me about your place. Start with the size and the number of rooms."

"Roughly one thousand square feet. A bedroom." Cute,

he listed that first. "Living room, small kitchen, small bath. And a patio."

"Appliances?"

"Oh sure. Pretty new." He shrugged. "They all work, anyway."

"How about furniture?"

"A bed." Funny how that topped the list. "A queen size. A guitar. A couple of plastic lawn chairs. A flat screen TV on a stand. It was a graduation gift. That's about all," he said, his expression telegraphing that the dismal list meant I'd turn him down.

"Now for the sixty-four thousand dollar question. How much do you have to spend?"

"Fifteen hundred," he said without hesitation. "For everything. I can't go over that figure."

As I studied him across the desk top, he paused, clearly torn about whether he should say more. He must have decided to go ahead for he added, "My trust fund doesn't kick in until I'm twenty-five. So until then, I'm on a tight budget. My dad thinks being strapped builds character or something."

He flushed yet again. An endearing habit, but I wondered how it would play out in the competitive world of investment counseling. Still, despite the boyish flush, he knew his fiscal limits and obviously had no intention of going over them.

"What was your major at Vanderbilt?" I asked, suddenly wanting to know.

"Economics with a business minor."

"Ah, so that's why you're with Harkness Investments?"

He nodded. "The Harknesses are old family friends. Norm's giving me a chance to prove myself, so to speak."

"Sounds good," I said, though after what I'd overheard

at Chez Grandese, I wondered if working with Norm *was* good.

"It's excellent training, and Norm is a great teacher except that—" On the edge of a verbal cliff, Nikhil skidded to a halt. "I'm not such a swift learner."

I smiled. He hadn't finished his original thought, but his cover-up had been lightening quick. Nikhil was a lot brighter than he let on and a lot less innocent than his frequent flushing indicated. I liked him. I liked him a lot.

I eased back in the ergonomic chair and swiveled for a moment before hitting him with the facts. "Fifteen hundred isn't much to work with."

"I know."

"Out of that I take twenty percent off the top. So…" I leaned over the desk, "…that leaves twelve hundred to convert an empty, dated apartment into a…" My turn to skid to a halt.

"…love nest," he finished with an outsized grin. "Can you do it?"

Yes, I did like this kid. And I liked the way he'd just challenged me.

"As they say in Harvard law school, 'You bet your sweet patootie I can.'"

He laughed, didn't flush, and said, "Done!"

I held up a palm. "But only with sweat equity." I pointed a finger at him. "Yours."

"I'm not afraid of hard work."

"Good. You're going to have a chance to prove it. So… when can I see your apartment?"

We set a viewing date for early the following Saturday morning. I confess the project intrigued me. One of the reasons I'd opened my own business, in addition to making money—no sense in being a hypocrite about that—was to help people with modest budgets create lovely environments. To make their lives better, more joyous—happier, I guess is what I mean. While that didn't make me Sister Mary Deva of the Order of Heavenly Designs, it went a long way toward boosting my morale and giving me the feeling that my work was meaningful. Nikhil's project was a variation on that theme. In his case I'd also be playing cupid. I loved the very idea.

While Lee wrapped a Steuben bowl for a customer needing a wedding gift, I rose and strolled toward the door with Nikhil. Before we reached it, the bells on the handle jangled, and Rossi stepped into the shop.

"What a nice surprise," I said delighted to see him. He looked heavy eyed and harried like he hadn't had much sleep. Or any at all.

"Nikhil Jamison," I said, "this is Lieutenant Victor Rossi of the Naples Police Department."

Nikhil shot a startled glance my way before reaching out to shake Rossi's hand.

He seemed so taken aback, I explained, "The lieutenant is a friend of mine."

"Oh, I see."

Why was he so relieved? "Nikhil is an investment broker," I told Rossi. "He's with Norm Harkness's firm."

"Interesting field," Rossi said. "For those who know what they're doing. Afraid I don't have that talent. Congratulations."

Nikhil reddened at Rossi's compliment. "I'm just learning the business. Norm took me in as a favor to my dad."

"Is that right? Know each other, do they?"

Baggy eyed or not, Rossi segued right into detective mode, staying low key, non-threatening, letting the suspect talk until he revealed something significant.

Wait a minute. What suspect?

His ploy worked. Nikhil said, "Yes, the families go back

a long way. Mrs. Harkness and my mother were roommates at Miss Porter's. And her father and my grandfather were business partners for years."

"Investment banking?" Rossi asked, offhand like he was only casually interested, only making polite conversation—the fox.

"No, jewelry manufacturing. Costume jewelry for the most part."

Anyone who didn't know Rossi well wouldn't have noticed his whole body stiffen for an instant. A millisecond only, and though he quickly stifled his surprise, from his reaction in that one split second I knew he'd heard something revealing. But what?

"Are they still in business?" he asked, his voice disarmingly soft.

"No, they sold it a few years ago and retired. Foreign imports did them in."

"The way of the world," Rossi said with a shrug.

"Yes, well, I'd better get back to the office. Good to meet you, Lieutenant, Mrs. Dunne. See you on Saturday."

"I'll be there," I said.

When Nikhil left, Rossi sent a quick glance Lee's way. She was deep in conversation with the Steuben customer. "How's Lee doing?" he asked quietly.

"What can I say? She's lonely."

"Do you think a one-way ticket to Paris and four thousand in cash would be enough to reunite those two?"

"Yes, I'm planning to—"

"Good." He actually smiled. "I'll get to the bank and take care of it but not today."

"Wait up a bit, Rossi, I have an idea."

"Tell me later, sweetheart, I have to run. I came in to tell you the coroner contacted me this morning. Donny was poisoned. Cyanide."

"Murder?"

At my stupid question Rossi just shrugged. "Until proven otherwise." His jaw tightened. "I want you to drop Grandese as a client."

"You know I can't do that."

"Can't or won't?" He cocked an eyebrow. "For me?"

"Aw, Rossi, that's not fair."

"True, but I had to try one last time. Enter that house as little as possible, and above all, do not eat or drink anything while you're there."

"Fine. I won't. But if there's that much danger, what about Jewels and the baby? And Francesco? What about him? I'm convinced he was the intended victim. Nothing else makes sense."

"Is that so?" Rossi treated me to a maddeningly superior grin. Which I guess I deserved. Me and my theories. "At the moment their welfare is out of my hands," he said. "However, as soon as I leave you, I'm heading for Rum Row to talk to them."

"How about Chip and AudreyAnn and Bonita? What does this mean for them? Norm and Cookie too?"

"They're all on my call list. See you sometime next week," he said wryly, giving me a distracted little nothing of a kiss on the cheek.

"While we're on the subject, why did you stiffen up when Nikhil was talking?"

He glanced down at himself. "Did you do that?"

Men.

SEVENTEEN

DESPITE HIS FLIP parting comment, Rossi had looked harried when he left the shop. No wonder. He not only had a crime to solve, he had a career to protect—his own. Once again, the realization that I was responsible for our involvement in the case ate at me like acid.

Mea culpa.

Slumped next to me in the passenger seat, Lee kept sending anxious glances my way. She looked tense, poor thing. She hadn't had any fun since arriving back in Naples, only work and sleep and longing for her love.

I returned her worried looks with a smile. The biggest, most dazzling I could muster. Even faked smiles are better than frowns, and she rewarded me with a timid one in return.

"What do you say we go out for dinner?" I asked. "My treat."

A little light leaped into her eyes, but she said, "Yesterday y'all bought a barbequed chicken from the Publix deli. There's a lot left."

"Screw the chicken, Lee. Let's shake our moody blues."

She shook her head. "You sure are using colorful language."

"Damn right. That's why we have to get you back to Paulo before it rubs off."

She smiled, and I pulled a U-ee and headed back into town.

"How about the Irish Pub, our old watering hole? The

food's far from gourmet, but the people watching is great, and they pour a mean glass of cheap white wine."

She giggled. Music to my ears.

"Young lady, you're going to be in Paris with your husband before you know it. Guaranteed."

"Oh, Deva." Lee heaved a sigh. "If only I could be."

She could, if Rossi had anything to do with it. Unless I beat him to the punch, but first I had to carve out some time to get to Treasure Island Antiques. Then, not only would I surprise Lee, I'd knock the socks off Rossi with a little secret I had in mind. I was as sure of that as I was of my own name. It felt good to be sure of something for a change.

As we cruised along Fifth Avenue South, a parking slot opened up—a minor miracle—and I eased the Audi into it.

In the warm April evening, the flower-perfumed air hinted that summer was ready to muscle its way into southwest Florida. Another month and the humidity would be relentless. But for now the palm fronds waved in the balmy breeze like fans, and the tourists strolling the open square wore the satisfied look of travelers who had hit perfect weather.

We sat at a table on the pub terrace overlooking Sugden Square and ordered two house chardonnays and an appetizer plate of nachos. After sipping our wine and snacking on the nachos, we decided on two of the house specials, Black Angus burgers. Bad for the hips, good for the soul.

I had a second glass of chardonnay so Lee drove home, chatting about Paulo all the way. Back at Surfside, quiet prevailed, not even a gecko scurried along the walkway. With no hope of seeing Rossi that evening, I slid a DVD into the player and settled down with Lee to watch *Titanic* yet again.

An hour into the show, just when Leonardo DiCaprio in

a borrowed tuxedo bent over to kiss Kate Winslet's hand, a scream rent the quiet spring night.

Then another. And another. Lee and I leaped off the couch.

"AudreyAnn," I said, racing out of the condo. With Lee right behind me, I tore across the lawn and barged into Chip's lanai.

"He's dead," AudreyAnn screamed. "He's dead."

"Who?" I asked, knowing, knowing.

"Chip." Her voice rose to a banshee shriek. "He's dead, I tell you. Dead!"

"Where is he?" Lee asked quietly, somehow realizing that calm was the best antidote to hysteria.

AudreyAnn pointed a trembling finger. "In there. The bathroom. Omigod."

We made a mad dash through the condo, careening to a stop in the bathroom doorway. A raw iodine odor clogged the air, and on the floor, the tiles, the bath mat, every garment Chip wore ran slick with blood. On his left wrist, a gash like an open maw oozed more blood.

"A tourniquet," I shouted. "We need a tourniquet. AudreyAnn, get a tie."

Shocked lifeless, she stood without moving.

"A tie, a tie!"

Lee ran into the master bedroom, yanked open the closet and came back with a silk necktie. Grabbing a pair of bath towels off a wall rack, I flung them on the blood-soaked floor and knelt on them. I wrapped the tie around Chip's forearm, shutting off the blood flow, hoping to God I wasn't too late. His face was as white as one of his chef's aprons.

I glanced up at AudreyAnn hovering in the doorway, wringing her hands. "Did you call 911?"

Her mouth hung open. "No. I never thought—"

"Get to the phone!"

She didn't move.

"Hurry up! He's dying."

She just stared at me. Without waiting for her to snap to, I jumped up and dashed into the kitchen. I yanked the phone off the hook and gave the emergency responder the vital information, begging her to hurry.

"I'll go out to the street and flag them down," Lee said.

I nodded. Every second counted. Trailed by a catatonic AudreyAnn, I hurried back to the bathroom to keep a vigil over Chip. His face had turned from white to gray. The seconds were eternities, though I knew only a few precious minutes had passed before the familiar siren wailed onto the Surfside tarmac.

"This way," I heard Lee call. "In here."

I stood and took AudreyAnn by the arm. It felt like a piece of wood under my hand. "Let's get out of the way," I said as two male ERU medics rushed into the bathroom.

I don't think she heard me, but she allowed me to lead her like a meek little lamb…*AudreyAnn?*…into the living room. I eased her onto Chip's oversized lounger and perched on the couch beside Lee, my fists balled in my lap.

Dear God, not Chip. Not sweet, lovable Chip.

While the medics attended him, AudreyAnn gazed straight ahead, eerily unmoving. She didn't even blink. I eyed her uneasily for a few minutes then finally asked, "Are you all right?"

She slowly turned her head in my direction and looked at me without recognition as if I were a stranger who had somehow, for some unknown reason, decided to pay a social call.

"He killed himself for me," she said, her voice filled with awe. "For me. Imagine a guy doing that."

I stared at her, unbelieving. So Chip's suicide attempt

was a tribute to her ego? A notch on her gun? Disgusted, I shook my head and got up to pace away my nervous tension. One of the medics, the one with *Bill* sewn onto his shirt pocket, strode into the living room.

I hurried over to him. "How is he?"

"He's lost a lot of blood, but his vital signs are steady. We're giving him a plasma transfusion before we move him."

"He's going to make it then?"

"His chances look good."

I turned to AudreyAnn. "Did you hear that? Chip's going to live. He didn't kill himself after all."

Hiding her face in her hands, she collapsed over the arm of the lounger and, shoulders shuddering, wept like a baby. In between sobs, gasping for breath, she blurted, "Thank God, thank God. I don't know what I'd do without him."

Lee sent me a little knowing glance that said maybe, just maybe, Chip had done the right thing—convinced the love of his life that she needed, really needed, him.

"Can someone answer a few questions for me?" Bill asked, shifting from one foot to the other, looking like the deluge was making him a little uncomfortable.

"I can," AudreyAnn said, wiping her eyes with the back of a hand. "I'm the patient's next of kin."

Wrong. But who cared about the legalities? To Chip, AudreyAnn *was* kin, and if she thought so too, this might actually turn out to be a win-win situation.

"Do you know any reason why the patient…" he consulted his clipboard, "…Mr. Salvatore, would attempt suicide?"

"Yes, I do," AudreyAnn said, her chin rising. "He thinks I don't love him." She smiled, more to herself than anyone in the room. "But I do. I just found out."

Bill flicked a male eye over her Junoesque form and

continued writing. No comment, just that eye flick. But I read flicker very well. So apparently did Lee. She winked at me.

Bill took down the rest of the information he needed and went back to the triage site in the bathroom.

AudreyAnn sniffled a few times, but continued to sit straight as an arrow in the hideous defecation-brown lounger. When Chip recovered, I'd have to speak to him about getting a new chair.

"There's another reason he fell to pieces," AudreyAnn said, glancing over a shoulder to see if Bill was anywhere in sight, "but I didn't think the medic needed to know."

"What was that?" I asked.

"Lieutenant Rossi came by today. Told us Donny was poisoned. Did you know that? Poisoned."

I nodded as a sole tear trickled down her cheek.

"Chip said even though he was innocent, when word got out he'd be finished as a chef. How could he reopen the restaurant with a poisoning hanging over his head? So whoever killed Donny, killed Chip's dream." She heaved a shuddering sigh. "If only Lieutenant Rossi had stopped there. But he didn't. He probed and probed…he wouldn't let up."

"What do you mean, wouldn't let up? That's not his style." I'd seen Rossi's questioning technique. *Sotto voce*, calm, quiet. To be interviewed by him was to get the velvet glove treatment…but I had to admit the velvet glove covered a verbal fist of iron. "I guess he had to get at the truth. But what more could Chip tell him?"

She pointed a finger at her chest. "Not Chip. Me."

"Oh?"

She heaved another sigh. "He asked how well I'd known Donny before the…uh…murder."

"And you did know him well, didn't you?"

"Yes, I knew him all right."

"I'm curious. How on earth did you two meet?"

Her eyes misted over, whether with memory or regret I couldn't tell. "At the Island Grill on a girls' night out. Donny bought me a mai tai and stayed to talk. Said he had come over from Miami with his boss. Francesco had business interests here and was looking for a house. Thought he might relocate to Naples. Donny wasn't happy about that idea until he met me…then everything changed…for both of us. I drove over to Miami with him one night and—"

"The rest, as they say, is history," I finished.

She nodded then bit her knuckle to stifle yet another sob. "But our relationship was over weeks ago when he… when he…"

"Asked you to move out?"

She looked over at me, eyes widening in surprise. They were a striking shade of bright blue. Funny I'd never noticed before. Guess like everyone else I had trouble getting up above the *carpe diem* on her T-shirt.

"How did you know he kicked me out?" she whispered.

I shrugged. "Lucky guess. Obviously something happened to bring you back to Naples. Besides, I never believed you left to go live with your aunt."

"Chip did, though. He wanted to, I suppose," she said, a spark of insight that stunned me. "So he was shocked when he found out about Donny. I tried all afternoon to convince him the six months had been a disappointment, but he wouldn't listen."

"Well the night Donny died, you did give an Academy Award performance over his body."

"I know." She actually looked embarrassed, remembering. "His death tore me up. A guy with a build like that. But I meant what I told Chip. I was over Donny. For good. He had a lot of baggage, and I didn't need that."

"What kind of baggage?" While AudreyAnn was in a confessional mood, I wanted to keep her talking. She might say something that would help Rossi.

"Oh, I don't know. Nothing I could put a finger on. A bunch of phone calls. He'd walk outside to talk, but I heard Francesco's name come up a lot. And Donny had visitors he warned me not to mention to anyone."

"Visitors?"

"Yeah, always two men at a time. In business suits. Who wears business suits in Florida except lawyers and bankers? These guys didn't look like bankers. Toward the end, I wanted to leave anyway…I got scared. Something was going on, but I never found out what."

"Do you think they wanted to harm Francesco?"

She shook her head. "I don't know, but with those two I think anything's possible."

The medics wheeled Chip through the living room on a gurney. Suspended from a pole, an IV drip fed liquid into his intact arm.

AudreyAnn jumped up. "I'm riding in the ambulance," she told Bill and, bending over the stretcher, she kissed Chip's cheek. "I'll make everything up to you, honey, every day for the rest of my life."

Though flat on his back and semi-conscious, whether he knew it or not, Chip was sitting in the catbird seat.

Unless, of course, AudreyAnn was lying like a rug.

EIGHTEEN

I SPENT MOST of the night on the living room couch alert to any sound from next door. At 6:00 a.m. a car drove onto the Surfside driveway and stopped, leaving the motor running. I peeked through the blinds in time to see a weary AudreyAnn stepping out of a Yellow Cab. I opened my door.

She greeted me with a nod but no smile. "He's going to be all right," she said, and without another word, walked into her condo and slammed the door.

Back to normal.

No. *She's just exhausted,* I told myself, closing my own door and heading for the shower. I wanted to believe her devotion to Chip would continue, that she had meant every loving word. Of course if she really had gotten over Donny, that killed my crime-of-passion theory, at least as far as AudreyAnn was concerned.

As for Chip, his suicide attempt revealed one thing— that teddy bear exterior hid a heart of fire. Although I didn't want to go there, he had proven he was capable of murder. After all, he had nearly murdered himself.

I stepped into the shower and turned the cold water on high. The icy spray gave me goose bumps and woke me up with a vengeance, driving all negative thoughts out of my head. I toweled off the chill and dressed quickly. Lee and I had to get to the shop. There was work to do.

But when I finally got deep into Francesco's presentation boards, the shop phone rang and rang, destroying my concentration. I looked up from the drafting table, wondering why Lee didn't answer.

Oh. She'd gone to Starbucks to get a mocha frappuccino for herself and a cup of black dynamite for me. Neither of us had slept much last night. We needed an extra jolt of caffeine to get through the day.

But the phone. Couldn't the caller leave a message? I flung down my pen, hurried across the shop to the *bureau plat* and grabbed the receiver on the eighth or ninth ring.

"Good morning," I purred, kitty sweet, phony as hell. "Deva Dunne Interiors."

"I want to kiss you all over," Rossi said.

"Who's calling, please?"

"Very funny. And then I want to—"

"Are we having phone sex?"

He laughed. "I don't know. I'm a virgin in that department."

"Where are you?" I knew he wouldn't be so open on a Naples PD line.

"At home. I'm going in a little later today. Worked most of the night."

"You heard about Chip?"

"Yes. The hospital faxed the report to the station. I would have called but I thought I might wake you."

"You wouldn't have, actually, but the big news is he's okay."

"Or will be after some therapy. We don't want an act two."

"No, but I think AudreyAnn has seen the light."

"If that's what he wants."

"She had a few secrets to share, but I'd rather tell you in person."

"What say I pick you up after work? We'll go to my

place. I'll grill a couple of steaks. Then I'll think of something else."

"Sounds heavenly, but no need to sweeten the pie, Rossi. I'll be there even if you have peanut butter and jelly sandwiches."

"Are we back to phone sex again?"

"Now who's being funny? See you at five. I'd better go. I'm trying to finish a project."

"Wait, don't hang up. I got to the bank yesterday and transferred some funds. If you ask Lee when she wants to leave, I'll buy her a plane ticket. And can you find out if she has a checking account? If not, I'll open one in her name and make a deposit to it. Once she stops by and provides her signature, the money'll be available when she needs it."

"That's wonderful, Rossi. I had a solution in mind, too, but you've solved the problem before I could. Lee will be beyond thrilled. Do you want to tell her the good news or should I?"

"Good Lord, you tell her." A typical guy, avoiding an emotional scene at all costs.

"As soon as she returns."

"Great. Pick you up at five."

At least I think that's what he said. A great screeching of brakes echoed up and down the alley. Outside the shop window a familiar black limo lurched to a halt, started up again, rolled a few more feet then came to another stop so suddenly, the driver lunged over the steering wheel, his head barely missing the windshield.

Francesco.

"Rossi, I have to go. Someone's here. See you at five," I said, hanging up before he could protest.

As I peered through the window, Francesco barged out of the limo, leaving the ignition running and the driver's side door wide open. He thumped his way into the shop with what looked like triumph on his face.

"Nothing to it," he said by way of greeting.

"You mean driving?" I asked.

"Yeah, a piece of cake."

"Francesco, not to be irreverent or anything, but you want another death in the family?"

"What's that supposed to mean?"

"It means do you have a driver's license?"

"No. That'll take weeks."

"A learner's permit?"

"I guess you're not listening. You know I lost Donny." A shadow darkened his face.

"Yes, and I'm sorry for your loss."

"Thanks. I miss the guy big time. But until I get another driver, what am I gonna do?"

"Get arrested?"

"Don't take that attitude, Deva. I'm not looking for trouble. I'm a businessman. But I gotta get around."

"Hire another driver."

"I am. Jewels's brother up in Rhode Island. He's taking driving lessons even as we speak. As soon as he gets his license, he comes down, and my problems are over."

"Are you sure you want to wait that long?"

"Hiring a stranger's not the answer. The job's delicate. I don't want just anybody knowing my business."

I heaved a sigh. "I don't have that problem, Francesco. I *want* people to know about my business. But right now, with your car clogging the alley, nobody can get to me."

He peered out at the block-long limo…a Bentley? "Oh yeah. I'll move it, but where the hell do you park around here?"

"Tell you what. Why don't you have a seat and I'll move it? There's a parking lot in back of this building. When

I return, after shutting off the motor, removing the key and locking the door, you can tell me what brings you here today."

"Sarcasm ain't ladylike," he said, slumping onto the zebra settee.

"Ha!"

"Hurry back. We gotta talk business. The wrecking crew gutted the kitchen and the baths. And that painter you sent over with the movie star name?"

"It's spelled differently."

"Whatever. He's through with the ceilings and the priming. Now we're waiting on you."

Guilt surged through me. My proposal should have been presented to Francesco days ago. My only excuse was murder. Literally. Well, I'd also had a lovelorn bride to deal with. An attempted suicide. And my own personal life.

Not a single valid excuse in the lot. Not for a professional.

"Be right back," I said, hurrying out to the alley.

Driving the Bentley proved more complicated than I expected. After a few lurchy fits and starts, I rolled the beast around to the rear of the building, parked and went back inside. Lee had arrived with my Starbucks lifesaver.

"They gave me a giant black Sumatra, but only charged me for a large." She handed me a tall cup. "I think the boy behind the counter was just being nice."

"Not surprising." Francesco eyed her appreciatively as I handed him his keys.

The cornflower blue dress matched her eyes. In blue with her blond hair cascading over her shoulders and a face like a Botticelli Venus, she would be a sensation in Paris. I could hardly wait to tell her what Rossi had wrought. But first Francesco.

"I'll split my coffee with you," I told him, hoping he'd refuse.

"Deal! Jewels didn't make any this morning. Makes her gag."

"Morning sickness?"

"Yeah, poor kid. But she don't complain. She's got the right name."

I nodded and poured half my Sumatra blend into a plastic cup and gave it to him. We sipped in amiable silence for a few minutes and then I said, "Let's get started, shall we?"

"That's what I'm here for. I want to get this house stuff settled." Again that cloud across his face. "As soon as they release Donny, Jewels and I are heading for Providence with his body. We're laying him next to our *nonno*. It's what they'd both want." His eyes filmed over, but to my relief no tears leaked out.

"Lieutenant Rossi's one of the best detectives in the world," I said. "If anybody can find out who...ah—"

"—stiffed Donny," Francesco finished.

"Yes, well, Rossi can," I ended somewhat lamely. How did anybody talk to this guy? I had to change the subject. "Have you ever heard of Zuber wallpaper?"

He shook his head. "No. What's it like?"

"Expensive."

"Good. I don't like cheap."

I guess he wasn't so hard to talk to after all, and as Lee took off for the post office, I wasted no further time getting down to business.

All was go, go, go. I had seldom had a client who grasped design concepts as quickly as Francesco did. He adored the Zuber murals and understood the wisdom of neutral surfaces in the living room and a vivid effect in the dining room. He agreed that the new case goods—primarily chairs and sofas—should be comfortable but minimalist. He even okayed a glass coffee table, realizing it wouldn't vie for visual space with his antiques.

He was a dream client.

The ashes of roses toile paper for his baby daughter's bedroom with a rose and green silk canopy over the crib fascinated him. Ditto for the nautical-themed cobalt blue and taupe scheme for little Frannie's room. He even laughed, delighted at the idea of spelling out Frannie's name with semaphore flags and hanging them over his crib. Every detail of the children's rooms he approved, right down to the custom-designed carpeting by Stark.

"I like your spin on the preppy colors for the kids' rooms," he said. "No Pepto-Bismol pink and no wimpy blue. So far terrific. Now what about the workshop?"

"The workshop? I don't rem—oh…the master bedroom suite."

"Yeah, where Jewels and me hang out together."

"In there you need both yin and yang," I said, sliding another presentation board across the drafting table.

His brow furrowed. "Who the hell are they?"

"The male-female principles."

He grinned. "Sounds about right."

Ignoring the grin, I soldiered on in my best starchy Boston manner. "I envisioned your private suite as serene."

His eyes narrowed. I guess serene isn't the word normally applied to his workshop. "I see it as largely monochromatic," I added.

"Yeah?"

"Yeah. I mean yes. *You* supply the color with the force of your, ah, personality."

"Got it!"

No question, he had mentally substituted the word *sex* for color, but whatever works.

"So in keeping with a serene atmosphere, I see the bedroom wall treatments in a pale shade of almond."

As if a switch had been thrown, Francesco's mood changed. "Almond, huh?" he said, frowning. "You know Donny was poisoned?"

I nodded. "The lieutenant told me what happened."

"Cyanide. I got a whiff of it when I bent over Donny. At least it smelled like almonds to me."

Uh-oh.

"So I got a favor to ask. Call that bedroom color beige or something. Anything but almond."

"Of course. Sorry. I didn't mean to be insensitive."

"You're not insensitive. You're just not up on your poisons." He took a linen handkerchief from a back pocket and wiped his eyes. "Poisoned. In my own house. My own kitchen. He ate my shrimp. So what does that tell you?"

"That he died by mistake?" I whispered. "Somebody wanted to kill you?"

Francesco ran the handkerchief over his eyes. "Yeah. Looks like somebody got the wrong boy."

"Why would anyone want to kill *you?*"

He shrugged. "Like I told the lieutenant, I got no enemies. But Donny, yeah, he made a few. All's I know is I'm never getting over it. Donny was family."

"Time helps, Francesco. It really does. I know that from personal experience. And now you have a new family."

He smiled and put away the hanky. "I do and I don't. Jewels is scared to death. When we get to Rhode Island, she wants to stay there with Frannie until this business is settled. I don't want her to but she can't eat, she can't sleep."

"Well, for a while that might be best."

He nodded and pointed to the presentation board. "Let's

hear the rest of this yin and yang stuff. I gotta get home and make some phone calls."

I pointed to the drawing of the king-sized bed. "The al—uh...ivory upholstery on the headboard is for serenity. It's soft and quiet, the yin principle. To emphasize the masculine element, the yang, we'll keep all the fabrics tailored. No ruffles, no frills. Greek key appliqués on the bed and window treatments, in Windsor Blue, and on the ivory carpeting as well. But the Greek motif on the carpet will be much larger. We'll exaggerate it, make it dramatic."

"I like it all. Every damn thing."

With that he stood and stuck out a hand. I took it— warm and sweaty though it was—and we shook on the deal.

"A handshake's usually enough for the guys I do business with, but I won't put you to the test." He reached into his jacket pocket and removed a single piece of paper. A blank check.

I breathed a sigh of relief and swiveled the daylights out of the ergonomic chair.

"How much to start?" he asked.

"The Zuber paper is nonreturnable and nonrefundable."

"So?" Pen poised over the check he waited.

"Fifty thousand to be on the safe side."

He didn't bat an eye. "What else?"

"I need to put half down on the case goods. So that's another twenty-five. Kustom Kitchens will bill you directly for the kitchen and bathroom installations. That leaves the orientals, the artwork and the accessories. But those can be taken out on approval and returned if need be."

"One hundred thousand to start?"

"That should be enough."

He scribbled in small tight handwriting and slid the check across to me. "We're doing a classic take on the house, which is what I want. But no fake ancestor pictures. You know, the ones with the stiff-looking guys in black suits."

"You don't care for them?"

"Do I look like my people came over on the Mayflower?" He scoffed. "Like Norm's?"

I laughed and locked the check in the drafting table drawer. "I'm taking the Fifth, Francesco."

"Smart broa—lady."

"Instead of portraits, how about landscapes? You could start a Hudson River collection. Echo the Zuber scene, establish a theme."

"Sounds good. I like woods. Show me a few. Now I gotta go. Jewels don't like being alone these days."

"Isn't Bonita with her?"

"I gave her a check and let her go. At least for the time being. I don't want to see anybody else get hurt. Besides, she was in the kitchen that night." He shrugged. "She lost her husband, and now Donny's dead. I figure if she hates my guts who could blame her?"

Who indeed?

"Chip and that salad girl won't be back either. Not till we get the goods on whoever did it."

I stared him straight in the eye. "I was there that night. What about me?"

He shook his head. "You got no beef with me. Same for the lieutenant. The other two, that's different. But I'm trying to make it up to Chip. The money he found is his. I'm not going after it. The restaurant was one thing. I would have helped him rebuild. But a poisoning? Who the hell will eat in his restaurant after that?"

"He didn't do it," I said, more out of affection than certainty.

"You guaranteeing that?"

"Sorry, Francesco, no guarantees. That's why it's so nice of you to let him keep the money."

"Yeah, it's his as long as nobody else comes after it. You don't stash money in walls without a reason. And here's a guarantee—the reason ain't good." He treated me to the shadow of a smile. "Hey, maybe Chip'll get lucky. According to the lieutenant, the money's been there a long time. The guy who stashed it might not be around anymore."

"Then it's Chip's and that's a good thing. He needs it. Thanks for looking out for him, Francesco."

"No sweat." He stood and pulled the car keys out of his pocket.

"You want me to drive you home? My assistant will be back in a few minutes. She can follow us in my car."

"How can I learn if I don't practice?"

Who could argue with logic like that? Well, I could have, but I knew it wouldn't do any good.

After he lurched off I sat at the drafting table for a moment mulling over our conversation. Then, feeling like a complete rat, I called the Naples police. To the deep voice that answered, I said, "There's a black Bentley limousine heading west on Fifth Avenue South. The man behind the wheel doesn't have a driver's license. He needs to be stopped."

"Your name?"

"That's unimportant. Just stop him before he kills somebody."

I hung up telling myself I had done the right thing. And that if Francesco found out, I could kiss the hundred thousand dollar check goodbye—before I even cashed it.

Despite all, I hoped I could keep him as a client. When finished, the house would be a showstopper, and his willingness to pay upfront with no haggling and no argument was just what Deva Dunne Interiors needed. In short, he was a godsend. He'd impressed me in so many ways…his taste in interior design, his generosity, his good spirits, and up till now anyway, the fact that he didn't take offense easily. He could have over my almond gaffe, but all he'd said was, "You don't know your poisons."

Right, I didn't. I swiveled around to the computer, and working fast, while the shop was empty, I entered the Wikipedia site and typed in *cyanide*.

A few minutes later I sat stunned in front of the screen, my mouth rounding into an O. *Omigod*. No wonder Rossi went on full alert when Nikhil told him Cookie's family had been in the jewelry business. Cyanide was used in the gold plating process.

Before Daddy sold the plant, had Cookie helped herself to some poison?

NINETEEN

"HEY, DID YOU call the cops on me?"

Francesco. Oh God, why hadn't I just let the phone ring?

"Where are you?"

"Never mind that. Answer the question. Yes or no."

I blew out a breath. There went the Rum Row house, the hundred thou, the chance to lift Deva Dunne Interiors out of the red.

"Yes," I said, trying to sound confident.

"Thought so. I no sooner go around the corner, the cops are swarming all over me. What did you do that for?"

"I was afraid you'd kill yourself." I didn't bother to mention the public at large.

"You were, huh?" A moment of silence. "You were saving my life?"

"In a manner of speaking."

"You know what I like about you, Deva?"

"I'm afraid to ask."

"You don't lie to me. So in case you're wondering, go ahead and cash the check."

"Thanks, Francesco, I will. Now maybe you'll tell me where you are."

"I'm in the goddamn police station, waiting for my lawyer to give me a ride home."

I stifled a laugh. "I'll be in touch soon," I said and hung up, shaking my head.

You really had to love the guy. No wonder he had no

enemies. But he admitted Donny had. *Hmm.* Did that include the two guys in suits AudreyAnn mentioned? She said they'd talked about Francesco. Something else Rossi needed to know.

I was on the phone with the painter setting up a meeting at the Grandeses when Lee walked in from the post office.

"The line stretched all the way out the door," she said. "I declare, everybody in town had a package to ship."

I cradled the receiver. "Lee, please sit down. I have something to tell you."

My tone must have scared her. A stone sinking into a pond, she dropped onto the little gold Chiavari chair by my desk. "What's wrong?" Her face paled to a frightening shade of white. "Is it Paulo?"

"No, no. I mean yes. Yes!"

With eyes like alarmed blue pools, she sat statue still waiting for the axe to fall.

God, I was bungling this badly. "You're going to Paris. Rossi's making the arrangements."

A light leaped into her eyes, and she went to rise, but her legs gave way, and she fell back onto the seat. "I don't understand."

"Watch my lips move. You. Are. Going. To. Paris."

"That can't be true." Her fingers gripped the edge of the *bureau plat,* clinging to the wood as if it were a life raft. "Y'all are playing games with me."

"You know I wouldn't do that. It's true. I'll miss you terribly, but think of what's ahead. Paulo. Paris." I spread my arms wide. "The world!"

She remained scary white, her lips trembling, looking so stricken I hoped she wouldn't faint.

"But I have no money," she said, her voice a whisper.

"It's Rossi's gift to you. A plane ticket and enough to live on for a year."

She stared at me, unbelieving, her whole body rigid. "Paulo and I can't accept a gift like that."

"Rossi will be crushed. You can't refuse. You'll hurt his feelings. Terribly," I added, knowing that would cement the deal. Lee would never hurt a living soul, not if she could help it.

A smile tugged at her lips, broke free and swept clear to her eyes. Her whole face aglow, she leaped up and hugged me. "I'm going to see Paulo?"

"Yes, yes and yes."

"When?"

"As soon as you give Rossi the word."

"Oh, I will. I will! I'll call him right this minute!" She danced a little jig around the display tables, jostling one in her excitement, just catching a teetering glass candlestick in the nick of time. "Forgive me, Deva, I'm *so* excited."

"That's the nicest part," I said, the smile on my own face beaming at two women who came in to browse. They must have felt very welcomed; they stayed nearly an hour and bought a pair of mirrored sconces and a hand-painted tray. Before they left, one said the interior of her house had the "blahs." Would I make an appointment to come take a look? I certainly would and did. *Yippee, a new design client!*

Between customers, Lee texted her happy news to Paulo and received an instant reply. She blushed a rosy red and didn't share the message, but I could guess what it said.

At five o'clock a beat-up Mustang rolled down the alley and moments later the Yarmouthport sleigh bells jangled like it was Christmas.

At the sight of Rossi, Lee burst into tears. He stood inside the door, his hand on the knob as if he weren't sure whether to stay or leave.

I turned the sign in the window to Closed and snapped off the overheads.

"Lee is absolutely thrilled," I told him.

"I can see that," he said wryly.

"Oh I am, Mr. Rossi, I am. It's just that I'm so beholden to you. Paulo is too. We both are," she finished, wiping her eyes with a tissue. "But we'll repay you. Every penny. Just as soon as we're able. Paulo said to tell y'all that. I'll get me a job as soon as I can speak a little French."

Rossi let go of the door handle and stepped into the shop. "Don't worry about that. Consider the money a gift."

"No, sir, we simply couldn't."

I smiled inwardly. *The iron man meets the steel magnolia.* Rossi shrugged resignedly and said, "How about an alternate plan then? Maybe Paulo can paint Deva's portrait for me someday. I'd like that. You know, to look at and talk to."

Lee grinned at me through her happy tears, no doubt remembering our conversation about Paulo's first big commission.

Looking sheepish, as if he'd given too much away, Rossi changed the subject. "So, young lady, when do you want to leave for France?"

"As soon as I can, Mr. Rossi. Just as soon as I can."

He laughed. "I'll go online tonight and buy you a ticket on the first plane to Paris."

We locked up, and Lee left for Surfside in my Audi. Rossi and I swung by the SunTrust Bank to deposit the day's receipts then headed for his place in Countryside. As he drove, I snuggled next to him, a hand on his thigh.

"You created a lot of happiness today, Rossi."

Violating his rule of never taking his attention off the road—though actually he'd been doing that quite a bit lately—he glanced over at me.

"I hope that trend continues. There's something you need to know."

"Sounds serious."

He nodded, his attention back on the road. "I should have told you sooner. The money I'm giving Lee is the money I was saving for Hawaii." He cleared his throat. "I was kind of hoping we could go together sometime. But after this, Honolulu's out for a while."

He looked so worried I gave his thigh another squeeze. "Oh, Rossi, what matters is who you're with, not where you go."

His dark eyes glowing, he took his hand off the wheel to grip mine. A driving first. "You mean that?"

"You know I do. Besides, we could drive to Key West for a weekend. That's a great destination. When you're with somebody who's fun." I glanced across at his stern, rock-hard jaw. "Someone like you."

Not fooled for a second, he barked out a laugh. "What a woman," he said, lifting my hand to his lips for a kiss.

He didn't know it, but I was planning a surprise for him. I'd decided to sell the rose medallion collection and the Tabriz rug. I wouldn't miss the porcelain too much, and as for the rug, well, it was a stunner, but a simple, inexpensive sisal would also work well in my living room. Anyway, making Lee and Rossi happy was more important than any rug in the world. Above all, I knew Jack would approve.

"You did the right thing, Rossi," I assured him. "Lee is over the moon."

"Good. She's like the daughter I never had. I'm glad I could make her happy."

A daughter. "Since she's twenty-two, you'd have been a teenage daddy."

He glanced over again, a glint in his eyes. "Could have happened."

"You mean that?"

"Of course I mean it."

I pinched his thigh. Hard.

"Hey, that hurts."

"Chicken." For all his assurances that he didn't see children in his life any time soon, and neither did I, I resolved to call my GYN back and say this *was* an emergency. I wouldn't wait two months to learn the truth about myself. Though that was all I wanted from the visit—just the truth for its own sake.

With evening not yet night, we settled on Rossi's living room couch, merlots in hand.

"To us," he toasted. We clinked glasses, and in that quick, chameleon way of his, he morphed from lover into detective. "You said AudreyAnn had a few secrets to tell."

I took a sip before answering. "You know she was living with Donny and that he asked her to leave?"

"No, she told me she wanted to leave. Couldn't wait to get back to Chip."

"A lie. Donny threw her out. All the while she was gone, Chip thought she was living with an aunt."

Rossi raised an eyebrow.

"I know. Even AudreyAnn said Chip was kidding himself on purpose. That your questioning forced him to recognize the truth."

"That why he cut himself?"

"She seems to think so."

"My fault then, hmm?" Rossi sipped his wine, frowning into what remained in the glass. "Chip may have more to live for than he knows. So far that money he found hasn't had any takers. A few more weeks and he could be a wealthy man. But I guess that isn't what matters to him."

He finished his drink and put the glass on the coffee table. Ever the detective, he said, "What else?"

"Donny had callers. Two men at a time in business suits. He'd walk outside to talk to them so AudreyAnn couldn't hear what they were saying. But a few times she did hear them toss Francesco's name around. Donny also went outside to take certain phone calls." I shrugged. "So maybe she *was* telling you the truth. Maybe she really did want to leave. Toward the end she was getting scared."

"Two men in suits, making periodic visits." Rossi was talking more to himself than to me. Nor did he seem surprised by what I'd told him. He acted like it reinforced something he already suspected...he was on to something. So was I.

"By the way, I looked up cyanide. Found out it's used in jewelry plating."

"Oh?"

"As if you didn't know."

"Common knowledge, Deva."

"Really? Well, what about the fact that Cookie's family owned a jewelry factory?"

He took my glass and set it on the coffee table next to his before reaching out and wrapping me in his arms. "Don't you dare."

"Don't I dare *what?*"

"Jump to conclusions. There's a murderer on the loose and until he—or she—is apprehended, I don't want you meddling in the Grandese case. Or going into the house alone. Only when the contractors are there." Holding me at arm's length, he added, "I'm serious, Deva. Be careful. I'm talking life and death here."

TWENTY

Tom Kruse's panel truck was parked on the Grandese's brick drive when I arrived at the house the next morning. I unlocked the front door, turned off the alarm system and ushered him into the empty dining room.

"In here, Tom, the walls should look like a ripe mango. Just before it rots."

He stared at me, his brow furrowed.

"It's a color you can't describe in one word."

"Right," he said, and then he laughed. "That's a first, Deva. And I've been at this for thirty years."

I rummaged through the canvas tote hanging from my shoulder. "There's no single word for the shade I have in mind, but I brought a mango with me."

"That'll help," he said, the edges of his eyes crinkling suspiciously.

I held the fruit in my palm. "See this soft spot over here? That's the shade exactly."

He plucked the mango from my hand and carried it to a window flooded with morning sunshine. "Okay, I see coral-tangerine with rose overtones underlain with a greenish-yellow. Not chrome yellow, more like daffodils in bloom."

I slid the tote off my shoulder and dropped it on a work bench in the center of the dining room. "Very funny."

"Sort of," he admitted, breaking out into a laugh again. "But you used Putnam Ivory in the living room. That was easy, so I owe you one. Let me keep the fruit, okay? I'll cut the coral with warm rose, add a dab of yellow to soften both and a drop or two, no more, of black for depth. How's that sound?"

"Confusing. But you're the mixologist."

"I've been called worse," he said, still smiling, obviously undaunted by coming up with a perfect, unnamable shade that at the moment existed only in my mind. And in the sky on that Zuber wallpaper. "Let me get the base mixes out of the truck and give me a few minutes. When I think I'm close, I'll call you back for a look."

While Tom went for the paint samples, I toured the house. With the living room redo now complete, Francesco had some of his antiques installed in place. In the quiet perfection of the room, they shone like the jewels they were. Especially the magnificent Townsend. In awe, I worshipped the desk, my breath catching in my throat, my hands behind my back in case I'd be tempted to touch it.

But finally, the lure was too strong. I had to caress the sweeping grain of that wood, just a little, a finger stroke or two. I reached out, the mahogany silk under my fingertips. Then the temptation took on a life of its own, and I ran a hand over the front panels. A brass key had been left protruding from a lock. What did the desk look like inside, were there cubbies and clever little drawers and small, fitted compartments? I had to know.

A single turn of the key and the panel doors opened. A mixture of dried rose petals and old potted ink came wafting out. I peeked inside and released a long, pent-up breath. The interior was a cabinetmaker's marvel, with rows of fitted drawers and cunning miniature cabinets. What did they hold? Precious little somethings put away for safekeeping? Love letters? A vender's bill from the eighteenth century? I opened a drawer. Empty. A second one. Empty. I pulled on the brass knob of a tiny little cabinet door and peered closer.

Made of clear glass with a metal screw top, the bottle was small, a vial really, and half filled with a clear liquid. An ordinary little container that could hold three or four ounces of fluid when full, no more, it was nothing special.

Then why secreted in the cubby of this magnificent desk as if it were an object of value? There was no label, no marking of any kind. Obviously the liquid wasn't ink, and a perfume bottle would be far more elaborate.

I reached into the miniature cabinet and removed the container. The top twisted off easily enough. I raised the open neck to my nose and sniffed. Almonds.

Omigod, cyanide.

Heart beating fast, I screwed the cap back on, replaced the vial and closed the desk. Poison wasn't an illegal possession, but still Rossi needed to know about this. Before I could pull the cell out of my pocket, the chimes rang. Tom must have locked himself out. I hurried to let him in, but the front door was already half open.

Oh no. "Cookie, what a surprise."

"I saw that little car of yours, so thought I'd stop by and say hello. I'm dying to see what you're doing with the place."

"Well, the project isn't finished yet."

"That's all right, dear. I'll just peek around and leave as quiet as a mouse. Don't stop what you're doing for me," she said over a shoulder as she strolled toward the living room.

"Wait—"

"Deva, want to take a look at this color?" Tom called from the dining room.

"Be right there."

He'd dabbed a twelve-inch swath on one of the walls.

"Close," I said, peering at it carefully. "But a tad too coral. We want more richness, more sophistication. More mango."

He didn't even sigh. "Less coral. More sophistication. Got it."

"Keep that mango spot in mind."

"Right." This time he did sigh.

Like a latter-day alchemist, he went back to his mixing, and I went searching for Cookie. She shouldn't be running through the Grandese house in their absence. How did I know if they wanted her in here snooping and prying? For that was what she was doing. *As I'd been doing in the Townsend.* But that was different, wasn't it? I was here on official business. I tamped down the spurt of guilt and found Cookie still prowling the living room.

"This is quite a change from Drexel's concept," she said. "Rather colorless, if you ask me."

"A half-finished dress so to speak," I said, damned if I'd justify my design decisions to her.

"Well, good luck pulling it all together." She actually sniffed.

"Luck has nothing to do with it." I was pissed enough to use my Boston voice. A bad sign. Cookie was getting to me, and I shouldn't let that happen.

"Ta-ta," she said, waggling her fingers. "Do tell the Grandeses I've been by. They're living over the garage, you know. How quaint."

If she knew that, why hadn't she called on them there? I resolved to keep the doors locked whenever I worked on the property, and I'd tell Tom and the other contractors to do the same.

She'd no sooner left than on a hunch I hurried into the living room and unlocked the Townsend. I opened the tiny cabinet and looked inside.

The vial was gone.

The nerve of her!

I ran to the front door and yanked it open. Cookie was slowly strolling across Rum Row. "Cookie, I want to talk to you!"

Without even bothering to look out for traffic, I dashed across the street. Cool as glass, she turned to face me. "Yes?" One eyebrow lifted.

"What did you do with it?"

"Whatever do you mean?" She was a good actress, I'll give her that. Not a glimmer of uncertainty crossed her face.

"The cyanide, Cookie. The cyanide. Where is it?"

"I don't know what you're talking about. Have you lost your senses?" She flounced away and started up the paved walk to her front door.

In a moment of sheer bravado I said, "Stop right there, or I'll call the police."

She whirled around. "You're insane."

I pointed to her chinos. "Empty your pockets. Take everything out and put it on the walk." I eyed her chest. Flat as a tortilla. No vial hidden there.

"I'll do no such thing."

I pulled the cell phone out of my skirt pocket and poised a finger over the keys. "Your choice."

She glanced up and down the street. "I don't want the police here. What will the neighbors think?"

"Precisely. So come on, Cookie," I said, thinking a little pleading might go further than threats. "A man's been murdered. We're all scared."

She heaved a sigh. "You're creating a scene. Come around to the back where we won't be seen."

Armed with my cell phone, I followed her across the lawn to the rear garden, a lovely private oasis centered with a splashing fountain and a weathered stone statue of an angel in repose.

"This is beautiful," I said, momentarily distracted by the surroundings.

"Yes, I designed the landscaping myself. The women in my family all have impeccable taste. Though we've never made a business out of practicing it."

Don't bother responding, I told myself. *She's not worth the effort.* I held out a hand. "Give it to me."

She shook her head.

Index finger poised over the cell number pad, I raised the phone into her line of vision.

She held out for a long moment before the resolution in her steely jaw wavered. "Very well. Why not? If you tell anyone, it'll be your word against mine." She reached into her pants pocket. "May I remind you that my husband and I are pillars of society in this town?"

I dropped the phone into a pocket and held out a hand.

She placed the vial in my open palm but didn't let go of it. "Satisfied now?"

I shook my head. "I'm not sure," I said looking down at the perfectly manicured fingers still clutching the bottle. Though the sun shone through the glass, no fire ignited that rock on her finger. My glance traveled to her wrist. In the pitiless Florida sunshine, the fabulous tennis bracelet should have sparkled like a wrist full of stars. But it didn't.

I slid the vial from under her clinging fingers and pocketed it. "What happened to your jewelry, Cookie?" A rude question, but under the circumstances, good manners had to topple.

She gasped and folded her right hand over her left, covering the ring from sight.

"Nothing's wrong."

"Your stones are glass," I said in a not-so-wild guess. "You switched out the diamonds. Why?"

She sank onto a Chippendale bench and stared up at me with pleading in her eyes. In that instant my heart turned over with sympathy for this difficult snob of a woman. Something had gone awry in her life, something she felt powerless to correct. Something, I suspected, that might be connected to Donny's murder.

I sank on the bench beside her. Keeping my voice soft as Rossi did during his interrogations, I asked again, "Why the fake stones?"

She held out her left hand and stared at the dull ring that sat so flat and lifeless on her finger. "It's all Norm's fault."

I waited, hoping she'd go on. In the silence I sniffed the gardenia fragrance of the garden and watched a family of wrens splash in the fountain—and kept on waiting. Whether Cookie noticed anything other than the glass on her finger was doubtful.

Finally she said, "Norm's a gambler. I've been covering up for him for years, but this time he's gone too far. He's borrowed from that horrible Francesco person. For the horses." She balled her fists in her lap. "I hate them both."

The day verged on summer heat, and we were warm sitting in the sun. Whatever the cause, Cookie's face had turned the mango shade I wanted on those dining room walls.

"Now Francesco is demanding that the loan be repaid?" I asked, phrasing what I already knew as a question.

She nodded. "All of it, but Norm can't repay him. To make up the difference, I've sold nearly everything. My jewelry, my mother's, my grandmother's. My silver service…it was a wedding gift from the governor of Massachusetts." Her chin trembled. "Stock my father left me. Everything. I'm at the end of my tether. I have nothing more to sell. Except my Jaguar. It's an XJ," she added with a touch of her old arrogance. "Even the house is mortgaged."

"Why did you let the situation deteriorate like this?"

She looked at me with something like pity in her eyes. "You're not married, are you?"

"No."

"Then I can't expect you to understand. There are appearances. One's public image. The vows one took. The Anglican bishop of Boston married us," she said solemnly.

"The vows, yes, there are the vows." I sighed, understanding better than she knew. The wedding vows I'd exchanged with Jack were until death do us part. No other reason on earth would ever have separated me from him. Yes, I certainly did understand. Poor little Cookie. Poor little formerly rich girl. "So what will you do?"

Her jaw took on that steely edge again. "For openers, if you ever tell anyone about this conversation, I will kill you. Second, I'm going to appeal to Mr. Grandese to forgive Norm's loan. Divorce is not an option." She shuddered. "We'd be the first in the family."

"Suppose Francesco won't listen?"

"Then I'll threaten him."

"With what?" It seemed to me her options in that direction were severely limited.

"The night of the murder, Bonita gave Norm the cyanide bottle to hide. Norm didn't know what to do with it so he gave it to me. I stole out to the garage and hid it in the desk."

"What was Bonita doing with poison?"

Cookie shrugged. "She was frantic. Said Mrs. Grandese gave it to her. When Jewels picked the baby up she found the vial in his port-a-basket."

"You might find that hard to prove."

Jaw firm, she shook her head. "I won't have to prove a thing. I'll just threaten to cause a scandal. Then Mr. Grandese can take his antiques and his arias and his gaudy wife and leave town." Her voice had taken on its usual finishing school edge. She was clearly getting her groove back, and I was glad she was, actually.

"Can you believe I promised to sponsor him for membership in the Port Royal Club? He's panting to get in, but if he turns me down he never will. Never. Norm and I will see to that." She sat back on the bench and squared her shoulders. "Right now, he has everyone's sympathy. He was nearly the victim of a crime. But if people believe his wife tried to kill him, they'll both be finished here. That's the last thing that little upstart wants. He has social pretension. I can recognize the type a mile away."

"I believe you can," I said, trying not to smile, "but suppose the Grandeses sue you for libel? Besides, even if they don't, your story will expose Norm."

"Unless the money hemorrhaging stops immediately, he'll be exposed anyway. I have nothing…or everything… to lose." She stood and smoothed her pants over her slim hips. "Talking about all this helped, but remember number one on my to-do list. If you repeat what I've just said, I'll kill you. Now if you'll excuse me." She stood and back ramrod straight walked over to a patio door and disappeared inside, leaving me alone on the garden bench.

She'd kill me? Despite the heat of the day, a shiver raced over my skin. No, that would never happen. I forced the stab of alarm down and leaped up. Good grief, what was I thinking? Enough sleuthing for the moment. Tom was still back at the Grandeses mixing mango paint. I rushed across the street and found him dabbing on a fifth version of the shade. No need. The fourth try was perfect— warm and subtle, vivid and discreet. Mango and yet not;

tangerine and yet not. Too complex to define, it was, in short, perfection.

"This one, Tom. You've nailed it."

"Excellent. That means we can finish this room in a couple of days and then you can send in the floor polisher. Next we'll start on the children's bedrooms."

"Wonderful. You're ahead of schedule."

To tie the neutral-colored public rooms together, I planned to introduce mango and tangerine accessories in the living room. Pillows on those Montoya couches would do that. For sheer sassiness, maybe one or two in a tiger print velvet. But pillows could wait. Right now I had a call to make. If Cookie thought she had me intimidated, she thought wrong. In Dorchester, Massachusetts where I'm from, we don't kowtow to threats—

The front door chimes shattered my concentration. Somebody had come calling. Cookie again? Well at least I'd had the presence of mind to relock the door and reset the alarm. Heeding Rossi's warning, at the front entrance I peered through the side lights before opening the door.

No telling who—*Bonita?*

I turned off the security alarm and opened the door. "This is a surprise, Bonita. I didn't think you were working here anymore."

"I'm not, Señora Dunne. I work for Mrs. Harkness now."

"You do?"

"*Sí.* Mr. Grandese pays better. But she talks to me more. Woman-to-woman."

I'll bet she did. Probably pumping her for everything she knew about the Grandeses. I hoped Bonita would end up getting paid for her efforts, but didn't bring up that sticky subject.

"Does Mr. Grandese know you're working for the Harknesses now?"

"He knows or not, what do I care? Here, this is for him." She held out a glossy red gift bag stuffed with festive-looking purple tissue. "It is for his baby boy. His son."

"From you? How lovely."

"No. Not from me. Why would I give gifts to his baby? His baby has a father. My son, my little Tomas, he has no father. And who is to blame for that? That Donny. That Grandese *bastardo*. Here, take." She thrust the gift bag into my hands. Fairly heavy, it sagged a little under the contents' weight.

"I don't understand, Bonita. If this isn't from you, who is it from?"

She shrugged. "I don't know. A man came to my house early this morning. A stranger. He said give this to Mr. Grandese for his little son. So I bring."

"What did this man look like?"

"A man like any other."

"Young, old, fat, thin?"

"In his thirty years I would say. Big shoulders. Black hair. Well dressed. In my neighborhood we don't often see such nice clothes."

Could she be lying? I looked down at the gift then up into Bonita's dark eyes. "A man was killed in this house. This might not be safe."

She nodded. "Is safe. Mrs. Harkness opened it. She too was worried. Said it might be a…how she say…a practical joke. I see it. Is a funny gift for a *niño* but is safe."

"You're sure?"

"*Sí.*"

I gave the bag back to her. "Then open it. Here on the doorstep."

I had to give Cookie credit for guts. Or foolishness. In her place I would have called the local bomb squad, never mind examining the contents of this thing. Who knew, maybe she had a death wish.

"I tell you is safe," Bonita insisted.

"Go on, open it." I had no intention of bringing this mysterious package anywhere near little Frannie without knowing what it held.

Bonita put the bag on the stone entrance slab, bent down and lifted the gift out of its tissue paper cocoon.

"Oh, my!" was all I could think of to say.

"You think Mr. Grandese will like this?" she asked.

"No. Mr. Grandese will not like this, but he has to see it."

"*Sí.* He's a good man. I want to hate him for what happened, but I cannot. That Donny, him I hate."

"Be careful what you say, Bonita. You don't want to be accused of…anything."

"I am not afraid. Mrs. Harkness she told me in your country you need proof to accuse. Is that not true?"

"Yes, but—"

"So let your country prove I poisoned that Donny. Let them prove."

With the dignity of a duchess, Bonita turned on her heel and strode across Rum Row, leaving me holding the bag.

Literally.

TWENTY-ONE

As soon as Bonita disappeared inside the Harkness house, I dug the cell phone out of my tote and punched in Francesco's number. Jewels picked up on the first ring.

"Baby sleeping?" I asked.

"Almost. Francesco's rocking him now."

"Sorry to disturb him, but I have a baby gift here for you."

She related the message to her husband then said, "Frannie said to come up. He's putting the baby down now."

"Fine. Be right over." Leaving Tom and his crew working in the dining room, I grabbed the gift bag, reset the door locks and climbed the outside stairs to the apartment over the garage.

No attempt had been made to make it attractive. It was what it was, a convenient pad with a king-sized bed and a baby crib in a corner of the single bedroom. In the main room a couple of lounge chairs faced a flat-screen TV. Baby bottles and jars and cereal boxes littered the miniscule kitchen galley. No Federalist furniture anywhere in sight.

Francesco saw me glancing around and said, "Yeah, it's a dump all right. See why I want your guys on the job? We gotta get outta here before I go nuts."

"Oh, it's not so bad." Jewels quietly closed the bedroom door. "The baby should sleep for a couple of hours."

"Thank God. Kids are killers, you know that?" Francesco slumped onto one of the loungers and raised the foot rest.

"I wouldn't know." I held the bag out to him. "Here's your baby gift."

"Oh, Frannie loves packages," Jewels said. *A sweet girl.* He took the bag.

"Before you open it you should know that—"

"Hey, this was swell of you, Deva. We didn't expect no presents."

"It's not from me," I began, but too late.

He'd already ripped the tissue apart and, reaching in, pulled out a toy truck with a shiny aluminum grille, black headlights and a chrome yellow body. A small piece of paper had been taped to the body of the truck with the word *Propane* inked on in black.

"What the hell." He reached in again and yanked out a fistful of play money. Some of the fake currency fluttered from his fingers and fell to the floor. Every one was a replica of a thousand dollar bill.

Sitting up straight, Francesco dumped everything out of the gift bag. A card had been tucked into the tissue layers. He stuck a blunt fingertip under the envelope flap and ripped it open. A moment only and he turned white as the undershirt he was wearing.

"Somebody's after my kid."

"What does the card say?" Jewels hurried over to take it from his shaky hand and read aloud, "'Enjoy your boy for as long as it lasts.' Oh my God, they're going to kill our baby."

As quietly as she'd closed the bedroom door, she crumpled to the floor in a dead faint, her head barely missing the edge of the kitchen counter.

Faster than I would have thought possible, Francesco leaped from his lounger and rushed over to her. "Come on,

Jewels. Come on," he pleaded, crouching over her body, patting her hands, her cheeks. "Get some water from the sink over there," he said to me. "I'll splash her up. That might do it."

I ran to fill a glass with tap water and gave it to him. A few drops on her face and Jewels's eyes fluttered open. "Frannie? Is everything all right?"

"Yeah, sweetheart, everything's fine. Some asshole having fun is all. But we'll get him. Don't worry, we'll get him." He helped Jewels sit up, propping her against the kitchen cabinets. "You really love my kid," he said to her, awe in his voice. "Me too. I love him too."

Still kneeling beside her, he looked up at me. "Deva, call that lieutenant. Tell him to get over here fast."

I rang Rossi's number and quickly explained what had just happened.

"I'll see you in a few minutes," he said.

"No, I can't wait. I have an appointment. But before you hang up, there's something else you should know." While Francesco tended to Jewels, I stepped outside and told him about Cookie Harkness and the cyanide.

After I finished giving him the clue of the century, all he said was, "Deva, I am not pleased."

"God, Rossi, you sound like a grouchy parent. I've just handed you a fantastic lead."

A sigh heaved it way through the line. "What you've given me is a headache."

"But—"

"The veiled threat to the Grandese child bears looking into, but possessing cyanide is not against the law."

"Not even when a person is murdered with it in the same house?"

"Not even. Unless we can prove that a person with access to the house used the poison for an evil purpose.

Furthermore, are you certain of the contents of that vial? Or that Mrs. Harkness told you the truth?"

"Well, no."

Another sigh. "Keep the bottle in a safe place until I can get it from you and have some tests run."

"I put it in my purse. It'll be safe enough there. So this *is* a breakthrough."

"No, your word against Mrs. Harkness's is a stalemate. I have told you repeatedly to stay out of this. You're not listening."

"Not obeying, you mean, like some medieval housewife."

"No, like a modern, intelligent woman who knows her own limits."

A silence echoed through the line. Not even a sigh this time. He was right, of course. "I apologize."

"Accepted. Is there anything else you want to tell me?"

"That's about all. Oh, one other thing. Cookie said if I told anybody about our conversation she'd kill me."

"Deva, I—"

"Have to go. Sorry I can't wait here for you, but my appointment's in a half hour."

I hung up quickly without telling him who I was meeting. He didn't have to know everything. After all he had his secrets, and I had the right to a few of my own.

TWENTY-TWO

AN HOUR LATER, wrapped in a hospital gown, all thoughts of Francesco and Jewels and little Frannie fled my mind as I perched on the edge of Dr. Elizabeth Enright's examining table.

"When was your last internal exam?" she asked.

"A few years ago, before my husband's death. Since he died, I haven't had one." My voice trailed off.

"Are you aware that one ovary never developed?"

"Yes, but I was told that wouldn't be a problem."

She nodded. "Alone, no. But unfortunately it's not the only problem. From what I'm able to determine, the second ovary may be compromised as well. Without more tests I can't be certain, but—"

I took in a quick breath of antiseptic-laced air.

She quickly added, "There are no signs of malignancy or tumors. Simply a somewhat undeveloped organ. Was that never explained to you?"

I gripped the padded edges of the table. "Years ago, before I was married, I remember something being said about it. At the time, I didn't take the news seriously. Babies were far from my thoughts then. In later exams, the subject wasn't an issue."

"That's unfortunate, be—"

Unable to hold back, I burst out with, "Doctor, will I ever be able to have children?"

Her eyes, large and gray and fringed with paintbrush-thick lashes, took on a sympathetic sheen. "All things are possible, of course. I've seen women with reproductive organs similar to yours who did…on a few rare occasions…become pregnant and carry to term." She shook her head. "But realistically speaking, the odds are greatly against that outcome."

"Would hormone treatments help?" The desperation in my voice was clear even to me. The sympathy in Dr. Enright's eyes deepened.

"In my view I'm afraid the answer is no, but you might want to get a second opinion. In fact, I encourage you to do so."

I clutched the opening of the gown, nodding as if I agreed. A reflex action. I was staving off the blow she'd just dealt me. "It sounds like children aren't in my future."

Leaving the portable table that held her laptop, she came over to rest a hand on my shoulder, a gesture intended as a comfort, but wasn't. "Many people consider adoption a viable alternative."

"Yes, there is that possibility…but one other question, Doctor. I asked to have my late husband's medical records faxed to you. Have you received them?" Though the air conditioning was set low enough to make me shiver, my hands were sweaty. I wiped them on the wraparound gown.

"Let me check."

Dr. Enright left the examining room, closing the door behind her. I stared out the window at a sweeping view of a manmade lake and beyond to a stand of scrub pines that reminded me of Cape Cod. Jack and I had honeymooned in a beach cottage on Falmouth Bay. A month of utter magic. When I hadn't become pregnant then, I should have known…I shivered in my thin clinical gown.

"Here they are." Dr. Enright returned with a folder full of printouts and sat back behind her computer table. "What in your husband's history do you wish to know?"

"I wasn't getting pregnant, so he had a fertility test a few years ago. Can you tell me the results?"

She looked up, her heavy lashes sweeping wide open, her surprise telling me I should already know the answer. But without further questioning, she poured over the sheets, flipping back several pages. "Ah, yes…your husband consulted the Ranier Group at Mass General. They're considered the best in this field." She looked impressed and read on for another minute before glancing up again. "He had no fertility issues at all. His testosterone was in the high range. He would have had no problem fathering—oh…" She took one look at my expression and snapped the folder closed. "You didn't know? You believed he was sterile?"

"He lied," I whispered, my voice as cold as my skin.

She stood and quickly closed the space between us. "Are you all right?"

After two double whammies, no, I wasn't all right. "I'm fine," I said, fighting back tears.

She placed a hand on my shoulder. "You have every right to be upset. Don't hold it in. This is a women-for-women practice. We're not ashamed of tears in here." Her voice gentled to a murmur. "You have my permission."

Too numb to weep, I said, "Jack should have told me the truth. I deserved to know. He pretended our infertility was all his fault."

"*Fault* isn't the word," she chided softly.

"He didn't trust me with the truth. That's what it comes down to."

"Mrs. Dunne." Dr. Enright stood in front of the examining table where I was still perched precariously. "From what I've read in this report and from what you've told me, your husband's lie, as you call it, was an act of love. He was protecting you from a devastating realization."

"He had no right to do that."

"He obviously thought he did. Mrs. Dunne...?"

At the question in her voice, I glanced up from my fists clenching and unclenching in my lap.

"Your husband is no longer with us. Questioning his motives is fruitless. To dwell on the past will do no good. Look to the future."

She meant well. But she didn't understand.

"I trusted him completely. I believed he never lied to me. Not once. Not about anything."

She rose from the stool and extended her hand. We shook like two businesswomen settling a contract. "I'm sorry I wasn't able to tell you what you wanted to hear. If you ever want to come in just to talk, my door will always be open. Now I'll go and let you get dressed."

She left and, like a robot, I mindlessly pulled on my bra and panties, then shrugged into the outfit that Rossi liked best on me—a pencil skirt and matching tee in a tawny bronze silk. He said the color looked great with my hair. He loved me in skirts. And why with my legs did I ever wear slacks anyway?

Rossi. What would he think about all this? Would he tell me again that he didn't care? That it didn't matter? Could I believe him if he did? Could I believe any man?

I clasped on the chunky, faux gold necklace and slid into my Jimmy Choos. My one and only pair of Jimmy's, they were holding up well. As if that mattered. As if anything mattered.

Lower than the price on a markdown sale, I drove home. Inside the condo, I kicked off my heels, slumped on the living room sofa and dialed Treasure Island Antiques. A woman answered, and I asked to speak to Randy. A fifty-something Englishman with a Cockney accent and a sharp eye for a deal, he'd adore taking the Irish furniture off my hands. The sooner that happened, the better. I wanted to get rid of it all. Every damn piece. Not out of consideration for Rossi, not to finance a trip to Hawaii. To get every vestige of Jack out of my life. He'd lived a lie and betrayed me day by day for years. I'd never forgive him for that. Never.

After a pause, Randy picked up. "Treasure Isle."

"Just the man I want to talk to. This is Deva from Deva Dunne Interiors."

"Marvelous! 'Ow are you, luv?"

"Fantastic, Randy. I have some things to sell I think will interest you. Can you come to my home and have a look at them?"

"For you, luv, anything. When?" A little frisson of expectation had risen into his voice.

"How about now?"

"Give me your address and I'll be right over."

THAT NIGHT WAS Lee's last in Florida before she left for Paris. Rossi and I invited her to the casually glamorous Bayside Grille for a farewell dinner. We dined on the second floor terrace overlooking Naples Bay, the salty breeze wafting through the air and mingling with the calypso chords of a Caribbean guitar. Chatting happily, brimming with love and expectation, she kept the conversation going.

Pleased by what he'd wrought, Rossi smiled across the table at her, every once in a while sending an inquiring glance my way, wondering, no doubt, why I was so quiet, probably attributing that to Lee's departure.

Wrong. I was delighted for Lee but dreading what I'd have to tell him tomorrow, after we put her on the plane to Paris. Still, on the way back to Surfside I gave him the vial I'd found in the desk and let him quiz me about my conversations with Cookie, Bonita and the Grandeses. I answered as best I could, but truth to tell my mind was elsewhere.

THE FOLLOWING MORNING we watched the Boeing 747 roar down the runway and lift into the sky, carrying Lee into the future on silver wings. I would miss her in my life and in the business too. Her hugs and a whispered "I'll never forget this" still echoed in my heart as the plane disappeared, a glittering dot in the distance and then…nothing.

The time had come. I wanted to talk to Rossi in a public place while I still had steel in my spine. I drew him to a wooden bench near a glass wall overlooking the runways. A tall Royal Palm in a huge concrete pot cast a shadow over us as we sat on the stiff seat.

Rossi took my hand. "Feel sad about Lee leaving?"

I shook my head. "I'm happy for her, but not with some news I got yesterday."

Taken aback, he jerked upright on the bench. His hand tightened on mine. "What is it?" His eyes narrowed as he peered into my face.

I hesitated, not eager now that the moment had arrived to plunge a knife into our relationship.

"For God's sake, what's the matter? You know you can tell me whatever it is."

"I know." On the pretext of smoothing my skirt over my thighs, I slipped my hand out from under his. "I saw my GYN yesterday. She told me chances are I'll never have a child."

His chin snapped up. "That's all? Christ, you scared me. I thought you were dying." His shout caught the attention of an elderly passerby. She sent him a startled glance and scurried away from us.

"What do you mean, 'that's all?'" I snapped back.

"Don't you understand? Babies are out for me. No son.
No daughter. Not ever."

The anger ebbed from his face, and the fear. He reached
for my hand again, and though I tried to pull it free, he
wouldn't let go. "I understand what this means to you. The
finality of it. But this isn't the end. There are other options
for having a family. You could—"

"—adopt?"

"Yes. Exactly. You loved little Frannie the minute you
held him."

"True, but I'll never be able to give a man a child of
his own."

"That won't matter to any man who cares for you."

"Well, it does to me."

"To me, you're what matters. *You*." He shook his head.
"I can't believe we're having this conversation again. I
thought the subject had been put to rest."

No question he was beyond upset, but I'd come this far,
and I'd finish what I had set out to say. "The way our relationship has been heating up lately, I thought you should
know." I freed my fingers and balled my hands in my lap.
"I prevented one man from having a family. I will never
do that to another one."

"Oh, so that's it? You've cooked up a foolproof excuse
to keep me—or any guy—at arm's length. You lost Jack
and you'll never let anybody take his place. All this other
stuff is nothing more than a smokescreen." He stood and
flung his arms in the air. "So, the mystery's solved. One
anyway."

"Yes, it's solved. There was nothing wrong with Jack.
He kept me from knowing the truth about myself, but now
that I do—"

"You're going to push me away." His sarcasm had

turned cold and precise. I'd never seen him like this. Well, what did I expect, hugs and kisses?

I stared into his frozen brown eyes. "Try to understand."

He shook his head. "No. You can stop right there. I understand all right. What you don't understand is that you're putting a wall between us. A wall of your own making." His jaw clenching, he glanced out the window. Another glittering bird was about to take flight. An instant only and his attention swiveled back to me. "You're worth ten women put together. A hundred. A thousand. Why won't you believe me? Do you think I'm lying to you?"

With my fingers still clutching each other as if for support, I said, "Jack lied, and I never thought *he* would."

"I see." Rossi bent over me, his face level with mine, and spoke in his quiet detective's voice. "I never met your Jack, but I always thought he sounded like a hell of a guy. I still do. He protected you."

"I don't need protection," I yelled.

A couple of teenagers strolling toward Concourse D heard me and giggled. Rossi ignored them. "The hell you don't. Jack knew you better than you know yourself. And so do I. You're scared. Scared to live."

"I am not!" I leaped up, heart thundering. "I'm not a complete woman."

Disgust and disappointment mingling in his eyes, he said, "I'm beginning to think that's true. But not for your reasons. You don't need me in your life. So let's make the break starting now." He stood and shot me a little quasi-military, two-fingered salute. "It was nice while it lasted. I'll take a cab back to town."

He strode off, shoulders hunched, the pink and red blooms on his Hawaiian shirt looking anything but cheerful, his shoes hitting the terminal floor like echoing hammer blows.

TWENTY-THREE

"HEY, DEVA, WAIT UP."

Chip. I hadn't talked to him since he'd been released from the hospital. Though the week since I last saw Rossi had been a killer, and I didn't feel much like chatting, I slowed my pace across Surfside's parking lot. He caught up to me by my front door, wheezing and puffing but not as badly as I remembered. A bandage circled his left wrist.

"How are you?" I asked him.

He drew in a ragged breath. "Never better. Lost ten pounds. Been working out. I…uh…want to apologize for putting you through that bathroom incident."

I patted his good arm. "I understand. You'd had a lot of stress. It got to you."

"True, but it never will again. No need." He stopped talking and, forehead wrinkling, he stared at me for a moment. "You okay? You're kind of pale."

"I'm fine, Chip. Thanks for asking." *My buddy. He's worried about me. What a prince of a guy.* "Really. I'm fine." No need to add to his woes by telling him about mine. He didn't look convinced, so I tried for a smile.

"If things got to you too I wouldn't be surprised." He tilted his head, and with concern flitting in his eyes, he ran a finger down my cheek. "You sure you're not upset about anything?" His worry was challenging my reserves. Not daring to speak just then, I shook my head, relieved when he changed the subject. "You moving or something? I saw a truck here yesterday."

"No. I'm not moving. I just sold some stuff."

"Redecorating?"

"You could say that…my entire life."

"Hope that means good things. Sounds serious." When I didn't reply, he cleared his throat. "I've got some news for you."

"Oh?"

He inhaled then noisily exhaled. "I got married last Saturday."

"You did! Wow! No need to ask who the lucky girl is."

"Nope. AudreyAnn finally said yes."

I flung my arms around him and kissed his round, teddy bear cheek then let him go just as fast as I had grabbed him. "Uh-oh," I said, smiling for real this time. "I can't do that anymore. Your *wife* might object."

He grinned big time at "wife."

"I'm so, so happy for you."

"Me too." He blushed. "She's all I ever wanted. And you know the best part?"

His good news had lifted my spirits. "Tell me, I'm all ears."

"She wouldn't wait to see if I keep that hidden money. Said it didn't matter." His eyes shone like it was Christmas and Santa had granted his every wish.

"Well, somehow I think you'll have AudreyAnn *and* the money. No one's claimed it yet, have they?"

"No not yet. Grandese's lawyer contacted Simon Yaeger last week. Looks like he's not going to make a play for it either."

"Francesco told me the same thing, and I'm so pleased."

"Yeah, the restaurant building's a total loss then somebody tries to kill him and gets his cousin instead. Grandese could be pretty bitter, but I guess he's not."

"I'm just glad he's not going after the money."

"Me too. Simon said the legal fees would've chewed up

a lot, and I want to help Bonita and do things for Audrey-Ann. You know, give her luxuries she's never had." He drew in a raspy breath, his happiness clouding over for a moment. "I sure hope the police find that killer soon. I'm a cook. You know what happens to a cook when some-body's poisoned in his kitchen?"

I patted his arm again, hoping to telegraph that I understood. "I can guess."

"At first, the money didn't matter much, but now it does, especially if I can't get work as a chef."

"That money's yours. I saw you pull it out of the wall. So did Rossi. I'll testify for you in any court in the state." Unless a former owner could prove he'd hidden the money—which was unlikely—every one of those Grover Clevelands belonged to Chip. And I *would* be happy to testify to that. Rossi would, too, I was certain, but the time when I might speak for him was past.

"Thanks. I knew I could count on you."

I would also be happy to finish the Rum Row project. To get the Grandeses and their problems out of my life. Actually I had no choice but to finish it or risk losing Deva Dunne Interiors. And now more than ever I needed my business. It was the only thing I had left.

"Are you listening, Deva?" Chip asked, bringing me back to the moment. "Will you come?"

"What? Sorry, my mind was wandering."

"AudreyAnn and I are hosting a wedding reception next Saturday. Here in the Surfside Club Room. We hope you and Lieutenant Rossi can make it."

"I'd love to, but I don't know about Rossi." I took a deep breath before admitting, "We broke up."

His mouth rounded into a stunned O. "When did this happen?"

"A week ago."

He let out a whistle then paid for it with a wracking

cough. When he caught his breath, he said, "No wonder you're looking pale. That's a heavy decision, but on the upside, wait'll Simon Yaeger hears about this. He's always had the…he's always been crazy about you. And he's already said yes to Saturday."

I groaned inwardly. The last thing I wanted right now was a fix-up. Not even one with glamour boy Simon. "I'll be there too. Wouldn't miss your celebration for the world."

Though I didn't want to be rude and cut our conversation short, I'd had more than enough for one day. I needed to get inside and collapse on my couch. Tomorrow I'd start scouring the local art and antiques shops for Francesco's Hudson River oils, lighting fixtures, rugs and other accessories. The sooner I did so, the faster I'd be through with the whole project. In the coming days, the Closed sign would be in the shop window far too often. What a time to be without an assistant.

On the other hand, working around the clock would keep me too busy to dwell on Rossi.

Rossi. What have I done?

Before I could make an excuse and duck inside, a shiny black Lincoln Town Car with tinted windows purred onto the tarmac. Since Dick Parker sold the building to Simon, we had a few new condo owners, some I hadn't met yet. Maybe this was one of our new neighbors.

The driver turned off the motor, and two men in business suits got out and slammed the doors. Though they were blocking vehicles in the carport, they left the Lincoln where it was and strode over to Chip and me.

The younger of the two, a man of about thirty-five, his beefy shoulders straining the seams of his pinstriped suit, reached us first. Close behind him, an older man, early fifties maybe, in double-breasted black serge brought up the rear. Neither one smiled. Neither one said hello.

"We're looking for a woman," Pinstripes said to Chip. "An AudreyAnn Baranski. You know her?"

Uh-oh. AudreyAnn had said two men in business suits kept calling on Donny. Were these the same two?

I shot an alarmed glance at Chip, but except for a puzzled frown, he appeared clueless. AudreyAnn mustn't have told him about Donny's creepy visitors.

"Who wants to know?" I asked.

Pinstripes gave me a slow, insulting, head-to-toe eyeball check. Blood boiling, I gave him a slow body scan right back, deliberately moving my glance from his receding hairline—I let my eyes linger there—down his bristly face, along his torso where I stopped a second to smile. Let him figure out why. Then I then dragged my inspection from his legs to the toes of his pointy shoes. And up again into his eyes, which had narrowed into slits.

I was playing with fire and knew it.

Rossi would have had a fit if he'd seen me antagonize this hostile-looking stranger. I gave a mental shrug. He would never know about it, would he?

As Black Serge folded his arms across his chest, Pinstripes reached into his jacket pocket and removed a badge. He flipped open the leather cover and flashed a piece of metal at us. "FBI," he said. "Looking for a Miss Baranski."

Chip gulped. "There's no one here by that name."

"You sure?"

"There's an AudreyAnn Salvatore."

"Big woman. Big—"

He stopped short of using the T-word, but Chip flushed and said, "My wife's an ample woman, if that's what you mean. What does the FBI want with her?"

"A chat."

"What about?"

Black Serge moved forward. "Just tell us where she is."

Chip backed up a step. "She's out doing errands. Shopping."

"She got a cell phone?"

Chip nodded. "Sure, but—"

"You're going to give her a call."

"Is that so? You can't barge in here like this and—"

"You saw the badge."

"What's the penalty for impersonating a federal agent?" As if I were simply making polite conversation, I directed my question at Chip.

"We got a wiseass here," Pinstripes said, snarly all of a sudden. He upped his chin at Chip. "Which one of these doors is yours?"

Chip stood there, blank faced.

"Come on. Come on."

Chip pointed to 103. "That one."

"Let's go."

"I didn't invite you in."

"We're inviting ourselves. You too." Pinstripes grabbed my arm in a half nelson. At least I think it was a half nelson. Judging from his iron grip, he could have flung a tire chain around me.

"I'm not going anywhere with you goons." I tried to pull away, but if anything, his grip tightened. "This is kidnapping. A federal offense."

"Don't take that attitude. We're just waiting on Miss Bar—*Mrs.* Salvatore."

I could have screamed. I should have screamed, but that's when Black Serge pulled a gun on us, and with the muzzle pressing into my back, I followed Chip into condo 103.

TWENTY-FOUR

THE MINUTE WE were inside, Black Serge waved his gun in the general direction of the defecation-brown lounge chair. "You. Sit over there," he said to Chip.

His face ashen, Chip slumped into it.

Another gun wave. This time at me. "You over here."

Stiff as a plank, I took a seat on the couch. Pinstripes hunkered down next to me and flung an arm across the sofa back. "Relax," he urged.

I upped my chin at Serge. "Tell him to put that thing away and I might."

"Shelve it," Pinstripes said to Serge, his arm slipping around my shoulders. "They won't give us any trouble. Not the redhead anyway. Isn't that right?" He squeezed my arm. His touch made my skin crawl. I twisted away from him and balanced on the edge of my seat.

The gun disappeared into Serge's double-breasted jacket. "Give the little lady a call," he said to Chip.

"On one condition."

Chip had the guts to demand conditions? Good for him.

"Yeah? What's that?"

"You don't hurt her."

"You in love or what?"

His jaw like stone, Chip said, "Those are my terms."

"Yeah. Yeah. Just get her here."

"No way." Chip wasn't about to relent. Push a mild, peaceable man too far, and what you get is immovable stone. I didn't know whether to cheer or cry.

Serge shrugged. "One way or the other, the little woman's got a surprise coming. So we wait. Unless we speed things up." His eyes took on a gleeful shine. "Get rough with you. Or..." his glance swiveled over to me, "...her. Yeah, her." He took a step closer to me and pulled out the Glock.

My heart leaped into my throat. What was he going to do, pistol-whip me? Whatever he had in mind, no question he meant business. In the cool air-conditioned living room, beads of sweat broke out at my hairline, and my hands clenched into fists. *Right. Terrific weapons against an armed thug.* I glanced across at Chip. His lips were trembling.

As Serge approached the couch, Pinstripes pulled me against his chest. This time I didn't twitch away. "Take it easy," he said to his partner. "Don't hit her in the face."

"Don't lay a hand on her anywhere." Chip huffed out a sigh so deep he had to have dredged it up from his belly. "I'll make the call."

I knew he didn't want to. From the ashen look of him, I could tell he was scared he'd lose AudreyAnn, the most precious thing in his life. But to save me from harm, he was willing to risk endangering her. An act of love—*for me*—that I'd remember for the rest of my life—however long it lasted. I unclenched my hands and sent him a wobbly smile.

He returned it with one just as shaky then under Serge's relentless stare, he removed his cell phone from his pants pocket.

"Don't let on you got company," Serge told him. "Just tell her you want her home. You got a surprise waiting. That always brings the chicks running."

A muscle quivered in Chip's jaw, but he carried out Serge's order to the letter.

While we waited for AudreyAnn to show, his buddy tried to strike up a conversation with me. But I was having none of it. I didn't care how much he liked redheads. The creep. He had the personality of a dead weed. Or a rattlesnake.

So I kept quiet and kept shrugging away from his roaming hand, praying all the while that we would get out of this alive. I tossed AudreyAnn's name into the prayer, too, even though she was undoubtedly the cause of our terror.

We waited in morbid silence for what seemed like forever. Then flip-flops slapped the stone pavers, and a second later in came AudreyAnn, her arms filled with Publix Market bags, her face filled with anticipation at the surprise Chip had in store.

One peek around the living room and she knew. The groceries plummeted to the floor. A bottle smashed and red wine leaked out over the tiles.

Serge pointed to the widening red circle. "Too bad."

"What are you doing here?" AudreyAnn whispered, terror siphoning the blood from her face.

"You know these guys?" Chip asked in a voice no more than a hoarse whisper.

She nodded without looking at him.

Pinstripes eased off the couch and sauntered over to her. "You got something of ours. We want you should give it to us."

AudreyAnn's chins trembled. "I don't have anything of yours."

Chip hoisted himself out of his chair, ready to leap on Serge.

The thug reached into his jacket and brandished the Glock. "Stay," he snapped.

Chip eased back down. "Don't hurt her."

Serge cocked his head at AudreyAnn. "You hurt?"

"No," she said, sounding like she wasn't sure.

"We're looking for a notebook. Small. Black. Lots of numbers. A few names. A few initials. You take anything like that out of Donny's place?"

The blue in AudreyAnn's frightened eyes lit up. "I took Donny's little black book to kind of…well…get back at him. I thought it was full of his old girlfriend's numbers. I called a few, but nobody sounded like a girlfriend. A couple of guys said they never even heard of him."

"You still got the book?"

She sent a glance Chip's way, pleading for understanding. "I think so."

"Go get it," Serge said. And to his thuggy partner, "Go with her."

"It's in my underwear drawer."

"Should be fun," Stripes said, taking her arm and marching her into the bedroom. Chip followed them with his eyes, so pale and shaky he looked like he was ready to pass out.

"She'll be all right," I said with a confidence I didn't feel.

He didn't answer. Just drooped back onto the lounger and closed his eyes. In the bedroom, a drawer squeaked open, and a moment later, Pinstripes strode into the living room, AudreyAnn in tow, a black notebook in his hand.

"Got it," he said. "Let's go."

"Not so fast," Serge said. "Any pages missing?"

"Oh yeah." Pinstripes quickly flipped through the book. "Everything's here."

His hand on the front door handle, Serge turned to us. "Keep this little party to yourselves. Understand?" He shrugged. "Otherwise, who knows?"

His partner tucked the notebook in his jacket pocket

and winked at me. "I meant it, babe. Love that red hair. Why don't you believe me? Would I lie?"

I shot him a filthy look. "Why not? Better men than you have."

"Better at what?"

"Before you go, I have a question for you," I said, getting daring now that they were leaving.

"You want a date?"

"Franceso Grandese said to thank you for the toy truck. The baby loves it."

"He got it, huh? How the hell did you find out?" As something struck him, he stepped back into the living room. "Bonita tell you?"

Serge frowned and jerked his chin at the door. "Come on. Who cares about that? Let's go."

"Yeah, yeah, we're out of here," Stripes said, heading for the foyer.

The instant the door clicked closed behind them, I raced over and rammed the deadbolt home, though truth be told, Serge's Glock could shoot off the bolt, the lock and half the door with no trouble at all.

Before Chip could rise out of his lounger, AudreyAnn ran to him and climbed onto his lap, sobbing. His arms reached around her…with only a little difficulty…and they snuggled together, blocking out the world and everything in it. That included me.

I hated to intrude on AudreyAnn's moment of comfort—I wasn't jealous, I swear—but I had to say what was on my mind or bust. "Chip." No response. "Chip."

He peered at me over his wife's heaving shoulders.

"You need to call Rossi. Tell him about this."

"No. They warned us not to say anything."

"So what? They're criminals. You can't listen to them."

He shook his head. "I can't take the chance. They might hurt AudreyAnn."

"They might hurt *all* of us. You've got to notify the authorities. Donny was *murdered*. Maybe over that little black book. Who knows? This is too dangerous to ignore."

"No." His voice was as firm as I'd ever heard it.

"Be reasonable. You're a person of interest in Donny's death. So is your wife. Me too. I'd call Rossi in a heart-beat, but I can't right now. You have to do it. Or Audrey-Ann does. I insist." I plopped back on the couch. "I'm not leaving until you do."

AudreyAnn sat up, rubbing a sleeve across her watery eyes. "Deva's right. Those guys used to show up at Don-ny's place in Miami. I think he was scared of them too. Always jumpy as a frog around them."

"They have something on him?" Chip asked.

She shook her head. "I don't know. I never heard what they talked about, but I think they were forcing informa-tion out of him. I'd peek through the blinds when they stood outside. Donny did most of the talking. They did the listening." She wiped her eyes again. The sleeves of her T-shirt had to be soaking wet by now. "Sometimes he'd take out the book and read from it. They'd write down what he said. Numbers, I guess. Before they left, they al-ways gave him an envelope."

"An envelope?"

She nodded. "Money, I'm pretty sure. He'd take me out for a fancy dinner that same night. Every time." She glanced warily at Chip, assessing his reaction, but he sat poker faced, listening. "Those were the only nights that happened."

"The police need to hear this," I said. A delayed reac-tion to the danger we'd just escaped had me sweating again in the cool air. "We can't have thugs showing up on our doorstep. Maybe next time they'll do more with that gun than wave it in the air. We know they drive a black Lincoln Town Car. The police can trace it. Apprehend them."

Chip shook his head. "Do you know how many black Lincolns there are in Florida? Thousands."

"I'll bet they're heading for Alligator Alley and the East Coast. I could chase them while you call the police. They should be easy to spot."

"You'll never find them. It's pitch black outside, and we didn't get the plate number."

Clearly he had no intention of playing cops and robbers, but I wasn't ready to give up that fast. "We can describe them. Say we think they're from Miami."

"If they're smart, they'll switch cars before heading across the alley."

"Who said they're smart? Make the call. Ask for Lieutenant Rossi. Don't force me to do it, please. Tell him they're the ones who sent the toy truck."

"The what?"

"Just tell him what I said. Don't you understand? They could be Donny's killers."

TWENTY-FIVE

WITH BOTH AUDREYANN and me staring him down, Chip reluctantly made the call. Then, pocketing his cell phone, he said, "The lieutenant will be right over. I hope you're happy now."

"That's a stretch, but I am relieved." I headed for the foyer.

"Hey, where you going?"

"Home. If the lieutenant needs my input, he knows where to find me."

"But you have to be here," AudreyAnn sputtered. As I went out the door, Chip was already explaining why I didn't want to see Rossi just then.

My thoughts scattering like buckshot, I walked into my condo and careened to a stop.

Oh, that's right.

No more tall case clock.

No more hunt board.

No more five drawer chest.

No more inlaid mahogany table.

Gone were the Sheffield silver, the rose medallion bowls, the brass candlesticks, the Tabriz rug.

Gone was every vestige of John Douglas Dunne.

Gone, too, was the grace, the loveliness, the subtle sheen and polish of Jack's family heirlooms. A much-needed check had replaced them…though actually, nothing ever could.

I flung my bag on the living room sofa and dropped

onto the cushions. The sofa, the club chairs and the glass coffee table were all the furniture that remained. A pair of lamps stood on the floor. The Pembroke tables that had held them were gone too. The room was as barren as I was.

In the center of the floor where the rug had sat, the tiles were duller than the rest. On one wall a dark square marked the spot where Jack's portrait had hung. In what I admit was a childish fit, I'd hid it from sight in the back of my clothes closet. Now, after all these changes, the living room needed to be repainted and the floors polished, but that wouldn't happen any time soon. For the foreseeable future, the effort of getting through my days—and nights— would take all my energy. The condo could remain stripped and bare forever. What did I care? It matched my mood.

Heartsick, I stared at the dull tiles, unable to stop wondering if Rossi would ring the bell and ask a few questions about the mysterious visitors. It would be a perfect excuse to see me. I half feared, half hoped my chimes would ring, that he'd stand on my doorstep, dour, glowering, eager to see me. If that happened, I knew I'd melt. My resolve of last week was already turning into slush.

Motionless as a stalked mouse, I sat still listening to the tomblike quiet of my empty home without the strength or the will to move. I had parted from a man I was crazy about. Yes, I'll admit it—Rossi had gotten under my skin. But that didn't make the loss easier to bear. Worse, lingering in the back of my mind was his crazy accusation that I was afraid of life. *Wrong.* For once Rossi was dead wrong. Honesty and doing the right thing were what this was about, not fear. Or were they?

The more I stared, the more I realized the tiles *had* to be polished. They'd drive me crazy if I left them like that. And the walls should be repainted. Maybe I'd go for a dif-

ferent color scheme. Something fresh and new. Off with
the old. On with the new.

Well, if I had any fear in my heart at all, it was for
Rossi, not for myself. I couldn't bear disappointing him.
As I must have disappointed Jack. I lowered my head to
my knees and cried the tears I'd held in all day, soaking
my skirt right down to the hem.

In a while, deep voices exchanged a few words outside…Rossi and Chip…then a door closed, plunging me
back into silence.

I sat like that for over an hour until once again footsteps
sounded on the pavement then faded into nothing. So Rossi
didn't want to talk to me. Just as well. A clean break. But
I knew how diligent he was about his work. No matter
what his personal reasons for avoiding me might be, if he
thought I could add anything to what Chip and Audrey-
Ann had told him, he would have knocked on my door.

His judgment, as usual, was correct. The night before
Lee left—the last evening we were together—I'd told him
everything that had transpired at Rum Row. As for the un-
welcome visitors to Chip's condo, I knew no more than
Chip did. Less than AudreyAnn. Interviewing me would
have been a foolish waste of Rossi's time.

Wouldn't it?

In the gathering gloom, the damn tiles merged into a
single, featureless mass. Maybe I should drag myself out
to the kitchen and fix something to eat. Except for black
coffee, I'd had nothing since last night's dinner.

But I sat without moving, trying to put Rossi out of
my mind, and also trying to unravel the skein of events
I'd been entangled in since the day Tomas died. His death
might have been a tragic accident, but no question about it,
Donny had been murdered. Whether the victim of a fatal

error or not, he was dead nevertheless—the unlucky one
who had unwittingly saved Francesco's life.

No saint, in the past Donny had had several skirmishes
with the law and obviously knew the two men who ha-
rassed us today. And they obviously knew Bonita. What
could the connection be? The night Donny died, they
weren't present to slip him the cyanide. Furthermore, their
weapons of choice were guns not poison.

So what about the cyanide? I revisited the Cookie possibility. If she'd gone into her father's factory and stolen
some, when had she done so? The business had been sold
several years ago. Would she have kept poison on hand for
years in case she ever needed to commit a murder? No, too
weird, the act of a deranged mind, and Cookie struck me as
totally rational. And totally rigid. Except when in her cups.

And then there was Norm, who liked the ponies. By
loaning him money, Francesco had fed his habit, perhaps
to keep Norm under his thumb. But if Norm were the murderer, killing Donny was a stupid mistake. Had he erased
Francesco, he would likely have erased his debt along with
him. Maybe that had been his original intent but somehow
the dirty deed got botched.

I slid farther down on the couch, kicked off my sandals
and stretched out.

It was silly to even consider Bonita a killer. In the first
place, how would she get her hands on cyanide? Besides,
even if she had, I couldn't believe she was ruthless enough
to use it. Nor Jewels either, pregnant with Francesco's baby
and loving little Frannie as if he were her own.

That left my friend Chip and his brand new wife. Warm
and unassuming, Chip was no murderer. Though in his
overwhelming love for AudreyAnn, he'd kill in a heart-
beat to protect her. Or if in despair at losing her, he'd kill
himself. Something he'd already proven.

As for AudreyAnn—the final piece of the puzzle—could she kill in either cold blood or hot? Doubtful. She'd fallen to pieces just looking at the two goons. To paraphrase a Texas saying, she was all chest and no cattle.

I shivered, wishing I had something to toss over me. But though I felt chilly, listing so many dead ends must have numbed my brain, for I fell asleep on the couch in my damp silk skirt and top, the tawny bronze outfit Rossi liked so much.

At dawn, while I hovered between wake and sleep, a pall of depression settled over me like a thick, black blanket. Before I could snuggle into it, my grandmother's voice echoed in my ear as loud and clear as if she were in the room. Quite a feat for someone who'd passed away fifteen years ago.

"Devalera Agnes Dunne," she said.

Shocked, I bolted upright. Nana only used all three of my names when she was angry with me.

"Get off that sofa, lass, and get hold of your life. Use what God gave you. Stop whining about what He didn't give."

"I'm not whining." I swear I spoke out loud.

"Well, Jesus, Mary and Joseph, you've fooled all the saints in heaven and meself as well. Look at you. Sleeping in your day clothes and putting nothing in your stomach for the last thirty-six hours."

"I've had coffee."

"Don't be after toying with me. You'll lose your strength carrying on like this. Then where will you be?"

I fell back against the cushions. "My life is a mess, Nana. I don't think I can bear it."

"Pawsh, I say to drivel like that." She threw her hands on her hips and stared at me, arms akimbo. "You weren't named Agnes after me for nothing. I know you never liked the name, but we share it nonetheless. So don't go shaming me, lass. Get a move on now. Up with you. Up!"

When Nana talks, I move. I leaped off the couch and in a half hour, no more, I was showered, shampooed, made-up, dressed in green—in Nana's honor—and ready to roll. I chugged down a power drink and rushed through my sad-looking living room without letting it get me down.

I'd been named for a political hero and a wise woman. Nana was right. I had to put my complaints and my heartache aside, stop whining and get to work. After last night's fruitless analysis of potential culprits, I knew once and for all that sleuthing wasn't my strong suit. I'd leave that job to Rossi—this time I really meant it—and stick to the work I knew best. Interior design.

And young love. I knew a little bit about that too, and this morning Nikhil Jamison needed my help.

I went directly to the shop, spent two hours doing paperwork and straightening display tables. Lee had been gone less than a day and I missed her already, although on the upside she didn't know Rossi and I had parted ways. She liked Rossi and would be upset about our breakup. But now happy with her love, when she heard about our split, she'd take the news in stride.

A few minutes before nine I drove to Tenth Avenue South. Nikhil's apartment was located on the ground floor of the Azalea Building. He answered the bell on the first ring dressed in jeans and a ratty Ole Miss T-shirt. A glad-to-see-you smile lit his face, and he ushered me into his living room with an elaborate arm flourish.

At the sight of the drab, empty space, an "Oh my" escaped me before I could stop it.

His face fell. "See what I mean? The place is a dump."

I didn't disagree. "Mind if I walk through?"

"Please. Be my guest." He threw up his hands then let them flop down by his sides. "It only gets worse."

A five minute tour of the small kitchen, smaller bath, sizeable bedroom and the concrete patio adjoining it revealed all the apartment's secrets.

Back in the living room, I eyed one of the two plastic lawn chairs that faced the fifty-two-inch HDTV—except for a vintage Gibson guitar propped in a corner, the room's only furniture.

"Why don't we sit down and talk about what needs to be done?" I asked.

"Sure. Sorry I don't have a more comfortable seat to offer you."

I laughed. "You will soon."

"Great. This stiff stuff's awful. Usually I just sit on the floor, but that's not too comfortable either." He ran a hand through his hair and flushed in that charming, boyish way I remembered. I reached into my tote bag and removed the clipboard. "You wouldn't happen to have any coffee, would you?"

'Oh. Sure. Coffee's my specialty. Starbucks medium blend. No cream though."

"Black would be heaven."

After I'd downed a few jolts of excellent brew out of an Ole Miss mug with a big chip on the rim, I said, "Okay. Good news first?"

He nodded, a flash of surprise lighting his eyes. "There's good news? Hard to believe."

"For starters, you have an excellent layout. Nice tiles in the bath. Fairly new appliances in the kitchen. Big bedroom closet. And I love the French doors leading out to the little private patio." With a finger I described a circle in the air. "This is a good-sized room too. Tall, wide windows overlooking the lawn."

I pointed at the blinds. "Verticals aren't my favorite, but they'll do, and the ivory color goes well with the rug. In other words, you have a lot to work with here."

He sat across from me, cradling a mug between his hands, his face a little brighter than it had been a few minutes earlier. "What's the bad news?"

"There isn't any."

"You're kidding me."

I shook my head. "Nope, not unless work is bad news to you."

As if his adrenaline didn't need another boost, he put his mug on the floor and sat up straight in his plastic chair. "Work isn't a problem. Not at all."

"Good. What you need, in addition to some basic pieces of furniture and a few well-chosen accessories, is cleaning and brightening. Sweat equity. We're not going to build for the ages. We're going to be practical."

He grinned. "Practical. My middle name."

"Forget about the ceilings and the woodwork. They're both white and in decent shape. The walls are what we'll concentrate on. And then the floors. Okay. For the walls, we need a color. Any preferences?"

"No, not really. Except no pink or anything."

"How about green?"

He shrugged. "Sure, whatever you say."

"Green would be symbolically perfect. It's the color of spring, of new beginnings—"

"Of money," he said laughing.

"True. Spoken like a bona fide investment broker. So how about a pale wash of lime green? It's bright and youthful. And in the bedroom—"

He leaned forward. "Yes?"

Cute.

"Well in there, a deeper lime green on one wall, the one

behind the bed. Make the bed a focal point," I said, resisting the urge to grin.

"I like that idea."

"I hoped you would." I kept a straight face but it wasn't easy. "As for the floors, this beige carpeting looks to be in good condition. It just needs cleaning. Once the painting is finished, you can rent a rug shampooer. Then wash the windows. When that's done, we'll bring in some furniture. Now…"

I didn't need to say more. Nikhil jumped up and hurried into the bedroom returning with a check in his hand.

"Fifteen hundred," he said. "My limit."

"Trust me," I said, tucking the check into my purse. "We won't exceed this amount by one penny. "I'll keep a running tab on everything I buy. If I can come in under budget, I will." I held up a warning finger. "But don't count on that, please."

I removed four rolls of blue masking tape from the tote and held them out. "For you. A present. Use it around all the windows and doors, up by the ceiling and down around the baseboards. I'm going shopping for paint. Should be back within an hour." I slipped the clipboard into the tote and stood. "When is Melanie due to arrive?"

"In six weeks."

"That's a tight schedule, Nikhil. Nights and weekends won't give you much time to get everything done."

"Time isn't a problem. I left my job at Harkness Investments yesterday."

And I left my Rossi last week.

"Our lives seem to be on a parallel track," I told him, trying to smile.

Nikhil's brow wrinkled. "Pardon?"

I shook my head, not wanting to get into it. "Recently I made a momentous decision too."

"Yeah, momentous is the word. Wait till my parents hear what I did. They'll have a fit, but I had no choice. Not once I learned what Norm was doing with the books. It's worse than I—" He stopped.

One hand on the door handle, I said, "My lips are sealed, but if I can make a suggestion?"

He nodded, clearly upset by what he'd told me.

"Do you remember meeting a Lieutenant Rossi in my shop?"

"Of course."

"Well, if you'll get a piece of paper, I'll write down his number."

Nikhil's face, so quick to flush, paled. He backed up a step. "I don't want to get involved with the police."

I shrugged and opened the door. "Your decision, but look at it this way. Norm is a person of interest in a murder case. You must have heard about that. The news was plastered all over the local media for days. Anyway, Norm was present the night the victim died."

"What's that got to do with Harkness Investments?"

I shrugged. "Maybe nothing. But something's the matter if Norm's been cooking the books."

"I didn't exactly say that."

I slid the tote over a shoulder. "No but you came close. At the very least you need to protect yourself."

Nikhil gulped in some air. "I haven't done anything wrong." Maybe not but he looked like he could throw up anyway.

I stepped back a little, just in case. "If something illegal is going on, and you know about it, you can't just quit and walk away." I was scaring him, but on the theory that it was better to be scared than arrested, I went for the jugular. "You want to go to jail for something you didn't do?"

He stretched out an arm and leaned on the door, snapping it closed. "I shouldn't have mentioned anything about Harkness. That was dumb of me. I don't even know you. Not really." He ran a hand through his tousled hair again, rumpling away any resemblance to his fledgling, stockbroker image.

I smiled in what I hoped was a reassuring way. "Interior designers are like shrinks. Our clients tell us *everything.*" And here I was telling yet another person to make an emergency phone call to Rossi. Would he?

Nikhil's shoulders slumped, and he stuck his hands in his jeans pockets. "I've been awake every night this week trying to decide what to do. You're sure making it tougher for me."

TWENTY-SIX

WELL, I COULDN'T force Nikhil to make the call, but I gave him one of my cards with Rossi's number on it anyway, and drove over to Barley's Paints to choose some wall color. A flat latex in lime green with the creative name of Citrus Frappé spoke to me. Barley's master mixer diluted the shade to a pastel wash for the living room and intensified it for that all-important bedroom wall.

To zap up the bland ivory kitchen, I'd have Nikhil apply masking tape to the walls in vertical stripes then run a roller of Citrus Frappé over them. Let the paint dry, strip off the tape and *voila*—stripes, style, panache. And no more money spent.

In the equally bland bathroom, a soft apricot shade sponged on above the tiles would make Melanie's skin glow every time she looked in the mirror. Yup, I was a red-haired cupid all right—for another woman's love life.

I added paper buckets, stirrers, brushes, paint tray, roller with extra pads, and a giant sponge to my purchases, pocketed the receipt, and loaded everything in the Audi's trunk for the trip back to Nikhil's place.

But I didn't go in. Not with Rossi's dusty Mustang parked at the curb in front of the building. So Nikhil had placed the call after all, and whatever he knew about Norm, Rossi must have thought was worth hearing ASAP.

I sat, staring at his car for a moment, wondering if he missed me, if he had slept last night, if he'd had anything to eat. All questions I'd given up the right to ask. I finally drove away, forcing myself to remember I *had* listened to Nana, *had* gotten up off the couch, *had* gone to work, and wouldn't give in to self-pity or longing. Not if it killed me.

Rolling along the quiet Saturday morning streets, I gripped the wheel of the Audi as if I were in the Indy 500 and headed toward the Old Naples shopping district. Francesco wanted Hudson River oils, so I hit the big three galleries—Harmon-Meek, Sheldon, and DeBruyne's. No luck.

Not in Hudson River oils, though at DeBruyne's a stunning, drop-dead abstract took my breath away, literally stopping me in my tracks. Jagged bolts of purple, tangerine and vivid mango—yes, mango—thundered across a huge canvas. Here and there, narrow shards of gold glimmered in the light, the power of the composition alone holding their glitter in check. The tension between the two forces was electrifying. And perfect for that mango dining room. It generated so much energy, Francesco's guests would be eating the tablecloth.

I stood in front of the canvas, tapping my toe, wondering if Francesco would agree to include one avant-garde piece in his antiques heaven. Totally unexpected, it would be a knockout. A little sweep of excitement flitted through me for the first time all week. Yes, it was true, work did help alleviate misery. Maybe if I kept busy enough, the days would peel away in a blur of activity.

"I'm fighting a tight schedule," I said to the store manager. "Can you deliver the painting this afternoon? And send an art installer to hang it?" They absolutely could and would and understood the sale was subject to the owner's approval. As for the Hudson River oils, they would contact dealers around the country and get back to me.

On Third Street South, I dropped in at Tommy Bahama's for coconut shrimp and salad. Fortified by the food and the sunshine and the salty breeze wafting in from the

Gulf, I plowed on…determined to stay busy…determined not to think about Rossi.

Francesco needed carpets. At least two to start—one for the living room and one for the dining room. That meant a visit to Arabian Sights, a shop always piled high with luscious orientals.

Zayd, the proprietor, greeted me with a bow so low his hair nearly mopped the floor. "Delighted to see you again, my darling," he purred. "How may I help you?"

"Lovely to see you too," I purred back. "What is your largest Heriz?"

His eyes flared wide at that, and leading me to a hip-high stack of carpets, he snapped his fingers. As if he were Aladdin and they were genies popping out of a bottle, a pair of young men with in-your-face muscles rushed over and folded back rug after rug for my inspection. This time I lucked out and found exactly what I had in mind. A rare fifteen by twenty-two Kashmar for the center of the living room and a lovely faded nineteenth century Heriz for the dining room.

"Can you deliver these today?" I asked Zayd.

"For you, my darling, all things are possible." He reached out, seized my hand and kissed it.

I resisted the urge to wipe the wet spot on my jeans and managed a smile. "You never did that before."

"Never before, my darling, did you buy a thirty thousand dollar Kashmar."

I waggled the forefinger on my wet hand. "Subject to the owner's approval."

He raised his open palms toward the ceiling and shrugged. "But of course. Though how can he refuse gems such as these?"

"We'll see, Zayd, we'll see. Now I have a favor to ask."

His jolly demeanor disappeared as fast as chicken wings at a Super Bowl party. He uttered a wary, "Yes?"

"To enhance the beauty of these ah…gems, when your men deliver the rugs, could they move some furniture for me?"

"Certainly, my darling." He tried to conceal his relief with a quick smile. "That is no favor. That is part of Zayd's white gloves service."

"Thank you." I scribbled Francesco's address on the back of one of my cards and gave it to him. "Can you be there in two hours?"

"But of course." He made a grab for my hand, but I yanked it back in the nick of time. "For you—"

"—my darling, anything," I finished with a laugh and, reaching out, I took *his* hand and gave it a good sturdy Boston shake. No kiss. No wet spot.

After leaving Arabian Sights, I swung by the Azalea Building. The Mustang had disappeared, so this time I parked and went in. Nikhil had the living room pretty well taped up and ready for painting, but he kept mum about whatever he and Rossi had discussed.

"With luck one coat should cover well," I told him, as he helped carry the supplies into his apartment.

"Fine," he agreed but a look at his glum face told me wall paint wasn't what he had on his mind. His discussion with Rossi probably was.

Though I felt sorry for his distress, the police needed to know what was going on at Harkness Investments. The leap from embezzlement to murder wasn't a farfetched stretch of the imagination by any means. Not that I was ready to heap a murder rap on Norm, but somebody in the house that night had killed Donny, and Rossi needed to know everything about everybody who had been there.

Leaving Nikhil to his painting, I drove to Rum Row and

punched in the security code to Francesco's house. Shortly afterward, Zayd's truck arrived and within an hour both rugs were laid, their size and elegant fading exactly what I'd hoped for. That done, I directed the men into the garage and had them move the inlaid mahogany table into the dining room, flanking it on opposite walls with a matched pair of Hepplewhite sideboards.

I was concentrating so hard on making sure not a wall or a piece of furniture was marred that I jumped a little when a soft voice said, "Deva."

I whirled around. "Jewels! How nice to see you. You too, sweetie," I said, stroking little Frannie's cheek with a single finger. Snug on Jewels's hip, his baby powder and milk aroma was so seductive I could have dabbed it behind my ears. "You're getting big, you know that?" I asked him. He rewarded me by showing off two pearly white teeth.

Jewels, slim as ever, kissed him over and over. Hard to believe she was nearly five months pregnant.

Time to change the subject. "Well, what do you think so far?" I asked, waving my arms around the rooms.

"No comment," she said and laughed.

"No, seriously, tell me. Your opinion's important."

"I don't have one," she said, wrinkling her nose. "Not about this old stuff."

"Oh. Right." She wasn't just being compliant, she really didn't care.

She shifted the baby to her other hip. "But Frannie can't wait to have everything finished. He promised the pastor at St. Anne's that as soon as the police find Donny's killer, he'd have a church fundraiser here."

"Really? I didn't know Francesco was religious. He's never mentioned it, not that—"

"He doesn't like to talk about it. He's shy that way. But he goes to Mass every morning. Don't tell him I told you.

He wants everybody to think he's so tough, but he's really a softy. Like you," she murmured into the baby's ear.

"My lips are sealed."

"He prays for Donny. I pray for him too, but mostly for Frannie." She lowered her voice though we were alone. "Someone tried to kill my husband, Deva, and I won't have a moment's rest until they find him."

"Or her."

Jewels shook her head. "No woman would do that," she said. "We create life. We don't kill it."

Francesco a churchgoer and Jewels a philosopher? I would never have guessed. My knowledge of people had to be seriously flawed.

"We tried to reach you this morning," Jewels said. "But we kept getting your voice mail."

"Sorry about that. My shop's been closed all day. I should give you my cell number." Though if I did, Francesco would probably call day and night...maybe Jewels wouldn't take me up on my offer.

But she nodded. "He'd like that. We're leaving for Providence tomorrow." Her face clouded over. "For Donny's funeral. Before we go, Frannie wants to ask you something."

"What's that?"

She couldn't wave her arms, so she tossed her head from left to right. "You know how he loves all this old stuff. Well—"

"Who loves all this old stuff?" boomed from the doorway. Francesco.

"You do," Jewels and I said in unison. Then we both laughed.

"You girls wanna have a chuckle on me, that's okay." In a cloud of macho musk, he strode around examining the rugs. "They look terrific. I won't ask how much they set me back. Surprise me with the bill."

"Ready for another surprise?" I asked. A discreetly lettered DeBruyne panel truck had driven onto the driveway. Stan, DeBruyne's art installer, and Larry, his helper, slid a heavily padded rectangle out of the truck's back doors and carried it carefully into the dining room. They unwrapped it, and as the padding fell away, my heartbeat quickened, and a long "Ooooh!" escaped from Jewels.

She loved it. Not a good sign.

Francesco blew out a breath. "This is Hudson River? Where's the trees? Where's the grass? Where's the water?"

"Try to keep an open mind," I said. "Think of the excitement this piece generates."

"Excitement I save for the bedroom." He waved a hand at the painting. "You're killing me with this."

My turn to blow out a breath. While the installers shifted from one foot to another, waiting for the verdict, Francesco stepped up to the oil and peered at the signature. "What's the guy's name?"

"Diego Pina," Stan replied. "He's not well known. Yet. But I predict he will be."

Francesco spun around. "You got a crystal ball?"

Alarmed, Stan backed away from Francesco's hairy hands.

"We have it on approval," I said, forcing my voice to remain calm. "We can send it back."

"I like it, Frannie," Jewels said.

"Is that right?" Francesco spat out the words. "What did I tell you? When it comes to the house, no comments."

"What am I, dumb or something?" No longer the passive little flower of a month ago, Jewels turned on her heel and stalked off with the baby in her arms.

"She's pissed," Francesco said to everybody and nobody in particular. He upped his chin at me. "You think this Diego guy's got the goods?"

"No guarantees. But the painting's a stunner."

He heaved a sigh, sending a waft of garlic across the room. "Okay, hang it up," he said to Stan. "Let's see what we got. The mother of my kids likes it. For this," he said, eying me and stabbing a forefinger at the oil, "you owe me one."

"What do you want, Francesco?"

"I want you should stay in the house while I'm burying Donny."

"What?"

He threw his arms wide, shrugging at the same time. "You said it yourself. I love all this stuff…except *that*." The abstract. "I can't leave the place alone for a whole week."

"A *week?*"

"Yeah. Somebody has to be here to make sure everything's safe. And what about the contractors? Who's gonna let them in? I don't want delays. As it is, building the kitchen's taking longer than the pyramids."

"Custom work takes time."

As if he were swatting flies, he waved a hand at my words. "I know. I know."

"I'd like to accommodate you, but I have a business to run. I can't just hole up in your house for a week." What nerve. Who did this guy think he was?

"No, no, no. Not days. Nights. You already got the entry code. You turn on the security system and you're okay. Mornings you let in the workers and then you leave." He arched an eyebrow. "That detective boyfriend of yours? Have him stay too. Though on second thought, maybe that's not such a hot idea. He needs to concentrate on the job. So far he hasn't nailed anybody for killing Donny. That's taking longer than the kitchen. He doesn't even know who sent us that goddamn dump truck."

Francesco wasn't alone in his frustration. I had no idea

how Rossi was progressing with the case. But about the toy truck incident, at least he knew Bonita was involved. I wondered if he'd stopped by to question her. At best he used to say very little about his work but now—nothing.

A flurry of movement caught my eye. I glanced over at Stan and Larry. They were lifting the abstract into place on the long wall opposite the archway into the dining room. As they straightened the canvas and stepped away, my heart sang. The space was perfect, the size of the painting was perfect, the colors were perfect. I turned to Francesco.

"What do you think?"

His eyes were shining. "I never woulda believed it, but it's sensational. It stays."

"Deal! So do I. Nights only. For one week." If Rossi knew, he'd have a fit, but he wouldn't know, would he? Or maybe he wouldn't care if he did.

Francesco gave me a celebratory pat on the back. I didn't see it coming, and it sent me reeling. "You can let these guys out and lock up," he said, oblivious. "I gotta go take care of Jewels." He shook his head with something like disgust. "Geesh, women. But I feel a hell of a lot better knowing you'll be looking after the place."

He strode toward the front door, then as a random thought struck him, he swiveled back for an instant. "While you're staying here, if anybody shows up you don't know, don't let them in. It'll only mean trouble."

"Hey, wait a min—"

Too late. He had ducked out, slamming the door behind him.

TWENTY-SEVEN

HOOT OWLS HAD invaded Rum Row. Sunday night I lay awake for hours listening to them screech from the tree-tops. They were predators, weren't they? Flesh eaters? I shivered on the four-poster in the unfinished master suite, imagining flesh-eating creepy-crawlies clicking along the floor.

The feather-filled duvet was first too hot, then too cold. Cold or not, I broke out in a sweat every time I glanced at my snub-nosed Cobra on the nightstand. I usually kept the gun locked in the bottom drawer of my desk, but now it was just a fingertip away and gleaming in the moonlight. The thought that I might have to use it kept me awake too.

Worse, God help me, was my longing for Rossi. These few days without him had been hell. And I had a lifetime to go. Had setting him adrift been the biggest mistake of my life? I kept bumping into his accusation—I was scared. Scared of a new commitment. Scared of being hurt again. Scared of living. Every time the thought popped up, "No, not true," bonged in my head like an annoying bell.

I tossed off the duvet yet again. Was Rossi right? Was I so wimpy I was nothing but a bundle of fears? Scared to be alone in the dark. Scared I'd be alone in the dark forever. I'd better get a grip. I had no one to rely on but myself, and if the doors of Deva Dunne Interiors weren't open more often than they had been recently, I'd soon have something else to fear. Bankruptcy.

No. I sat up and dangled my legs over the edge of the

mattress. I'd be damned if I'd let that happen. After this week I'd get back on a normal track. In the meantime I did have to shop for Francesco and Nikhil and keep the shop closed while I did so. I'd also have to squeeze in a visit to the woman who wanted help with her "blah" house. I heaved a sigh and lay back down. After that, as soon as I had time for interviews, I'd hire a new assistant...but for Rossi there was no substitute and never would be.

At dawn I gave up on the night, flung back the duvet and dressed for trench warfare—jeans, a T-shirt and sneakers. Foot sloughing through antiques and collectibles shops and a raft of thrift stores didn't call for style. After a moment's hesitation, I dug in my luggage for a larger handbag and dropped in the pistol. Along with the usuals I added a bottle of water and some hand sanitizer to the bag. My hands were sure to be sweaty and soiled after a day in the antiques trenches. With everything stowed in it, the bag weighed a ton. No doubt the Cobra added its share to the overload. Should I take it with me or not? Yes. I didn't want to leave it here in the house for someone to find, even if it did weigh heavy—in more ways than one.

At eight, the Smallbone crew arrived. Hungry, I ignored Rossi's commonsense warning not to eat anything from this kitchen and yanked open the fridge, just in case something luscious and irresistible lurked inside. *Nada.* Tom Kruse strolled in carrying a giant black coffee and an Egg McMuffin. All smiles, he looked as though he'd had a good night's sleep too.

"Work on the children's rooms this week, okay?" I said. "The master suite is occupied."

"That was my plan, though one room's as good as another," he replied, between munches and sips.

I tossed the purse over my shoulder, trying hard not to list to starboard. One hand on the outer door, I said, "The owner wants you to keep the house locked during the day. Before you leave I'll come back and put on the security for the night."

If that sounded strange, no one said so, and I left, eager for a mocha latte and a fresh blueberry scone.

Intending to accessorize the house with old silver hollowware, I was hot on the trail of sterling silver boxes. After hitting five antiques dealers in a row, I came away with three superb examples and two pair of tall, multi-armed candelabra for the matching sideboards. Nor could I resist a large Canton bowl that had been salvaged from the famous wreck of the *Vung Tau*. Its cargo, including thousands of porcelain objects, had lain under the South China Sea for three hundred years. The porcelain, amazingly, had survived in perfect condition. Francesco would love telling that story to his dinner guests—if his gruff manner didn't drive all of Port Royal away. For its provenance alone I'd have been attracted to the bowl, but what really drew me was the subtle blue and white of the design, which would center the dining room table beautifully.

Flushed with success, I reached into my purse for a celebratory swig of water. My fingers locked on the Cobra. *Egads, that's right, I'm packing.* My treasure hunt had caused me to forget about it for a while. But I'd better remember and not run any red lights today.

In one of the thrifts, I had more luck. I found a nubby beige couch for Nikhil in excellent condition, a steal at three hundred dollars. I snapped it up. For five dollars each I added a few coral and lime green throw pillows. In a dark corner of the back room I spotted some white wicker pieces and two rattan end tables. And had an "aha!" moment at the sight of a glass-topped coffee table the dealer was anxious to unload. Best of all, he agreed to hold on to everything until Nikhil was ready for them.

My night gloom had all but disappeared. Even with the doors to Deva Dunne Interiors closed for hours, I'd accomplished a good deal today. Maybe things would work out all right after all. Then I thought of Rossi and my glow evaporated like pixie dust. Squaring my shoulders—though that gun didn't make it easy—I told myself no whining allowed. What had happened with Rossi was my own damned fault.

On the way back to Rum Row, I stopped in at the shop to collect my mail. The answering machine on the store phone pulsed red. I pressed the message button, and Lee's voice came through as clear as if she were in the room.

"Deva, hello, hello, hello! I'm here with Paulo and loving every minute. Sorry I missed y'all. Will call again. Love you and that darling man of yours. Hugs and thanks to you both for all our happiness. *Au revoir.*"

I settled the receiver in its cradle and fought back tears. That darling man was no longer mine, and I might as well get used to the fact.

Huffing out a sigh, I collected the mail and locked up. With protective booties over her shoes, Irma from the Off Shoots Boutique next door stood in her display window fitting a gorgeous purple cocktail dress onto a mannequin. She smiled and waved, beckoning me inside.

"This one has your name on it," she said with a grin, stepping down onto the shop floor and slipping off the cotton booties. "Just two came in and one's in your size. Guaranteed, the lieutenant will love this on you."

"You think?" was all I could bring myself to say.

"Absolutely." A curvy size-two blonde with a short Cameron Diaz haircut, Irma was a good ad for the resort wear she sold.

Emma, her twin, a tall brunette who packed a lot of voluptuous woman into her size fourteens, poked her head out of the back room. "Hi, Deva. Irma's right about that dress. Ten percent off for a friend and neighbor."

"You tempting me or something?"

"Yup."

I eyed the dress warily. Purple? And where would I wear something like that? Well, I *had* promised to attend Chip's party Saturday night.

"Okay, let's try it," I said, giving in to the moment.

The three of us crowded into a dressing room. I stripped to my bra and panties and slipped on the dress. The sleeveless silk jersey slid over my body like a caress. "Oh my," I said staring at my mirror image. "Cleavage City." The low, rounded neckline gave new meaning to the word *plunging*. Actually my Bs kind of looked like Ds. Snug at the waist with just a few tiny gathers to give some walking ease to the skirt, the dress fit where it touched, the way a dress should but seldom did.

With an I-told-you-so smirk, Irma handed me a pair of spiky purple slides in exactly the right size. The girl had an eye.

As I twisted and turned in front of the mirror, she said, "What did I tell you?" She looked pleased with herself and with the way I looked, apparently.

"I've never worn purple."

"Well, high time. Redheads look gorgeous in it."

"What about the neckline?"

"That's the whole point," Irma said. "Knock 'em dead."

"You have any idea how fabulous that dress is on you?" Emma asked. "Wait till the lieutenant gets a glimpse. The reaction's going to be intense."

"Sold," I said. Agreeing was easier than arguing.

"You won't be sorry," Irma said.

Irma could have been wrong about that, but I took the outfit anyway, and left Off Shoots feeling a tad cheerier than when I walked in. At least I could still *look* sexy even if nothing would come of it.

On my way over to Rum Row I stopped in at the Publix deli counter and bought a bag of grilled chicken tenders and some mixed salad for dinner. In his desire to have someone babysit his possessions, Francesco had forgotten about his dysfunctional kitchen. No matter. The aroma of the chicken had my stomach growling. I paid for the food and slung the heavy purse over a shoulder. For the first time I couldn't wait to get back to Rum Row—to eat, and to get that gun out of my bag.

In the master suite a small portable TV had been set up on a stand at the foot of the mahogany four-poster. Most likely the TV had been Donny's. The fact that I was sleeping on a bed he had occupied hadn't made for sweet dreams so far. Neither had Francesco's warning not to let in any strangers. *What strangers?* But at least I had my cell phone, my Cobra and my chicken. What else did a girl need? Well, maybe a bottle of wine. I took care of that too.

AFTER AN ENDLESS stretch of busy days and restless nights—those owls!—on Friday morning I waited for Tom and his crew to arrive and then left for the day. Two more nights and I'd be out of there. I couldn't wait.

Before going to the shop, I swung by Nikhil's apartment. Love is a wonderful motivator. Distressed by conditions at Harkness or not, he'd already painted the living room and bedroom, cleaned the wall-to-wall carpeting and washed the windows. When I walked in, he was busy sponging apricot-peach paint on the bathroom walls.

"You've made amazing progress," I told him. "Melanie's going to love the place. Now we can have the furniture delivered and give you something comfortable to sit on. How's that sound?"

"Okay," he said, forcing a smile, his shoulders slumped.

He looked so dejected I decided to test the waters. "I've been meaning to ask you something, Nikhil. That conversation you had with the lieutenant last week? How did it go?"

He hesitated a moment before deciding he could trust me. "He thinks I'll be subpoenaed to testify against Mr. Harkness."

"Did you keep a paper trail?"

"Yes. I xeroxed everything. The lieutenant took a copy." Weighed down by what he'd just admitted, he sank onto the rim of the bathtub. "The police are ordering an audit of the Harkness books. On my testimony. If the discrepancies I picked up are accurate, Norm could face a stiff prison sentence. If not, I'm chopped meat." He went to run a paint-smeared hand through his hair but caught himself in time. "What being a whistleblower will do to my future is up for grabs. As of now, I'm out of a job. Suppose no one will hire me after this? Then what? Worse, what's Melanie going to think?"

He stared down at the sodden sponge in his hands, no doubt wishing he held a crystal ball. The sponge had dripped peach latex onto his jeans. I carefully plucked it from his hands with two fingertips, dropped it on the newspaper lining the sink, and turned back to him.

"No question, Nikhil, compost happens." It took him a second, but he did break out a wan smile. "Still I predict your future will open up like a flower. You're establishing a reputation as an honest, no-nonsense man fearless enough—gutsy enough—to protect his clients' assets. You're exactly what an investor wants—not a Madoff, not a Kozlowski, but a man of integrity.

"Furthermore, if Melanie is the girl for you, you'll be her knight in shining armor. Her hero. Fearless. A fighter of evil. Every woman wants those qualities in her man." I pointed a finger at his nose. "Just like in paint colors, you can trust me in that too."

His Crayola-blue eyes looked up at me. "That why you like the lieutenant?"

"Yes!" I shouted without a moment's hesitation. Then more quietly, "Yes. Also he has a great tush."

Nikhil laughed and got up from the tub. "I'd better finish here and start in the kitchen. I want to get this project over with. I have to go job hunting starting tomorrow." As he stood, his jeans slid down on his hips, and he gave them a hitch.

His lanky frame looked thinner than it had a week ago. "When did you eat last?" I asked him.

"Yesterday, I think."

"You want to lose all your strength before Melanie gets here?"

He blushed fever red. "That won't happen." He reached for the sponge.

"Darn right. Put that thing down."

He glanced over at me, startled.

"The project can wait for an hour. I'm inviting you for lunch. My treat. How about steak and eggs? Maybe some fries?"

He grinned ear-to-ear. "Sounds good."

"Then let's go. While you eat, I'll talk about what you need to do in the kitchen."

He glanced down at his paint-spotted jeans. "I'm not dressed for a...a—"

"Date?" I finished, laughing. "Not to worry. A guy I know wears Hawaiian shirts everywhere. Compared to that, peach-colored jeans are right out of *GQ*."

TWENTY-EIGHT

THE NEXT MORNING I fumbled through my purse for the shop key while inside the store the phone buzzed like an incessant swarm of bees. I wrestled the door open, and without bothering to close it, dashed over and snatched up the phone on the tenth or twelfth ring. Somebody was in a tear to reach me. *New business?* A little breathless, I said, "Deva Dunne Interiors."

"Good. Glad I caught you. This is the Second Time Around Thrift Store. Those items you bought a few days ago? We have to deliver them this morning. An unexpected shipment's coming in, and we're already jammed up."

Uh-oh. "That's not much notice for my client. He could use another day before—"

"The game's changed. Sorry. We'll be at the Azalea Building on Tenth in an hour."

I hung up and called Nikhil. He answered on the first ring and shot a hurried "hello" into the line.

"Your furniture's on its way," I told him.

"Oh no, not now. I can't wait around for a delivery. I have a job interview at Morgan Stanley." He sounded both harried and delighted. "I need this job, Mrs. Dunne."

As if I wasn't aware of that. I tried not to sigh. "Want me to come over and let the movers in?"

"Gosh, that'd be great. I'll leave the door unlocked. Nothing much to steal in here anyway. I better run. Have to put on a tie."

I hung up and this time did sigh. Another Closed sign

in the window of Deva Dunne Interiors. Not only was my personal life all screwed up, the business was sliding down the same slippery slope. Okay, Nikhil was in a bind. He needed me. Besides, what did one more morning matter?

The truck from Second Time Around arrived at his apartment shortly after I did. Putting everything else out of mind, I morphed into designer mode, zoning out my financial woes, my concern that Donny's murderer was still on the loose—even my longing for Rossi—as I directed the movers in placing the furniture.

The three hundred dollar couch with the extra coral and lime green pillows looked awesome against the pastel walls. The two rattan side tables fit on either side with inches to spare. Taking up no visual space, a good thing in the small room, the glass-topped coffee table added a little gleam. Even better, it would hold a pizza box, a beer can and a remote plus the enameled coral and green bowl I'd bought as a housewarming gift.

A white wicker dresser went into the bedroom along with the nightstands. And in the center of the kitchen, I placed the round white pedestal table and two chairs with zingy coral seat covers.

From the Audi trunk I retrieved four brass lamps. At ten dollars each, the bases had been a steal. With fresh parchment shades they were more than good to go. The heftier two I placed on the living room end tables and lit them. Even in the daylight they cast a cheery glow over the room. So far Nikhil had no artwork to soften the walls, but a safe guess was that Melanie sitting on the sofa leaning into the pillows would provide all the softening he wanted.

In the bedroom, as a foil to the deep green accent wall, I added a king-sized duvet in white splashed with vivid green ferns. Tossed over Nikhil's neatly made queen-sized bed, the duvet swept to the floor, a bit of boudoir drama I had a feeling he would love.

I set the other two lamps—lighter in feel—on the night-stands and turned them on as well. When Nikhil came back from his interview, for the first time he'd be walking into the semblance of a home. Leaving the lights on in the bedroom, I wandered out to the kitchen.

The movers had left black fingerprints on the shiny white table, a retro Saarinen look-alike. With showtime coming up, that wouldn't do. There had to be a cleaning cloth or a paper towel around here somewhere. I rummaged through the largely empty cabinets but no luck.

Under the sink then. I opened the cabinet door, crouched in front of it and peered inside. Like most under sink spaces, not a pretty sight, full of plumbing elbows and cleaning supplies, and in this case, a trash can stuffed with empty deli bags and dead soldiers. I pushed the can to one side, revealing a collection of pan scrubbers, dish-washer soap, and tile cleaner. Nikhil had been busy. And then I saw it, way in the back, nearly out of reach. A small, square bottle. Shipping tape secured a white paper label to its side. In big, black letters, the word on the label read *Cyanide,* and under it a crudely drawn skull and crossbones.

Omigod. My knees gave way, and I fell onto my fanny in front of the sink. Another bottle of cyanide? Unbeliev-able. First in the Grandese house and now here. Why? And in the kitchen of all places? Grandma's recipes, yes. Poison, no.

The more I stared at the bottle the less I could breathe. No matter how hard I inhaled, the air wouldn't pump into my lungs. I hung my head between my knees and took shallow breaths. *Ah better.*

Why was I so upset anyway? If Nikhil had used the poison for an evil purpose, wouldn't he have hidden it better? At least put it in a bag or something, not in a cupboard where anyone could look in and see it?

Furthermore, he hadn't been in the house the night Donny was killed. As far as I knew he hadn't met Francesco or Jewels, or AudreyAnn and Chip. Not Bonita, either. Of everyone who had been there that night, he was acquainted only with Rossi and me...and Norm and Cookie. Still, on the floor on my fanny, I hugged my knees and told myself to slow down, not jump to conclusions. Most important of all, Nikhil had probably never laid eyes on Donny. Having the same poison that killed him was simply a random coincidence.

I blew out a breath. Who was I kidding? That was as likely as seeing two pigs run down Fifth Avenue.

I closed the cabinet door, grabbed the leg of a chair and pulled myself to my feet. There had to be a reason for that hidden bottle. But what reason? Guilt? Not wanting to hyperventilate again, I tried to squelch the idea, but couldn't. I kept going back to the same question. What was a nice guy like Nikhil doing with cyanide? I couldn't get past it.

I dropped onto one of the kitchen chairs and sat staring at the fingerprints on the tabletop. Fifteen minutes passed as slowly as water dripping from a faucet. Another fifteen and I was sick and tired of staring at those dirty fingerprints. I rummaged in a utility drawer I hadn't gotten to earlier and—success!—two vintage tea towels, probably family hand-me-downs. I wet one and washed off the tabletop then sat back down to play more of the waiting game.

All morning I'd been dying for a latte and maybe a chocolate-covered donut, but the sight of the poison had stripped away all hunger and thirst. Now I just wanted to ask Nikhil why he kept such a deadly secret in his cozy little love nest.

Worry about my closed-up shop had brought me to the

brink of leaving when a key turned in the lock. I hurried out to the living room. Nickel strolled in, tie in hand, shirt collar unbuttoned. Two steps into the apartment, he stopped and glanced around. "Wow, the place looks great. I can't believe it!"

He needed a chance to check things out before I hit him with my discovery, so I said, "Why don't you take a peek at the bedroom?"

He walked in, eyeballed the fern-strewn bed and whistled. "Wait till Melanie sees this."

I had to smile. His eyes shone with pleasure, and after all, that was what being a designer was about—making people happy. Or happier. "You worked hard for this effect."

He shook his head. "No, the choices were yours, Mrs. Dunne. I just carried out orders."

"It's still pretty Spartan." I waved at one of the walls. "Some artwork would enliven the look, but the budget didn't—"

"Melanie can take care of that. She's an art history major." He tossed his tie on the bed, snatched it off with a laugh and hung it on the rack in the closet. "Thanks, Mrs. Dunne. Melanie's going to love the place. Things are shaping up all around. I got the job." He flushed and ran a hand through his hair in that signature gesture of his.

I was about to be a spoiler. Hating the necessity, I put it off with, "Congratulations, Nikhil. That's wonderful news."

"Yes," he said. "You were right. What tipped the scales in my favor was speaking up about what I saw wrong at Harkness. My new boss said the industry needs integrity. How about that? Integrity."

Whether I liked it or not, bubble-bursting time had arrived. I cleared my throat. "No question you're an honest man, Nikhil, so if I ask you something, I know you'll tell me the truth."

"Sure." My tone of voice must have been a giveaway. His eyes narrowed, wary all of a sudden.

"I found something. Under the sink. A bottle."

"The cyanide," he whispered.

"Yes. You want to tell me about it?"

He shook his head. "Not really but I will."

"Let's sit down, first. It's been a long morning."

He followed me out to the kitchen. "Nice," he said at the sight of his new/old furniture. But he didn't smile as he sank onto one of the chairs. I sat across the table facing him and waited.

"About three months ago when I took a few days off to visit my parents in Georgia, Norm asked if my dad had kept any of the chemicals from the business. Said squirrels had gotten into his attic and were racing around overhead, driving him nuts. He wanted to get rid of them.

"I was flattered that Norm thought I could help him. Guess I wanted to, well, suck up to the boss. Do him a favor. It was stupid of me, I realize that now. Anyway, I knew my dad kept some of the toxic stuff locked up in a shed out back. So I poured a few ounces of the cyanide into that bottle under the sink, and—"

"You gave the cyanide to Norm."

"I did. He took what he wanted and returned what was left. What you saw. I haven't known how to dispose of it safely, but I've got to get rid of it before Melanie gets here. She'll freak out if she sees it."

"Can't blame her. Norm should have known better. Ever hear of Truly Nolan?"

"The exterminators?"

"Yes. The ones who drive around town in VW bugs with mouse ears on the roof."

"I've seen them. It's a cool type of PR."

"Right. That's who you call when you have squirrels in the attic."

Nikhil's flush and his happy demeanor fled. Only his rumpled hair remained the same. "I know. It was a dumb move. When I realized Norm was working the books that was bad enough, but then I heard about that Grandese guy being poisoned. I knew Norm had been in the house at the time, and well, I got scared."

Pretending I had inside information, I acted on a hunch and asked, "Is that why you didn't tell Lieutenant Rossi about the cyanide?"

Slump shouldered and morose on his cute little chair with the bright coral cushions, he nodded. "Word of this gets out, it'll kill my folks. And what it'll do to me and Melanie? I can't even go there." He raked his long fingers through his hair again, this time standing it on end. I wondered, briefly, how he'd look with a buzz cut.

"You can't sit on this forever, Nikhil. The truth is bound to come out. Far better for it to come from you. Sooner rather than later."

Hands clenched between his knees, he looked up. Were those tears glistening in his eyes? I wasn't sure, but if so this was a new low for me. I'd made a grown man cry.

"Like I told you," he said. "I got scared. I gave Norm the poison. If he used it to commit murder, I'm implicated, aren't I?"

TWENTY-NINE

WITH NO ANSWER to give Nikhil, I left his apartment troubled that I caused him distress on what should have been a happy day. A week or so earlier I would have called Rossi and asked him to resolve the situation. But not now. Too bad. Still, Nikhil had already proven he was capable of doing the right thing, and I was confident that after a little reflection he would again. Armed with that thought I went back to my neglected shop and spent the afternoon paying bills and chatting with a few tourists who stopped in looking for baubles to bring back home.

At five I closed up and drove to Surfside. I wanted a full hour to shower and do my hair and makeup with extra care.

Who was I kidding? What I really wanted was to be a knockout in purple jersey. For in my schizophrenic little heart, I was hoping Rossi would show up even if I couldn't hold him. *Then what?*

Half-dressed, I sank onto the edge of my bed and the truth ripped into me. I had dismissed Rossi from my life. Whether for my reason or for his, I was no longer certain. But either way, playing games in purple dresses was ridiculous. The break had been clean and swift even if, as Rossi claimed, my motives were wrong. Whatever the reason, losing him hurt. It hurt like hell. Goodbyes bit into you with fangs of steel. When Jack died, they'd gouged deep. That had been enough for a lifetime. Now this…shredded again. But whose fault was that?

My shoulders slumped. Self-pity? Disgusted, I forced

myself to sit up straight. I'd made a decision believing it was the right thing to do. So why this nagging doubt? For the simple reason that if I were wrong and Rossi really meant adoption was fine with him, then I'd made the worse mistake of my life.

Rays from the late afternoon sun shone through the bedroom sliders and fingered the purple fabric.

I stared at the dress and sighed. Now that I'd bought it, I might as well wear it. Besides, Rossi probably wouldn't show anyway.

Wrong. He showed all right. And if I hoped to be the party knockout, I was wrong there too. *He* was the knockout. I couldn't believe my eyes. Freshly shaven and barbered, he was a sartorial sensation in a navy blazer, tan slacks, starched white shirt and maroon-and-navy striped tie. No Hawaiians, not even the one he usually wore on weekends with the Flying Fortress zooming over Oahu. I hadn't seen him as dressed up since Lee and Paulo's wedding day. He was so drop-dead gorgeous, he took my breath away.

So did the drop-dead blonde on his arm. How dare she wear purple tonight? The bitch.

With this Mother Teresa thought pumping blood through my system, I stomped over to the bar without stopping to speak to him. Or her.

"Scotch," I said to the bartender. "A double." I hated the stuff but loved what it did to me.

The party wasn't crowded or noisy yet, but it soon would be. To put everybody at ease, Chip had hired bartenders and a catering service, vowing he would stay out of the kitchen and go nowhere near the food or drink. Wise of him, but sad too. He was a masterful chef and needed to get back to his cooking without worrying that people were afraid to eat his food. Rossi needed to get back to work too. With the murder still unsolved, what was he doing out on a date anyway?

Glass in hand, I strolled over to congratulate the newlyweds. This was the first time I'd seen Chip at a party without his chef's apron. Tonight he wore a white ruffled dress shirt and black pants. AudreyAnn dazzled in a strapless white wedding dress with a foot long train, smiling by her new husband's side, a happy woman for once. It was good to see. I hugged them both without sloshing my drink and took a sip.

An expensive drift of musk and sandalwood floated around me. "So you still like scotch?" a deep voice asked. "I remember giving you some Dewars the day we met."

"Hello, Simon," I said turning around to face him. He drew in a quick breath. *The neckline.*

"You're stunning," he said. "Positively stunning. But then you always have been. Lieutenant Rossi is a lucky man."

"He might agree with you," I said, taking a gulp of my Dewars and trying not to shudder at the acrid taste. "We broke up."

Though skilled at courtroom maneuvering, Simon couldn't quite conceal the spark that leaped into his eyes.

I took another slug and didn't shudder a bit. "May I ask you something, Simon?"

"Anything," he said, struggling to keep his eyes higher than my neckline.

"Do you want to have children?"

In the act of swallowing, he choked a little and sputtered. "Not particularly."

"Did you want any with Cynthia?"

"Never had a chance to find out. She told me she was a solo act, take it or leave it."

"Really? You married her anyway?"

He studied the dregs in his glass. "Back then I was so enamored of her nothing else mattered."

"Do you regret not having a family?"

"Not at all. I enjoy my freedom." He glanced up, right into my eyes with no detour along the way. "Why the cross examination?"

I shrugged and glanced across the room, which was pretty crowded by now. Most of the people I didn't know. The athletic looking types were probably Pilates instructors who worked with AudreyAnn, and I guessed some of the men were restaurateur friends of Chip's. I searched through the throng for another glimpse of Rossi, finally spotting him in a corner, deep in conversation with the blonde. He looked like he was having the time of his life. He must have seen me come in—nothing ever escaped Rossi—but he'd made no attempt to speak to me. I guess we couldn't even be friends.

One of the caterers circling the room with a tray of canapés approached Rossi and his date. Rossi took one look at the endive leaves topped with chutney and squash blossoms and shook his head. I had to smile. His favorite *hors d'oeuvre* was pepperoni pizza cut into bite-sized triangles. The blonde took one. Why would Rossi go out with somebody who liked squash blossoms? Obviously they had nothing in common.

"Well?" Simon asked. "You haven't answered me. Why all the questions?"

I'd forgotten Simon was still standing there. "Oh, I don't know. Curiosity I guess. Forgive me."

"Always." His resonant courtroom voice pulsed with warmth. His glance slid over me then jerked back up, a guilty little boy eyeing the cookie jar but not quite daring to reach out and grab one.

Whoever had designed this dress was diabolically

clever. But was this my new career? Being a teaser? Causing reactions in men I had no interest in? The answer was so painful I chugged down the rest of the Dewars and plunked the empty glass on the bar top. I held out a hand. "Nice to talk to you, Simon, but I have to go."

His face fell. "You just got here."

"I know. Had to pay my respects to the newlyweds, but I do have another appointment." I faked a glance at my watch. "I'm late."

"A date?" From his tone, I could tell he was hoping I'd say no.

"Yes," I lied. Let him think so and forget about me.

He nodded. "I understand." Ever gallant, ever the soul of courtesy and civility, well dressed at all times—not just once or twice a year—why on earth couldn't I warm up to him? To top everything else off, he was brilliantly educated, rich and handsome. What the hell was the matter with me? I silently stormed as I wove my way toward the door between groups of noisy, laughing people. I'd make my excuses tomorrow to Chip and the bride. Tell them I was sick or something and simply had to leave early.

Truth be told, I was sick. Heartsick. To deny it would be lying to myself as I had just lied to Simon.

I had no sooner turned the key in my condo lock when Rossi murmured, "Deva."

My heart leaped into my throat. "Go away," I said without turning around. In that moment, I couldn't bear to look at him.

"No." He stepped closer. Lingering hints of his aftershave hung in the air. I definitely caught a trace of musk but no pricey sandalwood. His warm breath feathering my nape, he put a hand on my arm. A flash of longing tore through me.

Infuriated at my own weakness, I yanked my arm free and whirled around.

"That's quite a dress," he said with a smile that I felt like slapping off his face.

"Simon liked it."

"Every man on your radar screen liked it. Wasn't that your intent?"

Some things never changed. Rossi always understood my motives.

I upped my chin. "What are you doing out here anyway? Your date must be looking for you."

A wall-to-wall grin split his face wide open. I wanted to kill him.

"What date?"

"The blonde you were having a *tête-à-tête* with. That date."

"Ah." He raised a hand, examining his fingertips as if he were admiring a fancy manicure. "You must mean *Mrs.* Michael Bennett. She's with her husband at the moment." He glanced up from his hand, piercing me with those dark, diabolical eyes. "Jealous?"

He was toying with me. I'd be damned if I'd put up with that. "Go away, Rossi. Nothing's changed."

I opened the condo door and stepped inside. Before I could push it closed, he strode in behind me and slammed it shut.

Heat flaming in my cheeks, I turned to face him. "You weren't invited in. I don't want you here."

"You're a liar. That's exactly what you want."

"How dare you?" Hands on hips, legs apart, I squared off ready to…what? Fight?

"And don't wear that dress again." He pointed a finger at my chest. "Look at you. You're hanging out of it."

"Oooh!" I rushed for him, ready to scratch out his eyes.

He caught me, and pinning my arms to my sides, he kissed me, his mouth a hard, unrelenting line.

Imprisoned in his embrace, I refused to give in. But then...but then...with a will of their own, my lips betrayed me. Yielding to his demand, they parted. Seizing that nanosecond of weakness, his mouth eased its pressure. His lips softened, and his kiss created the magic I had longed for all the nights I'd lain awake listening to the hoot of the owls.

A groan floated up between us. Whether from Rossi or from me, there was no telling.

His lips brushed my cheek. "We belong together, Deva," he said. "Don't keep fighting it."

Weak kneed, I leaned against the foyer wall, my resolve to cut him loose, to be noble, to be self-sacrificing, exposed for the sham it had been all along. He was right, and every part of me, body and soul, knew it.

Would he forgive me?

With his eyes inches from mine, he smiled and asked, "May I come in?"

I had my answer, and my heart leaping up with joy, I took his hand and led him into the dimly lit living room. The sofa lamps on the floor beside the couch sent narrow arcs of light beaming up toward the ceiling.

Two steps into the room, Rossi came to an abrupt stop and glanced around. "What happened in here? Where's your furniture?"

"I sold it."

"Why? You loved those things." He was clearly astonished at the sight of the half-empty room, and no wonder. How many times had I told him how much I loved Jack's furniture, that they were beautiful old pieces? And though I never said it, Rossi knew they were also silent reminders of a life I had lost.

Still wobbly kneed, I sank onto the couch. Rossi settled beside me and took my hand again. "So? Why did you get rid of Jack's things?" A superb investigator, he would wait patiently for my explanation no matter how long it took.

"Well," I began, folding pleats into the purple fabric with my free hand. "I had mixed motives."

He nodded, his eyes full of questions.

"I was so damned mad at Jack, I wanted to get rid of everything that reminded me of him."

Rossi pointed to the light-colored rectangle on the living room wall. "His photograph too?"

"It's in the back of my clothes closet."

"I see." He rubbed his thumb over my fingers. "Did getting rid of Jack's things make you feel better?"

"No. I acted out of spite. That's never a good thing."

"Are you okay with it now?"

"Yes. The truth is I was clinging to the past. Maybe subconsciously I was searching for a reason to free myself, to move on with my life—" the shock of a sudden insight hit home, "—and Jack gave me that reason." I half turned to face Rossi. "Do you think that's possible? Jack wanted me to do what I did?"

"All things are possible if we believe they are."

I nodded. Though he was really telling me I was fantasizing, that was okay. The thought of Jack's benediction was healing, and an ease I hadn't felt in days flooded through me.

"There's more you should know," I said. "At first, before I saw Dr. Endicott, I had another reason for selling Jack's things. A more positive one."

"Oh?"

"You gave Lee and Paulo your Hawaii money. I know how you've been wanting to go there. So I thought—"

"I'd vacation on the proceeds of your furniture." His

eyes mysteriously dark, he kissed me. "A well-intentioned thought, sweetheart, but do you really think I'd take your husband's money?"

"But it wouldn't be like that."

"It would be exactly like that. No dice. Besides, you're underestimating me."

"Never!"

He waggled a finger. "I have the money for Hawaii."

"But how—?"

"Remember my mentioning an Uncle Beppe?"

My jaw dropped. "You're taking a trip on mob money?"

Rossi laughed. "What did I just say? Don't underestimate me. Uncle Beppe left me his father's gold pocket watch. Eighteen carat. Weighs a ton. Worth a small fortune. It came from Sicily, long before Beppe's…ah, career…blossomed. How a hundred years ago, El Pappa got his hands on a watch worth a whole Sicilian village is shrouded in mystery. But I'm giving the old boy the benefit of the doubt and—to make a long story short—the money for Honolulu is in my checking account. So…want to join me?"

From his big white smile, I could tell he already knew my answer, but I said yes anyway. "If you're sure," I added, staring at his face for telltale signs of regret. There were none that I could see. Still, I had to be certain. "Nothing about me has changed."

He groaned. "Good. I don't like change. You're perfect as you are. Stay that way." His arms snugged around me, holding me close. "Not only are you perfect, you—"

His cell phone rang, as always at the worst possible time. And as always, he answered it on the first ring, instantly morphing into detective mode.

He listened for a second then eased off the couch and stood, phone tight to his ear. "When?" he asked. "Where are they? Stay on it. I'll be there in ten minutes. Whatever you do, don't lose them." He hung up and pocketed the cell. "Sorry sweetheart, I have to go. Call you later tonight."

He kissed me quick and hard, hurrying away before I had a chance to tell him I wouldn't be at home tonight. I had a final date with Rum Row.

THIRTY

Once I was sure Rossi had left the Surfside parking lot, I stripped off the purple dress and slid into jeans and a T-shirt. I locked the condo and headed for Rum Row, my guilt growing stronger the closer I got to the mansion. No question Rossi would have a fit if he knew I'd been sleeping there alone all week. But a promise was a promise, and as uneasy as I felt about walking into the Grandese house in the dark, Francesco remained my most valued client. Besides, the security system was state of the art. I had nothing to fear. I'd complete my week in Donny's bed, and that would be the end of it.

The neighborhood was quiet when I drove onto the driveway, a lush velvety quiet scented with night-blooming jasmine and warm salty breezes. Even the owls were silent as I punched in the alarm code.

As soon as I entered the foyer, I reset the security system and tamped down my unease. Without even the murmur of the Gulf in the distance or the brush of leaf upon leaf, the silence was deeper inside than out.

Two hideous lamps cast pools of light over the living room's treasures. Colored beads hung from the shades and lumpy clay goddesses cavorted on the bases. Donny's choice? As ugly as the lamps were, I was grateful not to walk into a totally dark house.

I blew a kiss at the Townsend on my way to the master suite. No lamps in there, so I clicked on the overheads. The first of the week Tom Kruse and his crew could start in here. When they were finished, I'd have the new Stark carpeting installed, relocate the bed onto the opposite wall, bring in the Federal highboy and bureaus from the garage. Maybe to enhance the yin and yang, a round skirted table on one side of the bed. A masculine block-front chest on the other...

What was that? I turned down the monologue in my head and listened.

Hoot. Hoot.

Oh, just the owls having a party outside the windows. My heartbeat eased out of its panic mode...a Greek key design in silvery blue would work well on a round table...

There it was again. Not owls, a creak. Nothing to be disturbed about. All houses creaked. I was imagining things. *That's what happens when you have a double scotch on an empty stomach.*

An emergency energy bar lurked in the bottom of my handbag. I emptied the purse on the bed and there it was, peanut butter caramel with a slightly crumpled wrapper and a hundred and fifty calories' worth of energy. I tore off the wrapping and finished the whole thing in three or four bites. So much for dinner. I placed the cell phone on the TV table by the bed, scooped everything else, including the gun, back into the purse and carried it into the master bathroom. Half finished with bare plastered walls and a rough concrete floor, it had the ghostlike appearance of a room in an abandoned building. I sniffed the air. Nothing but damp plaster. No fragrance of jasmine in here.

At least the shower, vanity sink and toilet had been plumbed, but the floor awaited a custom tile installation, and the full length wall mirrors were on special order. For days I'd put on my makeup and brushed my hair with only the aid of a compact. God knows what I'd looked like. Well last week had been a nightmare, and how I looked the least of my worries. This week—I checked my watch, Sunday, 1:00 a.m.—was unfolding like an American Beauty Rose.

Once I was out of here for good, I'd hire an assistant. Get a haircut. Have a pedicure. Buy a new outfit. At Victoria's Secret. In purple. Forget white and beige. Call purple my new neutral. Change the sheets on the bed. Make love to Rossi. *Live.*

A creak. Louder this time. Closer. Wood floors did creak, but these hadn't all week, not before tonight. Why now? And what was that? A voice? Somebody whispering?

Useless as broken rubber bands, my fingers fumbled in my bag for the Cobra.

A step, an unmistakable step on the hard, unfinished bedroom floor. Somebody out to kill me? My hand froze inside the purse. Not now, I wailed silently. Not now when all of life was beginning anew.

"Deva? Are you there?"

I choked back a scream and flung the door open. "Jewels! You nearly scared me to death. What are you doing here in the middle of the night?"

"We just got back. I saw the lights on, so I came to tell you we're home."

In the harsh overheads, dark shadows ringed Jewels's eyes, and her baby bump showed. Judging from her appearance, I guessed Donny's funeral had been brutal.

Heart pounding, I sagged against the front of the vanity. "Well, welcome home. I think you'll see quite a few changes since you left. Francesco should be pleased."

She nodded, as indifferent as ever to what the house looked like. But she listened as I nattered on. "The contractor has made great progress in the kitchen. This bathroom is nearly finished. On Monday, the painters can start in your bedroom, so by Friday, you and Francesco could move in if you like. The finishing touches can be added after you're settled."

"That would be good. My brother Joey drove us down. We'll be crowded over the garage."

"Then why not stay here tonight? I'm still dressed. I can drive back home."

She eyed the bed as if it were a chocolate cream puff and she was on a diet. "It's after one in the morning, Deva."

"Doesn't matter. I can be at Surfside in fifteen minutes. If you help me strip the bed, we can change it in no time."

"I don't care about the sheets. I just want to put my head on a pillow. It was a long drive from Rhode Island with two men and a baby." She patted her stomach. "Two babies. I was nauseous most of the way."

We were so busy chatting, I didn't hear them come in. Not a creak. Not a footstep. Neither did Jewels. But suddenly there they were—Pinstripes and Serge—blocking the door to the master suite, trapping us in the bathroom. I drew in a shocked breath. "Omigod, not you again."

Jewels spun around, took one look and screamed. Pinstripes grabbed her and put a hand over her mouth, stifling her outcry.

"Nix on that. No yelling allowed."

"Let her go, she's pregnant," I snapped.

"We know," Serge replied, a snarky smirk on his face.

"You *know?* Who are you, anyway?"

"We ask the questions. But since I'm a nice guy, I'll tell you. We're friends of Donny."

"Ain't that right, Jewels?" Pinstripes said in her ear.

"You know her name?"

He gave me a sullen, high-shouldered shrug. "We know a lot, lady. But there's stuff we don't know. Like who the hell are you?"

"Let her go, and I'll tell you."

"You'll tell me anyway. But like I said, I'm a nice guy." Again in Jewels's ear, he said, "Don't yell and you won't get hurt. Understood?"

She nodded.

"We just want to talk to Frannie. He with you?"

Another nod.

He took his hand away from her mouth but held onto her arm.

"I'm going to be sick," Jewels said.

"Let her go," I said.

Jewels moaned.

"She's going to throw up, asshole. You want it on your shoes?"

As if his hands were on fire, he released her. Jewels made a beeline for the toilet. I took a step toward her, but Pinstripes stuck out a foot, nearly tripping me. "Not so fast."

"How about giving us some privacy? There's no window in here. Where are we going to go?"

He glanced over at Jewels on her knees in front of the john noisily barfing up her bellybutton. "We'll be outside."

The two goons left, slamming the door behind them. Working fast, I dumped the contents of my purse in the vanity sink. No time for fumbling, just a few moments while Jewels did her thing. Once she stopped vomiting, they would be in after us.

Wrong. Not even that long. I'd no sooner tucked the Cobra into the front of my jeans and flipped the T-shirt over it when the door reopened and Pinstripes joined us in the middle of Jewels's performance. In this tight space, I couldn't do any more than hide the gun, never mind use it. He'd be all over me before I could release the safety and pull the trigger.

Intent on Jewels, he didn't notice as I scooped the rest of my stuff into the bag.

Barely able to breathe in my now skin-tight jeans, I took a chance, reached under the shirt and unfastened the button at my waist. With a shaky hand, Jewels flushed the toilet. I took a deep breath of the foul air and regretted it.

The same gray as the plaster walls, Jewels pulled herself to her feet, clinging to the edge of the vanity for support.

I dampened a washcloth and gave it to her. She took it with a weak smile and wiped her face and hands. "Why don't you let her sit down?" I said to Pinstripes.

"Yeah," Serge said, barging in and sniffing the air. "Let's get the hell out of here. It stinks."

"Lovely. Maybe if you hadn't scared her half to death, you'd be sniffing roses right now."

"What's your name?" Pinstripes asked me.

"Mrs. Dunne. What's yours?"

"Vito."

"How do you spell that?" My defiance was nothing but a flimsy sham, but I was determined not to show how frightened I was. I was also stalling for time. Surely any minute now Francesco would come barging in, looking for his pregnant wife, and give these guys whatever it was they wanted.

"Mrs. Dunne, huh? Like I told you before when we paid a call on *Mrs*. Salvatore, you're a wiseass."

Using his Glock like a baton, Serge waved us over to the bed. Jewels sank onto the mattress with a sigh. I stood at the foot holding on to the bedpost as if it were a merry-go-round pole. In a way it was. I'd circled around these two goons before. Like the first time in Chip's place, the reason for it baffled me.

Vito and Serge—I didn't bother asking Serge his

name—stood in front of Jewels, arms crossed. "Where's Frannie?" Vito asked her.

Listless, wan, she shrugged her narrow shoulders.

Serge slid the gun into his jacket pocket and took a step closer. Even without the pistol in his hand, he looked tough enough to break her in two. "The man asked you a question."

She looked up, eyes wide. "Over the garage."

"Alone?"

She shook her head. "The baby's with him."

"Anybody else?"

Jewels hesitated, then shook her head. "No."

"You're a liar. Just like always." Serge leaned over the bed and gave her a slap that sent her spread-eagled across the mattress.

"Hey," I yelled. "Cut that out."

"You. Shut up," Serge said, then to Jewels, "Find a phone. We want you should get hold of Frannie."

Jewels lay whimpering on the bed.

"You need a phone," I said. "Feel free. Use mine."

Serge turned toward me with a snarl, ready, I was sure, to send me flying across the room. Not wanting him to get near enough to feel the Cobra at my waist, I held up my hands, palms out. "No offense. You want a phone? I have a phone." I pointed to the bedside table. "Right there."

Vito snatched it off the table and, grabbing Jewels by the arm, sat her up and handed her the cell. "Call Frannie. Tell him to get over here fast."

"It'll wake the baby."

He stared at her without saying another word. Just stared. And stared. With a trembling hand, Jewels reached out and took the cell.

While we all watched, she tapped in some numbers. Then, "Frannie, Deva needs to talk to you." A pause. "I know it's late. We have a problem here. A big one. Tell Joey to stay with the baby." She hung up and wordlessly laid the phone on the bed.

"Let's go," Serge said to her. "We'll meet him in the other room. Both of you dames shake a leg."

I let go of the bedpost, and he gave me a shove toward the door.

"What's the matter, you got a bug in your margarita?" I asked, playing with fire, but anger trumped my fear. Besides I had an ace, if not up my sleeve, down my pants, and that was comforting, as long as the safety didn't let go and the gun shoot out my appendix.

Nerves in shreds despite my bluster, I followed Jewels, whose complexion had gone from gray to ashen, into the living room with the thugs right behind us.

Vito glanced around, a disgusted expression on his face. "You got a problem with chairs? There's not one in the whole damn house." He pointed to the Townsend. "Just useless junk like that. I always heard Grandese was nuts, but this caps it."

"The design isn't finished," I said. "The chairs are on special order. Come back for the open house party. You'll be impressed."

"Enough out of you. Both of you, on the floor." Jewels squatted down in front of the Townsend, tented her knees and huddled into a crumpled ball. I was scared all right, but at the sight of the palpable terror in her eyes, I was worried for her.

"I'll stand." I didn't want to sit hunched on the floor in my snug jeans with the Cobra digging into my belly.

"Down," Serge ordered.

Down I went, hoping the damn gun wouldn't accidentally go off. Folding my legs to one side to ease the pressure, I waited for a chance to act. Serge's Glock was stashed in the pocket of his jacket, so I could probably risk going for my gun. But I hadn't used the Cobra in over a year. Could I release the safety, take aim and shoot fast enough? Or maybe shooting wouldn't be necessary. I'd just aim, force Serge to keep his hands in the air so he couldn't get at his own weapon and hold them at bay. Then Francesco could call the cops. Where was he, anyway? He sure was taking his time finding out why Jewels needed him.

The kitchen door opened and slammed shut. Serge reached into his jacket pocket again.

"Hey, Jewels," a voice called. "What's up?" The voice didn't belong to Francesco.

As sensuous as a tango dancer, a tall, limber young guy came striding in on the balls of his feet, looked at the Glock in Serge's hand and came to an abrupt stop. The tango was over.

"What—?"

"Who the hell are you?" Vito asked.

"Joey. Francesco's driver." He tipped his head at Jewels. "Her brother."

"Oh yeah? Where's your brother-in-law?"

"You all right, Jewels?" Joey asked, ignoring Vito's question.

She nodded, white-lipped and trembling.

"You scared her," Joey said to Vito, but with the gun leveled at him, he didn't move into any kind of attack mode.

"She's got reasons. Down on the floor next to Jewels. We want you should get Francesco over here. And we're not waiting all night."

While Joey hunkered down and gathered his sister in his arms, Serge kept his weapon trained on us and said to Vito, "Go get that phone off the bed."

He went after it, came back and handed it to Joey whose

initial assurance had slipped. These guys were serious. Though scared, I was curious too. Who were they? What did they want with Francesco?

The front door opened—Francesco was a front door kind of guy, no kitchen doors for him—and slammed shut.

"Jewels! I finally got the baby calmed down. That damned phone woke him…*whoa*." He came to an abrupt stop but recovered fast. "I wondered when you guys would show. Figured it was just a matter of time."

"You *expected* them?" I asked, indignation busting through my fear. "I've been alone in here every night this week. What did you do, set me up?"

"They're not after you," Francesco said. "Ain't that right, boys?" He stood defiant in what looked like a hastily pulled on pair of shorts, his muscular legs apart, arms folded across his hairy bare chest. His eyes never leaving the suits, he asked, "You all right, Jewels?"

She whimpered out a reply.

"So?" Francesco challenged. "What can I get you guys? An Amaretto? A cold beer? There's some Heineken out in the fridge. The one you passed in the garage."

"This is the nuttiest damn house I ever been in," Vito said, "but we're not here to hang out. We're here to talk business. Casino business."

Francesco nodded. He didn't look surprised. "There's casinos and casinos."

"Don't get smart. We're taking Emerald City. The owners don't like what you're doing out there."

"What's that, Vito?"

Over the weeks since I'd been working with Francesco, I'd gotten to know him pretty well, and though his stance hadn't changed, I could tell from the uncertainty in his voice that some of his cocky bravado had fled.

Vito took his time answering, examining his manicure—I hated shiny nail polish on men—hitching up his tight pants before saying, "They don't like you working with the Asians, helping them break into Florida gaming. The Florida boys got enough competition from the Seminoles. They don't want no more."

So Francesco was more than just a real estate investor. I'd had no idea, but guaranteed, Rossi knew. No wonder he'd wanted me to drop the project. Disgusted at my own stupidity, I blew out an exasperated breath.

Francesco simply put his hands in his shorts pockets and stood there quietly.

"Out where I can see them," Serge ordered.

Francesco took his hands out of his pockets. "No problem. The problem is you guys coming in here in the middle of the night, scaring my wife. She's got a kid on the way and—"

"Yeah." Vito snorted. "We know all about the kid."

"Yeah?" Francesco's eyes narrowed.

"Yeah. Donny told us." A nasty gleam shone in Vito's eyes. "He said it was his."

Uh-oh.

Francesco lost it. He lunged at Vito. No contest. Vito gave him a right hook that sent him flying across the room right into the block-front chest of drawers. Dazed but otherwise unhurt, Francesco scrambled to his feet. "You crazy? That chest's worth a fortune. You coulda ruined it."

Serge aimed the pistol at Francesco's head. "Don't move. We got more to say."

"You said enough." Francesco had gotten his groove back. "You're telling me my wife's having Donny's kid?"

Vito cocked his head at Jewels, who was sobbing into her maternity skirt. "Yeah. She's been Donny's squeeze since she was sixteen. Ain't that right, Jewels?"

Fists balled, Francesco strode over to Vito. "I oughta kill you."

"That's not nice." Vito waved a finger left to right in front of Francesco's face. "Just so you'll know we don't talk for nothing, I'm showing you something."

Vito reached into his breast pocket and removed the black book that I would bet was the same one he took from AudreyAnn. "In here's every name, every number, every contact you ever made in Florida. We've got it all. You been working like a mole. There's names here from Hong Kong to Orlando." He upped an eyebrow. "Rich pickings, huh? We know that's just the beginning. The toehold. Thanks to Donny."

"Yeah." Serge cleared his throat. "Donny sang for us. Just like Pavarotti."

Letting go of Joey, Jewels hoisted herself to her feet. "You killed Donny for that?" she asked Serge, her voice quiet as a snake moving through grass. "For some numbers?"

Serge laughed, an honest to God belly laugh. "Why the hell would we do that? Donny was the goose laying golden eggs. We didn't kill nobody." He waved the Glock in Francesco's direction. "He stiffed Donny. You didn't know that? You dumb or something?"

Ignoring the Glock, ignoring Serge's laugh, Francesco stared at her. "That true what they say? The kid's Donny's?"

Her eyes dull with untold sins, she nodded, just once. Once was enough. Francesco's shoulders slumped.

"Did you kill him because of me?" she asked.

Francesco let out a humorless guffaw. "I didn't know about you and him. I heard he was spilling his guts to these guys. He betrayed me. He betrayed his whole family. He was too stupid to live anyhow. Cost me plenty. Look how he tossed a butt and torched my building. A dumb move."

"You sure about that?" Vito's face wore a nasty grin.

Francesco's eyes narrowed. "Got something to say, say it."

Vito shrugged. "That torch job was no accident. You don't cooperate, this house is next."

Francesco was making an effort to control himself, but his hands were clenching and unclenching. He nodded at Vito, a thoughtful, evaluating nod. I wondered what he was thinking of—his furniture or his family?

Finally, his hands still grasping fists full of air, he said, "My wife and kids live here. You go after women and kids now?"

Family.

"Nah. We'd wait till Jewels was gone outta here. Why do you think she wanted to go up north a few weeks ago?"

Francesco swiveled his attention to Jewels. "That right?" he asked.

Wordless, she nodded.

Francesco's glance lingered on her baby bump. "I'm glad I stiffed Donny. He had it coming, more ways than one." He straightened his shoulders. "But who's gonna know? Vito and Carmine—" so that was Serge's name, "—ain't going into any court singing like Pavarotti. Not even like Sinatra. I'll lay odds on that. And you can't be forced to testify against me." He shot a glance filled with contempt at Jewels's brother cowering against the Townsend. "Guaranteed, Joey won't say squat." He upped his chin at me. "So that leaves only little Miss Decorator over here."

He swiveled his attention from Jewels to Vito. "We can work together. I leave the Florida casinos alone, you leave me and Jewels alone." He held out a hand. *"Capisce?"*

"Just like that? I dunno," Serge said, stowing his gun in his jacket again. "We got reports to make."

"Yeah, you guys are the messengers, not the capos. I got that. Well, go back to Lazzo with my offer."

Vito drew in a breath.

Francesco eyed him, smiling. "Yeah, I know all about Lazzo. You tell him he wins. He'll like that." He yanked up his low-flying shorts. "Yeah, he wins. Francesco Grandese is pulling out of Florida. The climate's not good for my furniture, anyway. So I'm out of here." He pointed a stubby finger at Jewels, who still sat huddled on the floor. "So is she."

Then he upped his chin at me. "The price for that is her. You gotta get rid of her or no deal."

THIRTY-ONE

SHOWTIME. I WHIPPED the Cobra out of my jeans and held it steady, both hands at shoulder level the way Dad taught me. One of Boston's finest, he would have been proud. Though even with my weapon at the ready, I wasn't sure I could handle all this. Suppose I had to kill someone? Could I do it?

Serge's hand crept toward his jacket pocket. *If I had to.*

"Make a move and I'll shoot your balls off," I said, sweeping the room with the gun.

"You ain't shooting nobody," Serge scoffed. "The safety's on. Get her, Vito!"

Vito hesitated. In that millisecond, I released the safety. He took a step toward me, and I shot him in the foot. He fell to the floor, the odor of gunpowder and his howl mingling in the air.

Ignoring the ringing in my ears, I leveled the gun at Serge. "Don't try it. I learned from the best." His hand, halfway inside his jacket, fell to his side. I glanced over at Jewels. "Call 911. Ask for the police."

She slumped against the Townsend and shook her head. "I can't. Frannie's my husband. I took a vow."

A vow? Wearing Donny's baby bump and she was talking of vows? Unbelievable. A tiny part of me wanted to shoot her in the foot too for being such a hypocrite.

"Murder trumps all, Jewels," I said, sounding like an Irish priest I once knew.

Hands on her abdomen, she gazed up at me as if she

were hoping my absolution was the real deal. "I can't call the cops on my own husband."

"That's right, baby, you can't," Francesco said, his expression lighting up as if he had just won the Power Ball.

Was she crazy? We needed help, and we needed it fast. I couldn't hold off four men forever.

"Joey, get the phone," I said. "Make the call."

Either too scared or too shocked to move a muscle, he stared at me blank-faced.

He was useless. I turned back to Jewels.

"Francesco killed your lover. The father of your baby. You don't owe him a thing." I wasn't sure that was exactly true, but in a room full of enemies, this wasn't the time for semantic fine-tuning. "Call 911, or I'll blast out the front window. That should bring the neighbors running."

"Let's talk this over," Serge said, a United Nations diplomat all of a sudden. "No sense getting hostile."

Vito moaned. "I need a doctor."

No one made a move to help him, including me, Annie Oakley, but I was worried. I didn't know how badly he was hurt, and I didn't want him to bleed to death while Serge pontificated.

"The phone, Jewels, the phone," I said. "You don't have a choice. Make the call or you'll be aiding and abetting. Helping a murderer. Think of your children."

That must have convinced her. She slowly nodded. "I know. I have to do it for them." Color returned to her cheeks. Ignoring me and my gun, she stared at Francesco as if he were a stranger. "Why did you kill him, Frannie? Your own cousin? What for? Casino money? Why did you need so much?" She raised her arms wide and waved them around. "For this junk?"

"Junk!" Like a man stabbed in the gut, Francesco

screamed out the word. "This stuff is priceless. There's only ten Townsends in existence. You know what that means?"

"No, and I don't care. Donny, I cared about Donny."

Francesco stared at her baby bump again as if he couldn't keep his eyes away from it. "Yeah. You proved that. But that don't matter to me. You're my wife. I'll pass the kid off as mine."

"No, you won't." She shook her head. "This baby isn't yours. She's mine. And Donny's. You're her father's killer. I don't want you near her." She jerked upright. "Where's the phone, Joey?"

"Over my dead body." Francesco lunged for her, moving so fast he was on her before I could stop him. If I shot now, I'd risk hitting Jewels.

In the confusion, Serge whipped out his Glock and fired. Either he was a poor shot, or he was rattled. He missed me. The bullet struck the front of the Townsend, ripping a hole in one of the perfectly matched mahogany panels. Before he could get off another shot, I took aim, squeezed the trigger and hit him in the arm. He screamed. The gun fell from his hand and slid across the polished floor.

Francesco leaped off Jewels. Howling like a banshee, he knocked Serge out of his way, dashed over to the desk, and ran his hands along the mutilated wood. "Look what you done. Look what you done! You wrecked it. Wiped out a million bucks. Or more. I oughta kill you for that." He swiveled away from the desk and, forgetting me, forgetting Jewels, forgetting everything but his own red hot rage, he went for Serge.

"Stay," I yelled. "Another step and you're a dead man."

Hands clenching and unclenching, face purple, Francesco stopped inches from Serge. He gathered his saliva, took careful aim and let go right in his face. *"Bastardo!"*

With his good arm, Serge swiped a sleeve across his cheek. "That goes in the book. Next to the numbers. You're a walking corpse."

"Speaking of corpses, Francesco," I said, "where did you get the cyanide? From Norm?"

Francesco blew out a lungful of sheer disgust. "*Norm?* I didn't get nothing from Norm. Not even good advice. I got my own sources. Norm ain't one of them." His glance swept the room, landing finally on the gun lying in a corner.

"That's enough," I said. "Jewels, get the gun. Hurry."

She jumped up and ran for the Glock. Poking a single finger into the trigger, she carried the gun back to me upside down and held it out. I took it and said, "Now get the phone. Call the police."

"That won't be necessary." Without a warning, there he suddenly stood, legs apart, gun drawn like a Deadwood sheriff. At the sound of his voice, a tidal wave of relief surged through me. I'd been scared stiff and hadn't even known it.

"Rossi. Thank God." My arms, unused to being held rigid at shoulder height, had tired. I gladly lowered both guns. "How did you know where I was?"

"That can wait. But I'm glad to see you're so well armed." His voice was bantering, his eyes smoldering. Which I took to mean he wasn't happy at finding me here, but would be damned if he'd let on right now. Later, he'd let on later. I heaved a sigh, the relief mingling with resignation.

In the distance, roaring closer by the instant, police sirens shattered the velvet quiet of Rum Row. Blue cruiser lights flashed onto the driveway and car doors slammed.

"I need a doctor," Vito said.

"Me, too," Serge echoed.

"We'll see that you're both treated," Rossi said. "Now can somebody tell me what happened here?"

Francesco pointed a finger at me. "She shot them. For no reason. She's crazy. Right, Jewels? Right, Joey?"

Obviously a company man, Joey gave him a scared little nod. *Great.*

But Jewels was no company man. "My husband," she hissed out the word, "is a killer. He poisoned his cousin Donny. With cyanide."

"She's making that up," Francesco protested. "The poison was in my shrimp. Not Donny's. Who knew he'd scarf it all down?"

"You did, Frannie. You knew that was his favorite. He always went for the shrimp first. Couldn't get enough of it. You knew he'd go out to the kitchen and grab yours before anyone else did." She paused for a second to brush away the tears streaming down her face. "You knew that. And you sat eating salami and listening to Puccini while he died. I swear if I ever hear Puccini again I'll vomit." Her voice cracking with outrage, Jewels stepped closer to her husband and thrust her wet face close to his. "You know something else? I'm glad he—" she pointed a shaky finger at Serge, "—shot that desk. I've always hated it."

Francesco snorted. "No comments allowed. You got no taste. No class either."

"That's enough." Joey grasped a handful of Jewels's skirt and tugged her back out of danger. Though regret at losing what Francesco could do for him was plastered over his sexy, tango-dancer face, he finally found the guts to come to his sister's defense. Blood kin must have meant more than money to him after all. "My sister's telling the truth," he said to Rossi. "I heard him confess."

Francesco shrugged, a nonchalant, I-don't-give-a-damn

shrug. Like a bully in a schoolyard he challenged, "Prove it. Prove I stiffed Donny. It's your word against mine."

"And mine," I added. I glanced over at the two patients who were slumped on the floor. "They heard you too."

"I was lying," Francisco said, jerking a thumb at Vito and Serge. "I knew they were packing. They had me scared. A guy'll say anything when he's scared."

Quietly, their guns drawn, two police officers entered the room. With a quick nod, Rossi indicated Francesco and told the first cop who strode into the room, my old friend Officer Batano, "Cuff him then read him his rights. And we need an ambulance." Batano's partner, petite Officer Hughes, hit the phone.

As Batano and Hughes sprang into action, Rossi lowered his gun and glanced around the living room. "Why are there no chairs in here?"

THIRTY-TWO

LATER, BACK AT my condo, with the sun already shooting fingers of light into the horizon, Rossi settled into a club chair. The emerging rays played off his face, emphasizing its cragginess and the fatigue he wasn't about to give in to. He removed his notebook and pencil stub from his shirt pocket and flipped the pad to a blank page.

"All right, let's hear it," he said. "Start at the beginning. Take your time. Don't leave anything out."

I squirmed uneasily on the sofa. Facing an annoyed Rossi made me more than a little uncomfortable. Besides, all I wanted to do was take a shower and go to bed, not relive a crime. Staying awake for twenty-four hours challenged my system in ways it wasn't used to. Worse, tired-eyed, but otherwise looking like he could go another twenty-four without any trouble, Rossi had no intention of letting up until I told him everything I knew. But first I had a question of my own.

"How did you know I was in the Rum Row house?"

"I didn't. Cookie Harkness was out walking her dog and spotted two men entering the Grandese garage. She called the police. Luckily Batano was on duty and recognized the address. He notified me immediately. I'm glad he did, though I damn near dropped my weapon when I saw you there. I thought you were home in bed safe and warm."

His update over, he sat with his brow furrowed, pencil poised relentlessly on the top line of the pad.

"Cookie helped out, hmm? Funny, there for a while I thought she might have been the culprit," I said.

"That so?" His expression, not to mention his tone of voice, telegraphed annoyance, but I ignored it and continued. Having this over with would be the fastest way to get some sleep.

"Years ago, she had access to cyanide and could conceivably have gotten hold of some. It seemed logical that she might have tried to kill Francesco in the hope of wiping out Norm's gambling debt at the same time. But if that had been her intent, when Francesco didn't eat the poisoned shrimp, she would have raced into the kitchen and made sure no one else did. She might be a snob, but she's not a monster.

"So my interest shifted to Norm. After all, he was the one Francesco was putting the squeeze on. Then Nikhil Jamison told me Norm had been cooking the company books, and I realized he had a gambling addiction. Also he'd persuaded Nikhil to bring him cyanide to kill the critters in his attic. Or so he said. At that point I was pretty sure he was the murderer. Of the wrong man, of course."

"Of course." Rossi did sarcasm well, but I didn't bother to challenge him on it. Too time consuming. I'd save my protests for another day. After I got some sleep.

"Earlier though, AudreyAnn had me worried. Chip too. After all, they were in the kitchen when Donny died and had plenty of opportunity." Not for the first time that night, I shook my head at my own stupidity. "But neither one had a strong enough motive. At the time of the poisoning, Chip didn't know Donny and AudreyAnn had been living together. Then—after Donny's death—he found out and tried to kill himself, not somebody else. At that point the finger of suspicion swung back to AudreyAnn...but when Chip nearly died, she admitted Donny had been a mistake. She had been glad to leave him and get back to Chip. Seeing how distraught she was, I believed her. There wasn't enough hatred in her heart to do the dirty deed."

"Anything else?" Rossi lowered the foot he'd slung across his knee and shifted in his chair, pencil stub still at the ready. I had a sinking feeling he could last several more hours.

"That only left Bonita, poor Tomas's widow. She was the X factor in all of this. The one I knew the least about. But with all those other hot leads, I put her on the back burner until the day she showed up on Francesco's doorstep with that toy truck and the threatening note. She might not have known about the hidden money, but she certainly knew about the propane explosion. So what that was all about, I couldn't fathom. Do you know?"

"Are you asking for my opinion?"

"Always. You're the pro. So what *was* that about?"

"Vito playing a head game with Grandese. Nothing more. The two boys had a job to do. Convince Grandese to either pull out of the casino business or to leave the state. Threatening his son was one way to accomplish that."

"So Bonita was just Vito's innocent messenger?"

"Correct."

"I guess it's a good thing I took her off my suspect list."

"Your *list?*" Rossi lowered the notepad and stared at me in disbelief as if nobody he knew had ever made up a list.

"Yes. After all, Rossi, even though a person is sweet and mild, you can't be sure of what's in their mind."

"Is that right?"

I could have made icicles from the tone of his voice. No wonder. My amateur theories were outrageous, and I knew it. While I had speculated about what had happened, Rossi, the forensic specialist, had investigated with the aid of an entire police department. But ever the good listener, he let me continue without serious interrupting—just the few jibes—and if he realized I was toying with him he didn't let on.

Sometimes, like now, it was hard to know what he was thinking. For sure he was a puzzle, and I would never have all the pieces to him. Maybe that was part of his allure, a man of enduring mystery. And fabulous pecs.

I slid along the couch and rested my head on the padded arm, signaling that I needed to sleep.

But Rossi was a bulldog after a juicy bone. "What else?"

More. He wanted more. I heaved a sigh to let him know this wasn't easy and soldiered on, either that or be here until high noon. "When Francesco and Jewels went to Rhode Island for Donny's funeral, Francesco asked me to house sit. He knew I valued his antiques...the Townsend alone is worth millions. Even with the damage, it probably still is. He wanted someone on the property to keep an eye on things."

Rossi snorted. Not a pretty sound. "Why didn't you suggest he hire a security guard?"

"Well, he already had the most expensive alarm system money could buy. It's state of the art, so I thought that was enough security. For the house and for me. Someone had to be there to let in the workmen each morning, and he knew I'd be coming and going anyway, purchasing things for the rooms. Besides I love his antiques as much as he does, and that made him feel good about leaving them."

Rossi shifted in his seat and frowned. *Excellent. Fanny fatigue at last.*

"Was making Grandese feel good a priority of yours?" he asked.

Despite the buzzing in my head, I bolted upright. Was Rossi jealous? I loved the possibility but didn't let on that I even suspected it. I could be cool too when I had to.

"For your information, Lieutenant, a big part of an interior designer's job is to make her clients happy. I always strive for that. If sleeping in Francesco's house for a few nights—"

"A week."

"—cemented our relationship—our business relationship—I was willing to do so." I waved a finger in the air. "Write that down too." I slid along the sofa cushions again and closed my eyes. The inquisition had gone on long enough.

"Deva."

I didn't even peek at him.

"Deva. Do you know you are a brave and wonderful woman?"

My eyes snapped open. "Really?"

"Yes, really. And stretched out on that couch, you make me realize all over again what sensational legs you have."

I arched an instep and glanced down at my calf. "Sensational, huh? Rossi, are you easily impressed?"

His gaze sweeping over me was like a long, breathless caress. "With you, yes. I'm always impressed with you."

"Thank you." I lowered my lids again. Actually they refused to stay open.

"There's more."

"More?" I forced my lids apart so as to enjoy the full effect of his next compliment.

"Yes, I'd like to wring your neck."

I winced.

"Oh. Sorry. I didn't mean to...a figure of speech."

Just a year ago, my friend and client, Treasure Kozlowski, had been strangled. To mention neck wringing, Rossi must be more tired than he let on.

"I mean it," he said. "I'm sorry. But the fact is your involvement with Grandese placed you in danger. I warned you about him, but you wouldn't listen. Are you always going to act like that?"

I nodded. "Probably. You want a floor mat, date a floor mat." I swung my legs over the edge of the sofa. "What you're forgetting is that I helped you solve a murder." I put my hands on my hips. "Say something about that, why don't you?"

"When I file my formal report, you'll be given full credit for your role in the case."

Mollified, I nodded though truthfully as long as I had been a help to Rossi, I didn't care about getting credit from anybody else. I had other, more immediate concerns. For openers, my biggest client was in the slammer. Though with Rossi's warnings echoing in my ears, whenever I'd placed an order for the Rum Row house, I covered the cost with Francesco's retainer. So I wouldn't have outstanding bills. Nevertheless Deva Dunne Interiors wouldn't profit from dealing with Mr. Grandese after all. Nor did I want to, knowing Jewels had two babies to raise alone. On the plus side, Francesco's collection of museum quality furniture was worth millions.

"Jewels *will* be able to keep the furniture, won't she?" I asked Rossi.

He nodded. "Under Florida law, she keeps her home, no matter what happens to her husband."

"Good. What's in that house will yield enough to support a dozen children. And I hope Chip gets to keep the money he found at La Cucina."

"I agree. So far no one has staked a claim. A few more days and the money should be his."

"Unless Francesco decides to go after it."

"He'll be fighting for his life. I doubt he'll want to tangle with any other lawsuits. But if he does go down that rocky path, I fully intend to testify on Chip's behalf."

That made me feel a little bit better, but not completely. I liked Francesco, his outrageousness, his wit, his enthusiasm. Killing his cousin in cold blood didn't seem to fit the person I knew, or thought I knew. Which told me I had a lot to learn about criminal behavior. More than I would ever master. My being in the house when the two thugs arrived and blew the lid off Francesco's cover was sheer, dumb luck, not detective work. Rossi had every right to be annoyed. Okay, angry.

"What's going to happen to Serge and Vito?"

"The two goons? They're being charged with breaking and entering. Possession without a license."

"That's *it?*"

"To get the charges lowered, they've agreed to testify against Grandese. They'll be singing like birds. Even misdemeanors on rap sheets like theirs will send them up for a long stretch. So with their testimony and yours, and that of Jewels and her brother, it's doubtful Grandese can wiggle out of this one."

"Norm can't wiggle out of his lawsuit either. Not with what Nikhil discovered."

"True." Rossi reached into his shirt pocket. "And you can't wiggle out of this."

"Out of what?"

With the same two fingers he used to extract his notebook and pencil, he removed a white envelope from his shirt pocket and handed it to me.

"What's this?"

He smiled a Cheshire cat smile, like he knew something I didn't, which most of the time was exactly the case. "You'll have to open it to find out."

With my pulse revving up, I slid a finger under the flap. This wasn't going to be an electric bill or a cancelled movie stub, so what could it be?

"Before I look, give me a hint, Rossi."

"Let me put it this way, there's a lei in your future."

"A *lay?*"

Without waiting another instant, I reached into the envelope and pulled out two airline tickets.

"Oh, Rossi," I said, leaping off the couch and flinging myself on him. "Aloha!"

* * * * *

REQUEST YOUR FREE BOOKS!
2 FREE NOVELS PLUS 2 FREE GIFTS!

HARLEQUIN

INTRIGUE

BREATHTAKING ROMANTIC SUSPENSE

YES! Please send me 2 FREE Harlequin Intrigue® novels and my 2 FREE gifts (gifts are worth about $10). After receiving them, if I don't wish to receive any more books, I can return the shipping statement marked "cancel." If I don't cancel, I will receive 6 brand-new novels every month and be billed just $4.74 per book in the U.S. or $5.24 per book in Canada. That's a savings of at least 14% off the cover price! It's quite a bargain! Shipping and handling is just 50¢ per book in the U.S. and 75¢ per book in Canada.* I understand that accepting the 2 free books and gifts places me under no obligation to buy anything. I can always return a shipment and cancel at any time. Even if I never buy another book, the two free books and gifts are mine to keep forever.

182/382 HDN F43C

Name _____ (PLEASE PRINT) _____

Address _____ Apt. #

City _____ State/Prov. _____ Zip/Postal Code

Signature (if under 18, a parent or guardian must sign)

Mail to the **Harlequin® Reader Service:**
IN U.S.A.: P.O. Box 1867, Buffalo, NY 14240-1867
IN CANADA: P.O. Box 609, Fort Erie, Ontario L2A 5X3

**Are you a subscriber to Harlequin Intrigue books
and want to receive the larger-print edition?
Call 1-800-873-8635 or visit www.ReaderService.com.**

* Terms and prices subject to change without notice. Prices do not include applicable taxes. Sales tax applicable in N.Y. Canadian residents will be charged applicable taxes. Offer not valid in Quebec. This offer is limited to one order per household. Not valid for current subscribers to Harlequin Intrigue books. All orders subject to credit approval. Credit or debit balances in a customer's account(s) may be offset by any other outstanding balance owed by or to the customer. Please allow 4 to 6 weeks for delivery. Offer available while quantities last.

Your Privacy—The Harlequin® Reader Service is committed to protecting your privacy. Our Privacy Policy is available online at www.ReaderService.com or upon request from the Harlequin Reader Service.

We make a portion of our mailing list available to reputable third parties that offer products we believe may interest you. If you prefer that we not exchange your name with third parties, or if you wish to clarify or modify your communication preferences, please visit us at www.ReaderService.com/consumerschoice or write to us at Harlequin Reader Service Preference Service, P.O. Box 9062, Buffalo, NY 14269. Include your complete name and address.

HIDIR13R

REQUEST YOUR FREE BOOKS!

2 FREE NOVELS
PLUS 2 FREE GIFTS!

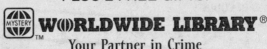

MYSTERY ™ **WORLDWIDE LIBRARY**®

Your Partner in Crime

YES! Please send me 2 FREE novels from the Worldwide Library® series and my 2 FREE gifts (gifts are worth about $10). After receiving them, if I don't wish to receive any more books, I can return the shipping statement marked "cancel." If I don't cancel, I will receive 4 brand-new novels every month and be billed just $5.49 per book in the U.S. or $6.24 per book in Canada. That's a savings of at least 31% off the cover price. It's quite a bargain! Shipping and handling is just 50¢ per book in the U.S. and 75¢ per book in Canada.* I understand that accepting the 2 free books and gifts places me under no obligation to buy anything. I can always return a shipment and cancel at any time. Even if I never buy another book, the two free books and gifts are mine to keep forever.

414/424 WDN F4WY

Name	(PLEASE PRINT)	
Address		Apt. #
City	State/Prov.	Zip/Postal Code

Signature (if under 18, a parent or guardian must sign)

Mail to the Harlequin® Reader Service:
IN U.S.A.: P.O. Box 1867, Buffalo, NY 14240-1867
IN CANADA: P.O. Box 609, Fort Erie, Ontario L2A 5X3

Want to try two free books from another line?
Call 1-800-873-8635 or visit www.ReaderService.com.

WWL13R

ReaderService.com

Manage your account online!

- Review your order history
- Manage your payments
- Update your address

*We've designed
the Harlequin® Reader Service
website just for you.*

Enjoy all the features!

- Reader excerpts from any series
- Respond to mailings and special monthly offers
- Discover new series available to you
- Browse the Bonus Bucks catalog
- Share your feedback

Visit us at:
ReaderService.com